Published in 2023 by FeedARead.com Publishing

A CIP catalogue record for this title is available
from the British Library.

A very special thank you to everybody who bought a copy of The Queen of Deadly Divas, it is greatly appreciated.

Also, thank you for all the support people have given to me, it really does help.

Finally, thank you to Lee, Sarah, Sue and Cathy – you have always believed in this project.

The Queen of Broken Hearts

Book 2 of the Divas Trilogy

Ricky James Rogers

The Divas Trilogy consists of:
The Queen of Deadly Divas
The Queen of Broken Hearts
The Queen of Devastation

For author updates and more information on the Divas Trilogy, follow me:
TikTok – @rickyjamesrogers
Instagram - @rickyjamesrogers
Twitter / X - @divastrilogy
Facebook – Ricky James Rogers – Author /
facebook.com/rickyjamesrogers1

I promise to tell the truth,
The whole truth and nothing but
the truth.
God, help me please!

PROLOGUE 01
Previously in The Queen of Deadly Divas

"...But first tonight, breaking news just in: A man was knocked down by a car which then drove off at speed. The incident happened on East Green Street earlier today.

"He was treated at the roadside for multiple injuries before being taken to the city hospital, where he was pronounced dead upon arrival.

"Police are appealing for witnesses and are requesting anyone with any information to contact them..."

PROLOGUE 02
Previously in The Queen of Deadly Divas

Inside the hidden room, motionless on the floor, lay her gorgeous drag queen son, Miss Tequila ShockingBird, whom they had christened James Taylor at birth.

Without hesitation, Wendy picked up the limp body in her arms and carried it quickly towards the exit, stepping over the stunning outfits, wigs, and shoes she had so desperately wanted to take with her just a few minutes earlier.

Ignoring her own pain, Wendy carried Tequila's body into the alley and then to the safety of the street at the front of the building, just as the fire engines began to arrive. But there was no sign of life from Tequila and no time to wait for the paramedics to arrive.

Wendy lay her dragged up son down on the chilly concrete pavement and pushed down on the chest, beginning the process of resuscitation.

You will live!

You will live!

I will not fail you again, I promise you that! But the body remained unresponsive. Wendy knew she had to keep going until the paramedics arrived, so she would, and she would never give up, and she would never succumb to defeat.

Through her own tears and pain, she momentarily looked up whilst she continued the compressions on her son's chest. What a sight she must have looked with her skin filthy from the smoke, no wig, no shoes, no dress, and no accessories to pull it altogether.

On looking up she saw Oliver standing there watching them, tears falling down his face, too.

But wait!

What the…?

There was somebody else there, just behind him, holding him tightly.

And it looked like Jake!

But Jake was dead, wasn't he?

She looked down at her lifeless son and then back up at Oliver but whoever or whatever she thought she had seen behind him was no longer there.

Damn it! Another young life will not be taken!

Damn it! You will live!

You! Will! Live!

You must live!

My beautiful son, who finally called me Dad.

CHAPTER 01
September

Impatient as always and still cruel, bitter and twisted, Chris Randall sat on the bottom bunk in his tiny prison cell with his feet planted firmly on the floor, listening carefully for any movement around him.

He was finally alone with only the wretched sound of silence echoing through the endless maze of corridors, the same corridors he had dreaded walking through when he had first arrived there, and still did.

As for those doors, those bastard doors... he still cringed or jumped every time he heard one slam shut. They disturbed his slumber, broke his peace, and invaded his thoughts. Mostly though, they altered his mental state in the most damaging way and intensified his constant craving to rest, to reset and rebalance his overwrought mind. He was never given the opportunity to do so.

But somehow, that endless maze of corridors which never led him anywhere he wanted to go, and those endless slamming doors that forever agitated him, both seemed like home now. Although this could never be his home because he did not intend on staying.

His freedom was calling him, loudly, and it would only be a matter of time before he was out of this hell hole as a free man, back in his world, ruling the Eastern Quarter, planning to take over the Northern Territory, and grabbing anything else the town he loved so much had to offer.

But, for now, he was finally alone, although the approaching footsteps of the prison officers or his latest cell mate never seemed too far away. Even though there was definitely nobody around, he listened carefully because it was imperative he was not disturbed, interrupted or overheard as he commenced his latest misadventure.

He stared hard at the whitewashed brick walls that always seemed to close in on him, even more so when there were two of them in there cramped up together. He particularly liked to stare at the part of the wall where he had scratched his initials, CR, into the paintwork in large letters. Perhaps done in a moment of utter boredom but with Chris was it that straightforward?

CR for Chris Randall?

No, nothing as ordinary as that.

CR for Connie's Revenge?

Maybe; a deliberate reminder to him of how he ended up here. But how could he be certain if his own cousin, Mark, aka drag queen Connie, was the mastermind behind his downfall? He'd had plenty of time to reflect on the situation in great detail.

CR for Chris's Revenge?

That was far more likely.

Understandably, he had feelings of pent-up anger and frustration within him that were just as keen to be released as he was. His overpowering negative emotions felt as trapped as he did and his long-standing paranoia was in constant danger of consuming him... he hardly knew how to cope.

He had plans to make and revenge to exact and now he had the time to do it. Anyone who had done him wrong in the past would be made to regret it and he intended to start with those whose actions were foremost in his mind: Mark... Oliver... Martin... Wendy... Security Guard... Tittie... The Maniac... Tequila... Jake... they all needed to pay.

These walls, the perimeters of the compound, the prison officers, they could not hold him for long. He would not allow them to. One day they would have to let him go and, unlike those who felt safer for him being locked away, he hoped that day would come soon.

Through soulless eyes, he stared at the heavy cell door which held him captive. It was scuffed and bashed in places, perhaps where previous occupants had tried to break through presumably without success; the heavy cell door that, like everything else, would eventually have to let him go.

He glanced at the water-stained hand basin in the corner of the room and the crude metal toilet, both of which he seemed to share continuously with an endless line of new cell mates - none of whom ever seemed to be in a hurry to wipe clean after use or even flush!

Vile, boring, obnoxious creatures, all with names he barely bothered to learn. He had no sympathy or interest as to why they were passing through his current place of residence – well, never altruistically.

On the inside, names and faces were easily forgotten but the nicknames he allocated to those around him helped him remember. First, there had been Skinhead Nutter who was always 'out of it' on whatever substance had been smuggled in that day, like Spice or Crack. Then, there was Cry Baby who had irritated him the most, especially during the night when it was time to sleep, and those bastard doors had finally stopped slamming. More recently, there was The Farter who, for obvious reasons, made him crave a window that would open widely.

This life was a far cry from his previous one as owner of Divas Cabaret Bar and the occupant of a lovely semi-detached house out in the suburbs, beyond the Eastern Quarter; that house was now on the market at a very reasonable price for a quick sale. Alas, the five-star luxury, the free-flowing champagne, and the fine dining all seemed so long ago although, in reality, it had only been a matter of weeks.

But it felt much longer.

He was resigned to the fact he was stuck there until everything was resolved and he wasn't exactly going without his home comforts; in fact, he really wasn't struggling inside at all - apart from in his mental health and that was to be expected.

He was far from being Top Dog on his block and held no aspirations to battle for that title - that just seemed like too much effort - but he had a fair idea how to play the game and was fiercely protective of the few comforts he had already secured for himself in there.

He had watched enough prison dramas to know if he scratched the backs of others they were more likely to scratch his, and he had plenty of time to earn favours, make demands, and implement his own version of the law.

Yes, he knew how to win and he would use his well-honed skills of cunning and manipulation to seize the opportunity to come out on top when he was ready. A handsome, confident businessman, Chris disarmed many of his fellow inmates and some of the less savvy prison officers, as well. The rest did not know what to make of him. They had never come across such an openly hard-faced gay man before who might turn around and clout them, so he was generally left to his own devices, which was exactly how he wanted it.

Initiating and grooming the newbies was no longer his priority: only he, himself, mattered, along with securing his freedom as rapidly as possible.

He stood up and stared out of the small window that overlooked the concrete wilderness beyond. The nights were beginning to draw in as autumn came ever closer. The sweetest of fruits would drop to the ground and decay; the vibrant leaves would desert their hosts, leaving them bare and gnarled beneath; the prettiest of flowers would curl up one final time as Mother Nature claimed them back to the earth for her own.

This gradual shutting down of nature would lead, inevitably, to Halloween, the time when the veil between the living and the dead was said to be at its thinnest. Who knew what ghosts from the past might be waiting in the wings to reveal themselves to an unsuspecting audience?

Bonfire Night would follow - *remember, remember the 5th of November* –shining victorious with its dazzling fireworks and blazing fires, screaming for attention, demanding to be noticed. Soon after - sooner than anyone was ready for - the bleak and cruel winter months would be back with their relentless bone-chilling cold. Mother Nature might freeze the ground into a stony blanket of white but, if Chris Randall had anything to do with it, cold dark forces of a different nature would conspire and join forces to supress the vibrancy of life in a more sinister way altogether.

Inside his cell, Chris continued to listen very, very carefully.

The prison officers had made their routine checks and, even though he was confident they would not be back again for a while, he remained on high alert because he had almost been caught out once before. As the silence stretched out around him his confidence grew: this seemed the perfect opportunity to implement the first of his plans to bring them down, those unsuspecting treacherous fools in the outside world.

CR... for Chris's Revenge.

As far as he was concerned, he could still exert control on the outside world from within the constraints of his captivity, albeit in a more limited capacity, and he had every intention of doing so. He had his cast of puppets to play with and, whether they liked it or not, he was still pulling their tangled strings.

One day he might cut them free but, for now, he was the master of destinies and there was very little anybody could do to stop him. All they had to do was survive.

With military precision, his index finger and thumb slipped neatly into a tiny rip he had made in the lining of his thin, tired mattress. Working in unison, they located a small hand-held device hidden safely within and, after listening once again for approaching footsteps, he pulled out a tiny fully charged phone. He shuddered violently as he recalled the repulsive favour he had been required to undertake in the shower block with an overweight and rancid opportunist to obtain it, an act he vowed never to repeat. But for what he wanted to achieve it was more than worth it in the bigger scheme of things.

He quickly returned to his bunk, sat down on the edge, dialled a number and, when it was answered, began to speak in a quiet, urgent voice. "It's me. Listen; do you know what you need to do?... Good, just leave it a while, okay?... Yes, let the trail go cold first. But soon, right?... Sometime around the grand opening or soon after would be ideal. I want him to suffer, and I don't care how you do it... Yes, then you can have exactly what you want, you have my word on that. Now, you're not going to flake on me, are you?... Good, because he doesn't deserve to live... Right, go now before anyone suspects."

Chris ended the call and again listened carefully at the door to ensure nobody was around to have heard those hateful words of revenge. He pushed the phone down the toilet and into the U-bend before flushing away any evidence of it ever having been in his possession deep into the bowels of the building and the overflowing sewers beyond.

It had served its purpose and he didn't expect he would need to use it again, although it might have been a useful commodity in there, something to trade for another forbidden object. But he was not prepared to risk it being found during one of the random cell searches which happened with alarming frequency, certainly not when his fingerprints were all over it and it was linked to the fate of a soon to be dead man.

Under no circumstances was he planning to stay in there for a moment longer than was necessary. As far as those in authority were concerned, he was a model guest and that was all they needed to know, all he wanted them to know.

More than satisfied with himself, he settled down for the evening. He switched on the small television that always seemed to flicker during the exciting bits, before plumping up his only pillow as best as he could and relaxing on his bottom bunk.

This was as far removed from the life he was accustomed to as possible but he had no doubt he would find a way to open a door out of there.

After all, he knew the truth, the whole truth, and nothing but the truth.

God help them all!

And his ripple effect was now spreading outwards, just as it had once done against him.

CHAPTER 02
Late October

It should have been the happiest day of her life but that was far from true.

Instead, her ruined dress and the chaos that surrounded her clearly reflected her failure to walk down the aisle hand in hand with her one true love after saying 'I do' on her supposed wedding day.

Here she was slumped awkwardly in her easy chair, both of them frayed and battered around the edges. Here she was alone in her empty room with her empty heart, trying to make sense of things. The meagre glow of a nearby lamp cast little comforting warmth over her tear-filled eyes.

What would become of all the lovely presents that her family and friends had so carefully selected for her?

She would no longer be able to open the beautifully coloured ribbons and tear apart the exquisite gift-wrap which covered new toasters, matching kettles, and fine china. But worse - worst of all - the hostess trolley that she had craved since she was a little girl, would have to be returned as well. It would probably all have to be sent back but she couldn't think about that now, she felt too weak, too broken, her heart destroyed.

Oh, the humiliation!

Her stunning, crisp white dress was as stained with mascara as her face, desolated like the delicate ringlets and French roll she'd had fashioned for the occasion, which she had tried to unpin and release back into a flowing mane with little success.

All around her music was playing, songs for broken hearts. Her beautiful bouquet of white lilies lay tattered on the ground, strewn around the white lace-covered shoes she had slipped her tiny feet into, earlier that day. To the side lay a once divine and mouth-watering three-tiered cake, pushed over, uneaten, no longer required.

She stared all around her as tears fell freely from her tired, aching eyes. This should never have happened. How had it come to this? She didn't understand, couldn't, and refused to.

She reached out for a handful of flower heads which had been spared from her earlier anger and, with tightly clenched hands, began to destroy them. He loves me... he loves me not.... he loves me... he loves me not!

No, he must love me! He must... he must... he must!

But how could he ever have loved her if he had been able to put her through this heartache so easily?

How could he have humiliated her like this in front of all her nearest and dearest? Hadn't they been happy? Were they not destined to be together? Had it not been love at first sight? What had happened to their fairy tale?

How could she face life now, alone and empty, when it had taken her so many years to find The One? She had always hoped she would find somebody... somebody kind, loving, special, tolerant. He had broken the mould, fitted the bill better than anyone ever could have dreamt.

And now he had broken her heart. Why?

He had told her he loved every face she showed to the world, every mask, every new frock, every stunning accessory. More opportunities to love all the sides to her remarkable personality, he had said.

And she had believed him, totally.

She no longer believed him. How could she? How could she ever believe anything again? She would never again believe in the miracle of falling under the spell of a wonderful man, falling in love, and being in love forever.

If only she could turn back the unfair hands of time.

If only she could lay her hands on the mould he had come from, she would wedge an eight-inch heel right through it and make him regret the day he was born.

If only she could make him understand how he had ruined everything... how he had ruined her.

She pulled off one false eyelash, then the other, and placed them both on the side table next to an expensive-looking decanter of brandy. Should she drink away her sorrows? Could she drown away all the tears and the pain? Would that help? The quarter-filled glass next to the decanter suggested she had already made a start.

Was he not her Romeo? Had she not been his Juliet? Had he not made his way up to her balcony on more than one occasion?

How would she ever get over this? Could she get over it? Was this her destiny, to replicate the ill-fortune bestowed upon the other Juliet?

She thought about Oliver... dear, sweet, unfortunate Oliver. Was this how much his heart had hurt as Jake drifted away at the roadside? Had he felt like self-destructing as she did now? My god, how could anybody face that much pain and heartache alone? How on earth had that poor boy coped with the loss of his one true love? How was he coping even now, some three or so months later?

She closed her eyes momentarily and slumped back into her chair. An object that appeared to be a large, empty bottle of pills, fell from within the ruffles and layers of her dress and rolled away across the floor.

Maybe the paramedics would find them if they were called in time, maybe not.

Was she slipping into a coma of denial? Was she already there? Was there any time left to save her? Did she even want to be saved? Her heart was broken, what was left to live for?

What she had done to deserve this she did not know. Her mind was too cloudy to recall. Still she could not help but think about Oliver and how he must have felt on that terrible, terrible day; how he must have felt the day after it had happened, and the day after that, and every blasted moment since that godforsaken day.

Oh, poor Oliver, that poor, poor boy.

She was channelling him now, consumed, totally, by his despair and grief as her emotions flooded from her. The tears continued to fall down her makeup-streaked face as she imagined how he must have been torn apart by the tragic death of Jake Robinson, and how he must miss him every single day.

Who would miss her if she was gone? Not her fiancé, not now, not anymore, that was certain. What would life be without him? Nothing, that's what it would be, absolutely nothing.

Then, suddenly, in the distance, over the sad, melancholy music, she thought she heard a sound. Was it him?

The doorbell rang. Just once at first, then again, repeatedly.

She looked up, weak, exhausted. Could it be him?

Had he changed his mind? Did he want her back? Could she take him back? Was he still her one and only?

She tried to stand. Perhaps she would have her answer when she saw him face to face, when she gazed upon his manly features and lost herself in his eyes.

Filled with hope, she felt sure she could forgive him. Yes, she wanted love and romance again! She wanted to be a wife, his wife! She just wanted him.

But her legs gave way beneath her for they were drained of all strength, and she fell helplessly back into her chair as another empty bottle of pills fell to the floor and rolled away.

Was it too late? Was she drifting away?

Her heart filled with the lost hope and despair of many an actress from an old movie. She tried to reach a hand towards the door where she imagined he was waiting penitent on bended knee, with flowers, chocolates, and pretty trinkets just for her.

But it was too late and she knew it. She felt it. The energy and the soul were draining from her limp, little body.

As the doorbell continued to ring, the sound inside her head grew ever fainter.

The music began to blur and swish, like the last dregs of water disappearing down a plughole, chewed up like an old cassette tape nobody wanted to listen to anymore.

It was him. It was absolutely and most definitely him. He was back. He wanted her back. He needed her. She knew it.

Out of view, he shouted to her. "I'm so sorry, my darling. I love you. Please take me back."

But as she drifted further and further away, his distant words became inaudible.

"Please marry me," he continued to say. "Just as we planned. Oh, please say you will."

She wanted to say she would, she really did, but she could barely move. She could barely speak. She had so little strength left. The end was all she could hear now, and it was whispering her name.

She made one final effort to stand and make her way towards him but she was unable to hold herself up. This time when she fell, she fell heavily to the floor amongst the torn-up petals and stalks.

This woman's work was all but done. With her dying breath she announced: "He loves me..."

Then the sad song stopped playing and silence reigned, and Wendy WolfWhistle lay motionless on the floor.

And, to the untrained eye, she was quite dead.

CHAPTER 03
That same evening - late October

Rather awkwardly, Oliver stood behind the bar at The Old Queen's Jugs cabaret bar, previously known as The Old Maiden's Jugs, on the corner of East Green Street. He tutted loudly, shaking his head as he watched Wendy WolfWhistle pick herself up from off the stage floor and stand tall and proud in her damaged wedding dress.

Amongst the ripped-up flowers and the ruined cake, she bowed and curtsied to the appreciative audience who had very much enjoyed her opening number, which she referred to as her rendition of the *Dying Swan*.

She had originally wanted to perform a ballet whilst wearing a crisp-white tutu that had once belonged to that woman who had named herself after a meringue-based pudding, but a line had to be drawn somewhere. Particularly after she had suggested the compulsory bun in her hair should be edible, so it could be eaten between performances.

Oliver continued to shake his head in disbelief as the crowd applauded and cheered her debut performance. Throughout the ruckus, she bent down to pick up handfuls of petals and threw them all over herself as if it were confetti.

Well, it was her wedding day, after all.

Seriously, had there not been enough death already without seeing it acted out on stage in front of him and around fifty other people, most of whom had forgotten about Jake and all that had happened to him.

Still, it wasn't about what he did or did not want to see, it was about the punters and they were getting their money's worth on the opening night of their town's latest and best gay and drag queen hangout. Whilst the venue was heaving from corner to corset, Oliver felt very out of place serving behind that bar and had never felt so lonely, even during any other day following Jake's demise that summer.

He would have hated it even more had he known Wendy was drawing on what she perceived to be Oliver's real-life emotions just to enhance her own performance. But, if nothing else, the audience and the restless tongues had loved it, and had remained silent throughout as Wendy played the jilted bride with a broken heart, delivering the best performance of her career thus far.

Martin Woodward, previously known as drag queen Miss Sugar Daddy and now the proud owner of this new cabaret bar, joined her on the stage and encouraged the audience to give her one final round of applause, which they were more than willing to do.

After all, she deserved it.

As Wendy took a final bow, she grabbed once more at the petals around her feet, threw them into the air and over her grateful audience before departing the stage for a costume change in the luxury of her very own dressing room.

At long last she had made it! She was a star! And if she could make it there then she could make it anywhere. Suddenly, poor deluded Wendy WolfWhistle was once again having dreams and expectations far beyond her own limited capabilities.

For the punters there that night, the restless tongues too, it had been weeks since Divas Cabaret Bar and its controversy had burnt down. Thankfully, the drag queens and the cabaret were back in their lives along with a sparkling new venue right on their doorsteps. Many of them lived in the Eastern Quarter, on or around East Green Street, and had been waiting patiently for this night to arrive ever since the posters had gone up telling them what would soon be coming to this former straight man's pub, which they had never before contemplated entering.

Whilst Wendy *untucked* backstage hoping television's favourite psychic drag queen, Miss April Showers, would say something extraordinarily wonderful just for her on the evening news, Martin stood proudly on stage with a microphone in his hand - just as he had seen Chris Randall do at Divas Cabaret Bar many times before.

He faced the ecstatic audience as the stage curtains closed behind him. For once, all eyes were on him. Oh, how he hoped he could maintain the momentum, his composure, his confidence. For once, he felt important and like he was needed in this exciting new venture. He had finally made a good decision.

He was no longer invisible to the entire world, although it wasn't easy knowing what he knew.

Martin found it hard keeping so many secrets, desperately hoping nobody suspected things were not as they seemed.

He couldn't help but wonder if everybody was questioning his every move and he spent his time worrying he might accidentally reveal the truth at any moment.

He was forever watching his back and his front, not knowing who or what might be coming around the next corner.

Martin had been suspended from police duty shortly after the Divas Cabaret Bar fire but in some ways it had come as a welcome relief to him. It had given him time to complete the sale of his late mother's house and to get this cabaret bar up and running, both of which were challenging and time consuming tasks.

But the truth of the matter was he had screwed up big time and he might never be able to step back into any part of his former life again, should he wish to do so. He had little choice but to make a bloody good go of this just in case it was his only remaining option... providing, of course, his many undisclosed secrets would permit him to.

Oh crap! Had he locked his office door before stepping out on to the stage? Nosey staff and prying eyes had the potential to cause him real problems, even if they seemed perfectly innocent, and he had to remain vigilant because this was his life now and it was one he really wanted, really needed. But the truth would out sooner or later, it always did, and it would undoubtedly have a huge impact on everyone in that town.

As soon as he got off that stage he would have to check his office door was firmly locked. He was sure it would be because it always was but this was becoming something of an obsessive compulsive habit for him, bordering on paranoia. But nobody – not a single living soul - could find out what he knew or what secrets he was keeping in there.

As he stood proudly on the stage in his smart new suit with the microphone in his hand, hosting the show, he couldn't help but wonder if this was all just another mask he was hiding behind.

Suddenly, he felt like a fake and a fraud, like he had no right to be hosting the show.

And yet the audience seemed to have no idea. They just listened to him and followed his lead, giving Wendy a further round of applause before she reluctantly left the stage purely because he had asked them to!

They had heard him.

God! What else might they have heard?

He always knew the restless tongues would be problematic for him, as they openly spread their poison and happily whispered their gossip at anyone daft enough to listen. Just as Chris Randall had been a sitting duck for their idle chatter, he was, without a doubt, their next target.

Oh, the paranoia of a troubled man!

Was this really how Chris Randall had felt night after night, trying to make a success of his cabaret bar whilst battling his demons and juggling the other pressures that came with the role? Although, when Martin had been a paying customer there, he had never truly appreciated how much was involved in making the place a success. From his perspective he had worked hard all week, deserved a fun night out, and expected Chris to pull out all the stops to make sure that happened.

Was that his role now, his responsibility? Was this a fun night out for everyone who had worked hard all week? Was everybody enjoying themselves? Had Wendy's *Dying Swan* act been more successful than he had expected? Was he a success too?

He glanced over to the bar staff who seemed relieved to have a moment of grace whilst the attention was drawn away from them, towards the stage. He couldn't help but notice how ill at ease Oliver looked... at least he wasn't on his own in feeling that way, then!

Martin had strongly believed this was not the right environment for Oliver to be in but, nevertheless had felt it safer to give him a part time job behind the bar so he could at least keep an eye on the younger man.

Wayne, the former landlord of the pub in its previous incarnation, was head barman and, unlike Oliver, seemed completely at ease with serving drinks and undertaking the other tasks that came with running the bar.

Wendy and Martin had been clueless about running a venue like this but Wayne had all the necessary expertise and knowledge they needed along with a very open mind. Plus, Wendy had had nothing but positive things to say about him when it had been suggested that he stay on there.

Wayne had needed to move out of his home above the pub because it was no longer his business and he had done so without a word or a single emotion crossing his face. It was entirely unknown how he had felt about any of the changes that had befallen him. Maybe he was relieved, although that was unlikely because his own business venture had failed. At least he could still make ends meet with a fixed income each month.

Martin, still holding the microphone in his trembling hand, pushed his reservations aside and addressed the audience once more. "Welcome to the grand opening of The Old Queen's Jugs," he said, and as the words came tumbling out his confidence grew. "It is wonderful to see so many of you here with us this evening, on our opening night. In a short while we will have more amazing cabaret for you but before that let me tell you about next weekend's charity masked Halloween ball. Tickets are available now from behind the bar, and it would be great to see you there."

"Are the rumours true?" shouted a loud voice in the crowd, one of the restless tongues.

Martin began to fear the worst. "Rumours?" he almost whispered back, dreading the response that might come back. What did they know? What did they think they knew?

"About the special guest appearances?" explained the same loud voice in the crowd.

"I reckon it is," replied his friend. "I hope so anyway."

Martin breathed a sigh of relief, gasped it almost. The audience must have heard him. "Yes," he replied, with new found confidence. "The rumours are true. Alongside our very own cabaret acts, there will also be special guest appearances by mother and daughter drag queens, Phero-Moan and Whore-Moan. It's going to be an amazing evening… you won't want to miss it!"

Turning off his microphone, Martin left the stage as the sound of pop music filled the venue and the punters returned to their drinks and discussions in their own little clusters.

Phew! He was relieved, partly because that was over but mostly because he could now check his office door was locked: it was.

He really did need to stop worrying about it so much.

But not on opening night.

Not when there were so many things he needed to keep under control.

But if he did stop worrying about it or became distracted by other things would that be when he accidentally left it unlocked?

Leaving the secrets hidden within to be revealed?

CHAPTER 04
That same evening

Naturally, everybody had an opinion on what Martin had just said, especially about the forthcoming special guest appearances.

"Oh, I just love Phero-Moan and Whore-Moan," a restless tongue announced, whilst nursing an empty wine glass which he hoped somebody would offer to refill for him. "I saw them last year and they were hysterical. They really should be on the telly."

"Unlike that useless psychic drag queen. Talk about generic... oooh, I can see a marriage proposal for a woman in love, and someone will celebrate a birthday soon."

"Hmmm," muttered another restless tongue keen to take the conversation back to the forthcoming drag act. "Well, I've heard they're not that good anymore. My ex saw them recently. He said they were trying out some new material and it was utter rubbish. In fact, he said the whole show was shite."

"And which ex was this?" asked Empty Wine Glass. "The one who stole from you or the one who slept with your hot cousin at your grandmother's funeral? Either way, I wouldn't trust anything they might say."

"Well, as you know," butted in another, who had an unfortunate tuft of hair sticking up at the back which nobody had told him to correct, "I'm not one to gossip or pass judgement..."

"None of us is," announced Unfortunate History of Ex-Boyfriends.

"...But I reckon it's about time the daughter, Whore-Moan, went solo. She's so much better than the older one."

"Well," announced Empty Wine Glass, finally putting it down onto a nearby table, much to the annoyance of the people sitting there, "it's going to be a great night out, probably way better than anything we ever saw at Divas Cabaret Bar."

"Oh yes, particularly towards the end," agreed Hair Tuft, also putting down his empty glass at the same table and making its occupants pout tighter than a ferret's arse. "I still don't know what Chris Randall was thinking putting that Connie into the lead role like that. She was no Tittie Mansag, after all."

"Oh, wasn't she awful," commented another restless tongue who had just returned from the bar with a tray of drinks, which were snatched up by the others with little gratitude or grace. "Well, it's just nice to have some normality back in our lives again. I was getting sick of going to that lesbian bar down the road from Divas. There was never any talent to look at in there."

"Do you know," interjected Hair Tuft, "I can't help but wonder what happened to that Connie. She just disappeared without a trace."

"Yes, and Tittie did too."

"You don't think Chris Randall killed them as well, do you?"

"As you all know, I'm not one to gossip or make judgements about anybody..."

"None of us is."

"...But I wouldn't put anything past him."

That they all agreed on. They clinked their glasses together, wishing they had some way of finding out for certain.

"Now," said no longer Empty Wine Glass, "why do we think Oliver has chosen to work behind the bar?"

At the bar, Oliver had seen them gossiping away and knew exactly what they were up to: bad mouthing people, not caring about anybody but themselves, and then questioning at the end of the night why they were still single. But Oliver had no time to think about them because a group of lads arrived at the bar with a large drinks order which he set to work filling.

As he was pulling a pint the barrel ran dry, with the few remaining drips spluttering noisily out of the beer tap and into the partially filled glass. "Wayne," he said, "the lager has gone. Can you change it for me please?"

"I'm really busy over here," he responded, slightly stressed, for he was not used to serving this volume of people, so quickly. "Can't you do it?"

"I don't know how to."

Wayne knew Oliver did know how to because he had shown him several times already, and he quickly reminded him of that. Oliver shrugged his shoulders and looked slightly uncomfortable about it.

"Oh, for goodness sake!" exclaimed Wayne, putting down the glass he was filling. "Why don't I just do everything?"

"I'm sorry," muttered Oliver. "I just need some help."

But the truth was he hated going down into the creepy, dark, damp cellar below the pub which stretched out like a labyrinth of lost hope, deep beneath the ground. The sense of foreboding that so openly presented itself to whomever set foot down there had a particularly intense impact on Oliver. It genuinely felt to him as though something bad had happened down there, or that it would at any moment.

Wayne looked out across the room at all the punters they had already served, who would soon be heading back for refills. He shook his head in despair and then said: "This place is seriously going to be the death of me."

He then paused, realising what he had just said out loud to Oliver. "Sorry, I didn't mean to say that word in front of you."

"It's okay," said Oliver, "What happened to Jake was an absolute tragedy but it happened. You can't sensor everything you say just because I'm around."

"But Martin said I wasn't to say anything that might remind you of Jake."

"Wayne, honestly, it's okay. I can't ignore it forever and I don't want to forget about him."

Wayne nodded sympathetically and willingly headed towards the cellar to change the lager barrel, hoping it might help make him feel better. Oliver knew he had to take his head out of the sand and begin to address what had happened, maybe even try to move on from it. If only he could find that extra strength he needed to start living again. He couldn't even imagine how his heart might begin to heal.

Once the lager was flowing again and the group of lads had been served, they picked up their drinks from the bar and moved out of the way. Their departure left a gap that allowed Oliver to see across to the seating area on the opposite wall. Sitting there staring at him was a stranger who immediately looked away as soon as he realised he had been spotted by the very person he was looking at.

Oliver was unsettled by this, agitated even, but it went with the territory of working in a place like this. Customers stared at the barmen, it was a fact; lusted after them, probably fantasised about them too. Heaven knows he had done just that to Jake many times before, whilst he had been at Divas Cabaret Bar.

He found himself thinking about Jake and, for a moment, he felt happy then sad as waves of grief engulfed him once more. Reality bit hard.

He looked at the stranger he thought had been staring at him but did not notice anything particularly significant about him. Possibly because he was wearing a cap pulled down low with his hair brushed forward to cover his face. His body language seemed closed but Oliver had only caught this man staring at him for a moment, so perhaps the situation had been misinterpreted. It very much seemed he didn't want people to see him clearly or to approach him.

Still feeling uncomfortable by this person's presence, Oliver turned to Wayne and gestured discreetly towards the stranger. "When did he come in?" he whispered quietly to him.

"Why, do you fancy your chances?"

"No, not at all, there's just something about him that's bothering me. I caught him staring at me. At least I think he was."

"Leave it to me," said Wayne, picking up a wet cloth from underneath the bar. "I'll clear some tables around him and see what I can find out for you. Believe me, if somebody is after you, I'll be the first to know about it."

Oliver watched as Wayne meandered through the crowd towards the stranger. He stopped to wipe down the table nearest to him and then returned to the bar with the empty glasses left by the restless tongues.

"Well, I said hello to him," explained Wayne, putting the used glasses on the countertop, "but he was quite unresponsive. I told him I was Wayne but he just mumbled back at me. I think he said his name was Jay, or something that sounded like Jay, but that was about it."

"Jay?" questioned Oliver, and without a moment's hesitation asked Wayne if he might have said Jake.

"He could have said Jake," replied Wayne, shrugging it off.

But Oliver was no longer listening.

Inquisitively, he looked back to where the stranger had been sitting to check if it could possibly be Jake. After all, the hair, which was now pulled forward and covered his face, could have grown since the last time he had run his fingers lovingly through it.

But Jay, or whatever he was called, was not there.

No, it couldn't have been Jake, could it? Surely, he would have recognised him. Jake would not have ignored him. He'd have come over to the bar and spoken to him, wouldn't he?

Jesus, what the hell was he thinking?

How on earth could it have been Jake sitting there, staring silently, looking so different from how he remembered him?

It was impossible, and he knew it.

Because Jake was dead, right?

Killed at the roadside, on East Green Street, right outside his first-floor apartment, right?

CHAPTER 05
Later that evening

Martin, now with a much calmer demeanour, stood on the stage once more and addressed the crowd of eager faces staring back at him. "Well, if you've enjoyed yourselves so far," he said, "then believe me, you haven't seen anything yet! Please welcome on stage, for the very first time tonight, and for the first time since her recovery, in her grand debut performance... you all know her and you all love her... our very own Miss Tequila ShockingBird!

The music started and Tequila, looking much healthier after being carried virtually lifeless from the Divas Cabaret Bar fire, appeared on stage amongst a haze of shimmery smoke which quickly faded away.

Most, if not everybody there, had observed neither sight nor sound of Tequila since that fateful night, and it was rumoured she had probably died.

Fortunately, and thanks to a combination of the relentless efforts of her father, Wendy WolfWhistle, and the incredible skills of the paramedics, she had made a full recovery in hospital as her male alter ego, James.

Now here she was back in drag as Tequila and back on stage where she belonged; beautifully ethereal like an angel, a shining vision in silver from head to toe, looking more radiant than ever before. Finally headlining the show, and she was more than ready for her close up.

Admittedly, she was sharing the spotlight with Father Wendy but it was she, Tequila, who was the more talented dancer and singer, wafer thin, the eye candy of the show. This was her moment, and she planned to relish every second of it.

♫ I'm ready for my close up
I'm ready to be swarmed by all the boys
If you want a taste of honey
Then you'd better have the money
Cos my best things in life don't come for free ♫

She couldn't help but stare at the crowd and smile widely to herself. This was exactly what she wanted, had always wanted: to be the star of the show and to feel these obscene moments of pure self-obsession, self-adoration, and self-indulgence.

She knew she looked utterly stunning in her outfit and she loved that she was the absolute centre of attention. In this moment, she was their whole world and she was sitting right on top, looking down upon them, all the power in her hands. Nearly losing her life had temporarily changed Tequila's priorities but, now she was fully recovered, she remembered how much she had missed this feeling.

As she performed nobody drank and nobody spoke. Spellbound, the hungry audience barely dared breathe in case the respiration disturbed the new drag queen goddess of their world.

♫ I'm bitching with my best girls
We're hanging out with all the mighty fines
If you think that you can buy me
Then I reckon you should try me
But if you can't, then get out of my way

That's right, tonight...
If you can't then get out of my way ♫

My god, this was amazing! Self-gratification had never felt so good. And to think Chris Randall had promised her all this at Divas Cabaret Bar but had never delivered.

In hindsight, she felt foolish ever to have believed he would. Thankfully, she had never stepped in too deep where he was concerned, and she had certainly never done anything that would compromise her or make its way back to her... right?

No, Chris Randall had never given her anything like this. Just like him, his words were fake, meaningless, and now firmly locked away.

Earlier that year, she had been willing to pay any price for the success she craved but a price had never been set. She thought perhaps it was almost losing her life because she didn't yet know the actual cost would soon be revealed.

Time would tell, and far more quickly than she ever could have imagined.

♫ *Cos sex sells, sex sells*
You can use me and abuse me
If you can flash the cash
Cos sex sells, sex sells ♫

She couldn't wait for the musical bridge to come after the third verse, when she knew the audience would go wild. As Martin had promised, they had not seen anything yet!

Then they would demand more from her. No, not demand more... beg for it. She intended to enjoy every single moment of her grand debut performance at The Old Queen's Jugs because she would not get another one there.

To think she had had almost died and missed out on all this! What a waste that would have been!

But that wasn't worth thinking about now because she intended to live forever.

♫ *New age wealth is so obscene*
But Baby, that's my dream ♫

Ha, screw you, Chris Randall, and your new age wealth. I hope you rot in hell, or wherever it is you've been dragged to.

Oh wow, there really was no better feeling than this.

Divas very own Miss Connie Lingus, or whatever it was she went on to call herself - Connie Luscious, perhaps? - had been the inspiration for this sexy little number.

Momentarily, Tequila couldn't help but wonder what had happened to that sex selling, drug taking, talentless witch who, for whatever reason, thought she could be the lead in a cabaret show.

Oh, who cared! Connie's reign was well and truly over. She, and all those who had so willingly sailed in her, could also rot in whatever hell they had slunk off to.

She had never really liked Connie much or felt she needed her in her life but then again she had previously thought the same about Father Wendy…

♫ *I want to call my agent*
I must insist all my demands are met
If you're freaking with me, Baby
Then I'm tweaking with you, maybe
I'm wreaking havoc everywhere I go

That's right, tonight...

I'm wreaking havoc everywhere I go

Cos sex sells, sex sells 🎵

Okay, so discovering Wendy WolfWhistle was her father had been far from ideal but she had really stepped up to the role not only by saving her life but also by being there for her throughout the recovery period. If that was not enough, Wendy had provided a place for Tequila to live, upstairs at the new cabaret bar, and a joint-headlining role in their new cabaret show, even allowing Tequila a lot of creative input into designing it.

Whilst Wendy remained the overweight, hairy, middle-aged, deluded, gender fluid (possibly), non-binary (possibly) drag queen who had abandoned him shortly after he was born so he could live the rest of his life in a dress, this definitely went some way towards making up for it.

Fickle and hungry for the spotlight Tequila most definitely was; vengeful and angry, not so much... not anymore.

Although the box-sized bedroom into which Tequila could barely fit was not her preferred choice, at least she and Father Wendy had a reasonably nice place to live in, together, alongside Martin who had understandably taken the biggest of the three available bedrooms for himself. It was certainly better than being homeless anyway, being hounded by all those horrible people to whom she owed money, including that hideous loan shark in the Northern Territory. Although any one of them could still be looking for her male alter ago, James, who had run up the debts. If only they knew where he was and that he hid behind a mask called Tequila ShockingBird.

Maybe some of them did know.

Still, at least it was comfortable and warm, and a tiny bed and a tiny wardrobe were always better options than sleeping backstage at Divas Cabaret Bar, or in that awful hospital bed with those tubes and machines and things attached to him.

But at that moment it was all about Tequila; her male alter-ego, James, might as well not have existed. All eyes had remained on her throughout and now the musical bridge, which she was longing to get to, was just about to follow the third verse.

♫ *I need a cash advancement*
I need more money than we first agreed
Now that I'm the superstar
Who the hell do you think you are?
Cos I'm the best you're ever gonna get

I'm the best you're ever gonna get... ♫

Without warning, the doors of The Old Queen's Jugs cabaret bar burst open quicker than the buttons on Wendy WolfWhistle's polyester blouse when she forgot to breathe in for a moment.

Then four burly policemen in perfectly fitted trousers with very handsome faces stormed in in quick succession, knocking over drinks, tables, and the occasional gay man who had been unable to move out of their way in time, or who had hastily stood up hoping to be frisked.

The audience was mostly amused by this, with the exception of those who had had drinks spilt over them or who had been knocked down - although the sight of one good looking guy in a police uniform after another more than made up for it.

Tequila remained on the stage trying to make out what was going on but the bright lights dazzled her, obscuring her view.

The backing track continued to play but was inaudible over the loud, heavy thuds of large, manly work boots on the wooden floor underfoot.

The first policeman reached the stage. "James Taylor, also known as Miss Tequila ShockingBird?" he asked the drag queen who stood tall in front of him.

"Yes," she replied nervously, shielding her eyes from the blinding stage lights with her hand so she could see him more clearly.

"I am arresting you on suspicion of selling illegal substances at Divas Cabaret Bar this summer. You do not have to say anything, but it may harm your defence if you do not mention when questioned something you later rely on in court. Anything you do say may be given in evidence."

Tequila stood motionless whilst she was surrounded and handcuffed by the officers. Still in full drag, she was ushered off stage through the shocked and surprised crowd. This was not the close-up she had been hoping for.

"What's going on? What are you doing?" screamed Wendy, running onto the stage in an over-stretched leotard which she had clearly not tucked herself into properly. She catapulted herself onto the wooden floor below and fell head over tit as one of her ill-fitting high heels buckled inwards under her weight. Her wig, in tragically predictable Wendy fashion, flew off her head and landed several feet away.

Bald, helpless, and legs akimbo, Wendy lay sprawled across the floor reaching out for her son but grabbing nothing but air and dust. She watched powerlessly as Tequila, the son she had helped nurse back to health, was led away by the police, out of the venue and out of sight.

Had there been a puddle of spilt beer underneath Wendy's over-sized man frame, it would have been just like the old days back at Divas Cabaret Bar.

The confused audience looked at each other and then burst into a huge round of applause and cheers. Wow, what a fantastic show this was turning out to be.

What an amazing opening night!

Their expectations had been more than met or even exceeded: they had been smashed! Watch and learn Chris Randall because this place was already so much better than your drag queen cabaret bar ever was! Some of them couldn't wait to personally congratulate Tequila on her literally show-stopping debut performance when she returned, hopefully with the uniformed policemen in tow.

Endless selfies would be requested and socials would be plastered with messages of her success, littered with hastily invented hash tags such as *#Tequila-Riffic,* *#Fabulicious* and *#WhyTheHellArentYouHere?*

Back in the office on Monday morning, everybody would say what a great night out it had been! What a show! And what a pity the people they were telling hadn't been there to witness it for themselves.

Some were posting messages about the four hot policemen strippers who would soon be back, with their truncheons and handcuffs on display for all to see – and hopefully touch! They wanted nothing more than to be very bad boys so they too might get arrested and towed off in their manly grasp.

Because that's what they thought had happened; they had no idea it was not part of a cleverly constructed act.

In actual fact, the policemen were not strippers and, just like Tequila, they would not be returning because this was about as real-life as things could get.

It could not have been any further removed from the version of events that should have unfolded during the musical bridge after the third verse.

And Tequila was in way too deep.

CHAPTER 06
Mid-August

The door to his prison cell burst open and a tall, mildly attractive prison officer with a seventies porn-star inspired moustache ushered Chris out.

"Randall. Visitor," were the only words he offered to justify his presence there.

Chris was unsurprised as he had personally orchestrated this visit from within his four walls; he had waited patiently for this visitor to arrive because this guest was a key player in his plan to survive, to re-emerge on top. He fully intended to manipulate this person as much as possible and make them jump through every hoop he held up.

This meeting was a small part of a much bigger plan that would require careful directing. He knew he could make it work, and he would make it work. It wasn't as though there was much else for him to do in there other than think and plot, and there were plenty of people out there who had either wronged him or had tried. He would have his revenge on each and every one of them, beginning in that very moment. He would make them suffer.

One by one, he would judge them all under the Law of Randall and dispense punishment.

Line up the soldiers and shoot them all down!

Unfortunately, this could apply to every person Chris had ever met, although some had behaved more heinously than others.

But they would each get their comeuppance when the time was right.

Nobody would be exempt. Exceptional circumstances would not apply.

Chris followed Moustache to the visitor's room, one security door after another opening with just a quick flash of a smart card against an electronic wall-mounted device.

Hmmm... that was easy.

Hmmm… just imagine the advantage he would have if he could get his hands on one of those cards. Rumours were rife there were already some in circulation amongst the prisoners but that was just hearsay and pretty unlikely. But not altogether impossible.

Chris spotted his visitor before he saw him arrive; it was easy because the reluctant guest had his head down as though he did not want to be seen and was trying to hide from the world. They certainly did not appear to want to be there and looked apprehensive as if dreading what might be said, fearful of what might be asked of them, terrified of what the outcome might be.

But they had played a dangerous game before and couldn't expect the rules to change now, just to suit them. Not now they had shifted to the opposing team.

Chris sat down opposite him at the small wooden table and smiled politely. "Good to see you again," he said to his visitor. "Perhaps less so from your perspective. And if I'm being honest, it's not good to see you at all but here we are, nevertheless."

His visitor shifted uncomfortably in his chair whilst seeking out anything to look at other than the cruel, cold person sitting in front of him, whom he despised.

If Chris's visitor had believed he had any choice in being there, he would never have come. But, sadly, he had little choice other than to obey the commands of his new leader because a debt was owed, and Chris was calling in payment. He desperately hoped he could afford the price and could live with the consequences.

So here he was, face to face with Chris Randall who held the winning hand yet again: a victorious royal flush compared to his pathetic low ace. In fact, Chris held all the cards and each one, like those within a tarot pack, would foretell a future. One card for each person who had worked against him or had helped him survive when he needed it the most.

The Death card.

The Wish card.

The Tower of Destruction.

But who would be presented with the most impactful card of all: the Queen of Broken Hearts?

"So, what do you want, Chris?" his visitor asked him.

He was visibly anxious about being there, temporarily trapped within those four walls, and hoped that a hasty conversation might bring this secret rendezvous to an abrupt and speedy end.

Their eyes met once more and Chris held his stare for as long as possible, burrowing right into the windows of his visitor's soul with his cold stare, freezing him from the inside out until the person facing him could bear it no longer.

Chris wanted his unwilling companion to know this was not a social visit; he meant business.

His visitor was painfully aware.

Chris remained silent and folded his arms, creating further hostility. His eyes alone communicated what needed to be said far more clearly than words could ever have achieved.

As he had suspected, his visitor couldn't bring himself to look at him and tried to distract himself by directing his gaze around the room and paying way too much attention to mundane objects, like a notice board with no notices posted and the unwelcoming interior design like a cobweb on a wall-mounted light fitting slightly to the left of where Chris was sitting; anything to avoid looking at his host.

"You want to know why I asked you here?"

"You hardly asked me here, did you?" replied his visitor, staring momentarily at Chris's chin as it seemed the benign place to focus; within seconds, his gaze had returned to the noticeless notice board.

"You can't even look at me, can you?"

"Of course I can't!" he replied. "Why would I want to?"

"You need to remember I know what you've done."

Unconvincingly, his visitor tried to shrug it off. In a way this was not the worst thing. The nightmares and the restless nights which drowned out what should be sweet, much needed sleep were much worse.

The inescapable dread of the past catching up with him was far worse; the paranoid certainty that Chris would find him one day, probably soon.

No, this, being here now and waiting to learn his destiny was not the worst thing; in fact, it was almost a relief to be getting the inevitable out of the way. He had always known Chris would bide his time, summoning him when he was ready. He just hadn't expected it to be quite so soon.

"And what exactly do you know?" asked his visitor.

After all, he could be bluffing, chancing his hand.

"I know you screwed me over," he replied, calmly. "And I also know you have something I want."

His visitor stared at the ground, studying his own footwear… the table legs… the hard, faded red plastic chair he was perched upon.

"Want me to elaborate on either of those things?" said Chris.

"No," he responded quietly.

"I didn't think so," Chris smirked. "You messed with me and this is what we are going to do about it." His visitor listened to every word and did not like anything that was said.

"No," he bravely responded once Chris had finished his well-prepared and overly rehearsed speech.

Chris stared back at him coolly, once more holding his gaze. He had fully expected this kind of pushback but knew it was not an outcome he would accept.

Chris always got what he wanted, and he knew this time would be no exception.

"No," responded his visitor again, trying to sound firm.

Chris glared back at him, his silence, once more, speaking volumes. He folded his arms again, tighter than before and repeated his demands. His visitor had something he wanted and he was going to get it.

"Let's suppose I agree to this..."

"Which you will," interrupted Chris.

"What do I get in return?"

"This may just go away for you. I may even go away for you too. Wouldn't you like that?"

His visitor sat silently for a few moments thinking about it and trying his hardest to look Chris in the eyes. If he could look deep into this monster's soul perhaps he could find the strength to do what was being asked of him, particularly if it meant finally being free of his debt.

He nodded his agreement. It was worth a try if he could walk away from Chris Randall forever.

"Well, it has been a pleasure," said Chris once their conversation was over.

He stood up and neatly tucked his chair underneath the table. Anything that made him look good in the eyes of the prison officers was a bonus for him.

He continued to speak: "Now if you'll excuse me, I want to get back to my guest accommodation as I have lots to do. I'll be in touch again soon."

His visitor stared back at him dejected, beaten, and utterly broken.

He watched the man with no moral compass leave the room knowing all the while he was about to lose everything that was dear to him, furious at how easily Chris had been able to take it all away from him.

Damn him! This world would be a much better place without the likes of Chris Randall in it.

Seriously, who would miss him, the obnoxious, twisted scumbag who ruined everyone and everything he ever came into contact with?

Seriously, why couldn't somebody just come along and shoot him down?

Why the hell couldn't Chris Randall be dealt a wretched hand for a change!

CHAPTER 07
Late October

It was a couple of days after the grand opening night when Oliver felt he was ready to start facing his past. He knew he would need to sooner or later and this day seemed as good a time as any.

He had tried so hard to put everything that had happened that summer to the back of his mind but keeping it bottled up inside him was not healthy, and it was affecting him every day, deeply.

He needed to release some of the pent-up tension within him and desperately needed closure, although that seemed a long way off yet.

He locked the front door to his one-bedroom apartment, which he had almost given up and had briefly shared with Jake for just a few days that summer, left the building behind and headed off along East Green Street. As he walked, he zipped up his jacket against the chilly autumnal weather and pulled up his collar.

This time, he headed in the opposite direction from The Old Queen's Jugs Cabaret Bar. His destination was the other end of town, the part nobody seemed to visit anymore because, since Divas Cabaret Bar had burnt down, there was little reason to go that way. But that was precisely where he was going.

He needed to see the building again or at least what was left of it. He needed to stand outside and remember what had happened.

Maybe some good memories would return, although he doubted it. Whatever might happen, he felt ready to face his demons and everything seeing that place again would bring.

He had not been back there since that terrible night when so much damage had been done and he needed to clear his mind. He needed to address the thoughts that were eating away at him, that haunted his dreams at night. He needed to allow hope into his heart once more so he could start to heal and begin to move on.

He had stopped to look at the section of road where Jake had been knocked over and killed, he always did. Every time he passed it, he vowed he would not look again but it was inevitable; he always looked. He always would. Ultimately, it was a memory of their time together albeit their very last one. And although it was a morbid event, it would never outweigh the memory of the love they once shared.

Oliver had tied a ribbon around the lamp post near to where Jake had been struck to secure the flowers he had left in honour of his one true love.

Of course, the flowers had long since gone but the ribbon remained.

It had been hard not going to the funeral, even harder not knowing where it had been held, or where Jake's body now lay, or even where his ashes may have been scattered.

He would have liked to be included.

He had waited in that hospital for so bloody long only to be told nothing.

He hadn't been able to see him.

Per police instruction, he had been denied entry beyond the pale blue chairs in the waiting room.

He recalled the overpowering smell of disinfectant, the old magazines which brought very little comfort or distraction, and the fake plants with the realistic dead bits.

Eventually, Martin had spoken to him and explained in minimal detail that Jake's family had been contacted and, at their request, the body had been appointed to their care. They finally had their son back even if he was no longer breathing.

The funeral was to be held where they lived and it would be for immediate family members only. Alas, Oliver did not know where they lived for Jake had rarely spoken about the family he had left behind.

Martin explained he had told Jake's family about his relationship with Oliver but they were not interested. His birth mother, like the rest of the family, was too distraught to listen. Their darling son, Jake, was dead and that's all they heard. They did not want to learn any more. They could not accommodate anybody else's emotions and grief on top of their own.

Perhaps if circumstances had been different they might have listened.

Perhaps if they had known how deep and pure their love for each other had been they would have let him be a part of it. But he had been left out, disregarded, and Jake been taken away from him again. And he was utterly powerless to do anything about it.

So, all that remained of Jake for Oliver was that ribbon tied around a lamp post, on which he had written his farewell message: 'Always be with me'.

It was no way to say goodbye to the wonderful, beautiful man he had planned to spend the rest of his life with and, as he walked towards the other end of town, his heart felt heavy and he blinked away persistent tears.

How would he ever get over this?

If anybody had cared enough to stop him and ask if he was okay, he would have told them the cold autumn breeze was blowing directly into his face making his eyes water.

Not that anyone would have stopped to ask. It had been weeks since it had happened, an entire season ago, and nobody in that godforsaken town ever asked if he was okay anymore; his mood seemed constantly dark to them, and he was probably best avoided.

He had constructed a wall around himself where once there had been love. His emotions were erratic and he was furious, angry at the world, at the system, the police, the hospital, and everybody else who had stood in his way or who simply dared to be happy and live their lives in front of him.

He was mad at Jake's family but most of all with Chris Randall. How he hoped their paths would never cross again.

He thought about working behind the bar at The Old Queen's Jugs. In all honesty he had not wanted to. He had only recently returned to his day job after an extended period of compassionate leave, which he knew he had been lucky to get as he had not been there that long. But Martin had asked him numerous times and eventually convinced him it might help him move on.

Somehow, being behind a bar serving drinks, clearing tables, and washing glasses did seem to make him feel that little bit closer to Jake. But he was still so isolated from everything else.

He passed the lesbian bar situated just down the road from where Divas had stood, less busy now a new venue had opened but guaranteed a dedicated supply of loyal regulars.

Ahead, he saw the canopy of the run-down, tired-looking newsagents and he remembered how he had once stood underneath it whilst he summoned up the courage to go inside Divas for that very first time. Oh, how different his life could have been if he had listened to his gut instinct that evening and stayed away, well away.

Perhaps Jake would still be alive. Probably still standing behind that bar with the weight of the world on his shoulders, counting down the hours until his shift finished for the evening.

Perhaps Chris Randall would still be roaming the streets of their town, hunting for his next great opportunity, seeking out the next innocent face to manipulate and scar for life.

Finally, he allowed his eyes to rest upon where Divas Cabaret Bar had stood, now covered with scaffolding and enclosed by wooden barriers as repairs had commenced to fix the damage and make it safe once more.

Higher up, there was clear evidence of the fire: bricks discoloured from the filthy smoke, windows smashed from the searing heat. It really was just a shell of its former self but, then again, so was Oliver.

He remembered Martin holding open the door for him and then later trying to make a play for him once he had eventually made his way inside.

Why did he ever go back that evening and fall in love with the place?

He remembered how he had stayed behind for late night drinks with Chris at a table set for two, even though he hadn't wanted to.

To welcome him into their family, Chris had said. But that had been a lie and just another one of his games.

He remembered the desperation in Jake's voice as he had asked him to meet with Chris. He remembered nodding through his reluctance, wondering what was the worst that could happen.

He remembered the fire vividly, although he had no idea how it had started. Of course, the restless tongues had their theories but he had never listened to them.

He shuddered deep inside, nauseated as he recalled the flames and the thick, billowing smoke. He remembered his rage as he confronted Chris in the dressing room and the agony he felt when Chris finally confessed to killing Jake.

All those feelings returned to him in that moment, crushing him to his very core.

But he allowed the feelings to flow because that was the only way he could purge them and allow other, better emotions in.

He had purposefully avoided this part of town since the fire, partly from fear, partly to avoid the past but now he realised the building in front of him was just a desolate, ruined entity that no longer had a soul or a purpose, and it couldn't hurt him anymore.

Granted, one day it might be something else and over time people might say, "Didn't this used to be that drag queen bar?" but then the foundations, the walls, the surviving rafters, and the remaining roof tiles would form part of a new venture, where happier memories might be made.

One day, this broken building might be somebody else's dream and Divas Cabaret Bar would be nothing more than a faded memory. But those who had been there would never forget.

A partial memory teased at the edges of his brain.

What was he was trying to remember?

Was it Wendy carrying her drag queen son, Tequila, out of the building before frantically trying to resuscitate life back into the weak, unresponsive body?

No, that wasn't it… he could remember that.

Was it the sirens going off, the screams of concern, and the relentless smoke filling the sky? Back then everything had seemed to move in slow motion, just like it did in the movies.

But no, that wasn't it either - he could picture those things clearly in his mind.

What was he trying to recall?

He could visualise Wendy looking up at him with terror etched on her face because Tequila would not respond. He remembered himself crying, broken after everything that had happened, emotions spiralling downwards, crashing, crushing, killing his spirit.

Hold on, that sparked the elusive memory he was grasping for… before trying to stir life back into Tequila's unresponsive body once more, Wendy had looked up at him and her expression turned from fear to surprise. Maybe even shock.

Why?

Suddenly, the memory leapt fully formed into his mind, in glorious technicolor!

There been a presence behind him, fleeting. Somebody there, resting their head on his back, right between his shoulder blades, arms wrapped tightly around him, warming him gently, loving him, providing a momentary feeling of safety.

But they disappeared just as quickly as they had appeared.

Who had it been? Connie? Tittie? Martin?

As he stood there, staring at the ruins of the place he had once loved most in the world, somebody silently approached him from behind.

They put their arms around him tightly and rested their head on his back, right between his shoulder blades, exactly the same as in his recently recovered memory.

This person felt familiar, smelt familiar, and their hug was definitely familiar.

They whispered softly in his ear and said: "Oliver, this was the last place I ever expected to find you."

CHAPTER 08

There had been speculation, rumours, and suspected sightings of Mark (formerly known as Connie) but none of them had ever been confirmed because none of them were true.

So, what had happened to Mark following the Divas Cabaret Bar fire that was entirely his fault?

Well, he had quickly fled that godforsaken town, taking with him only the bare essentials he needed to start a new life far away from there.

Nobody knew where he was and they were unlikely to find out because he had left no trail.

When he arrived at his new destination, nobody knew him, where he had come from, what he had once been, or what he had done.

It was largely unknown it was he who had created so much destruction that night, carelessly risking so many lives in the process. He had no idea whether or not Chris Randall suspected what had happened or the role Mark had played in the devastation of his bar, but it didn't really matter as Chris was locked up after confessing to killing Jake and there were many miles between them.

For now, Mark was safe, and he had no intention of worrying about things in his past.

The greatest and most irrefutable truth for Mark was that his drag queen alter-ego, Connie, whom he despised more than words could ever express, would never make an appearance again. She was dead, buried, gone, along with every carefully styled wig, stunning shoe, scrap of makeup, false eyelash, and exquisite gown she had ever owned.

Most of those things had been destroyed in the Divas fire anyway.

Connie had left town at the same time as Mark but, unlike him, she would never be allowed out to play again because neither of them could survive whilst the other existed, and it was time for Mark to live freely and openly as a happy, confident gay man.

It was a shame he had had to escape so quickly unable to say his goodbyes, although he wasn't sure to whom he would have bade farewell.

Who would have wanted to say goodbye to him?

If there had been more time maybe he could have reinstated his website and sold what was left of Connie's life to Wendy WolfWhistle, claiming it had all belonged to some girl group who had done really well on a reality TV singing show... for at least an album and a half anyway.

Still, it was not as though he needed the money anymore. He had more money than he had ever dreamt of even if, technically, it didn't belong to him and he'd had to endure some wretched times to get it.

But that was all in the past: now he could happily live off the proceeds of Chris's misfortune for a very long time to come. When all was said and done, it was only what Chris owed him for damaging his life. Compensation for all the times he had been forced to live in darkness, barely surviving, constantly suffocating.

For fuck's sake, his own relative doing that to him! Seriously, why would anybody ever do that mixed up, twisted shit to a helpless and vulnerable young person? Well, he got everything he deserved in the end!

But now, with a bank account overflowing with cash, he was finally free of his past and could be anybody he wanted to be. Although all he really wanted now was to be thought of as a nice, decent chap called Mark, and to be respected by the community within which he lived.

Gone were those hideous breast implants that the punters used to love and had once paid generously to explore. Now, they were surgical landfill and in their place sat a flatter, more manly chest, with two scars that the regrowing chest hair covered beautifully.

In time, they would be all but invisible.

In time, perhaps he would be able to lay confidently on a beach or in a park and sunbathe without a top on, not caring one bit whether people looked at him, judging him and his body.

For the first time in his life he was beginning to like who he saw looking back at him in the mirror. He had let his shaved hair grow back into a fun, trendy style. The new stubble on his chin and his updated wardrobe, hand-picked to highlight his tiny frame looked good on him.

For once, he felt attractive and thought others might think so too.

He could finally see a future for himself as Mark, and he couldn't wait to embrace his new start and explore every possibility it presented.

The money-grabbing, drugged up, dragged up whore he used to be had been obliterated in the Divas fire, along with the debilitating secrets he had lived with for too long.

With Chris safely locked up in prison, hopefully forever, he was beginning to build the foundations of a new existence where he could rise again, fully in control of his own destiny.

He was a phoenix, determined to rise from the smouldering ashes and live happily ever after in this new place of solitude, his dark and seedy past forever behind him.

Providing, of course, fate was willing to let him.
Could life really be that cruel to him again?

CHAPTER 09
Late October

Alone inside his prison cell, Chris sensed changes were afoot, ones which would soon sweep through the compound and overthrow the internal governance. He wasn't directly involved but he had heard the rumours, and he knew something huge was unfolding that would affect everybody in there.

Hushed words were exchanged and secret discussions took place in quiet corners, immediately stopping the moment the wrong person came too close.

There was a constant string of knowing looks and well-timed glances that could mean only one thing: the prisoners were planning a revolution. Perhaps that was too dramatic a word but, not being familiar with prison jargon, it was the only way Chris knew how to describe the situation.

The House of Randall was about to collapse once more and there was nothing he could do to stop it. But he didn't want to stop it. He needed out of there and the sooner the better. He needed to be free of the walls that held him hostage and felt as though they were closing in on him until he could no longer breathe.

He desperately needed to find that open door out of there. He needed to flee the relentless slamming doors, the endless rules and regulations he was never able to circumvent. But mostly, he needed to escape the screams of despair that kept him awake at night, some of which were his own.

Sitting on the bottom bunk, he stared hard at the television screen in front of him. It was switched off, but he could see his own worried reflection staring back at himself. Exactly when had he become the star of his own reality TV show? Audience ratings: one!

Prison was so much harder than he had anticipated. If only he had made different choices in his recent past. If only he had made different choices throughout his life!

Jake! Oliver! Divas! The drugs! The debts! The Maniac! The fire! Confessing to the murder!

He should have seen it coming, the nightmare he was setting himself up for. He had made so many bad decisions over so many years, and he hadn't considered any of the consequences, even once.

He had never seen the need to when he had always been at the top of his game, and the idea of taking responsibility for his own actions had simply not occurred to him.

It was very much occurring to him now.

He was stuck here, in this mess, in this excuse for a life directly because of the choices he had made. He was trapped behind the gates of hell, drowning without a lifeline, though his puppets in the outside world were still executing his evil schemes on his behalf.

This was no kind of life, certainly not for him; it was barely an existence. At any moment of the day some bossy bastard would pitch up, barking instructions at him: "Randall! Time to eat! Get in the showers! Go outside and get some exercise!" If it wasn't a guard, it was a pissing bell dictating what he should be doing, when, and for how long.

He had no control over his own life and he needed to remedy that. Being in control was the very thing that defined him, the magic elixir that enabled him to rule the outside world.

How could he have been stupid enough to end up here, enduring this miserable restricted existence in the arse end of despair? How could he have let himself be dragged to his hell?

But if a revolution really was in the pipeline, then somebody different would be telling him what to do and the ringing bells would sound louder and longer than ever before. And they would not be ringing to tell the inmates what to do… instead they would be trying to make them stop what they were doing.

After that, he would be right back to taking orders only from himself.

And then he would make it his business to drag some other people to their personal hells, too.

CHAPTER 10
Late October

The words echoed around his head, startling him, transporting him to the past: "Oliver, this was the last place I ever expected to find you."

The person who had spoken them was still holding him tightly from behind outside the ruined Divas Cabaret Bar, and she was absolutely right: what *was* he doing there? Why had he dragged himself back to that part of town, to that hell?

Oliver turned around as his mother released the arms that had been holding him.

"Seriously, what are you doing here?" she asked him, concerned.

All Oliver could do was shrug his shoulders because he genuinely did not know.

His initial intentions had been positive and fuelled by hope, if not more than a little naïve, but had he achieved anything by going? Seeing the charred carcass of Divas Cabaret Bar so soon after everything that had happened there had not been a good idea, in hindsight, but at least now he knew that.

His mother looked at her sad, lost, lonely son and tried to understand what he must have been coping with. Sympathetically she said: "Come on, let's go and get some coffee and something to eat, and you can tell me all about it. Do you know any nice places?"

Oliver nodded. He knew exactly where to go, although he wouldn't tell his mother his reason for taking her there because that would only open another wound from the past he was still fighting to close.

It was the first time he had been back there since Jake's death and, until he stepped through the doorway, he had not been sure he would be able to return without him. Despite the barrage of bittersweet memories that assaulted him, he led his mother towards a familiar table for two in the old-fashioned tearoom where the staff looked at least twenty years older than they probably were.

He wasn't even sure they were the same staff anymore, the ones he had always felt were rooting for his and Jake's relationship but, either way, they still looked twenty years older than they probably were.

There hadn't really been any point in going there lately but, with his mother at his side, he felt safe to revisit this part of his past… it seemed to be a good day to face up to his demons.

After collecting their order, Oliver set down the tea tray of hot drinks and little cakes on the table in the bay window where he and Jake used to sit, vibing and making secret plans to run away so they could spend the rest of their lives together, safe from Chris and all the other horrors that resided in that town.

As he thought about him, he felt touched by Jake's presence.

Oliver looked at his mother. "Please don't think it's not nice to see you because it is," he said to her, holding his steaming mug of hot chocolate in his hands to warm them up. "But why are you here? I wasn't expecting you."

"Oliver," she replied, picking up her own steaming mug of hot coffee to warm her hands, "I'm worried about you, even more so since I found you outside that wretched building. Has that place not brought you enough grief already?"

"It's the first time I've been back there," he explained, lifting his drink to his mouth and blowing it. "I just needed to see it again, that's all."

His mother took a sip from her cup before she continued to speak. What a nightmare this was. "With everything that has happened here, I do wish you would consider coming back home. Even for a little while."

"This is my home now," he replied, helping himself to the biggest of the little cakes because that is what Jake would have done. "My job and my friends are here. I have a second job, too, in that new cabaret bar I told you about. Only when they need me, but it's okay, so far."

He was trying, unsuccessfully, to convince her he was moving on. It was no surprise considering he didn't believe it either.

"Oliver, I stayed in a hotel near the train station yesterday, and I visited that new cabaret bar last night. I'm not happy you are working there. From your descriptions, I spotted that Wendy WolfWhistle immediately."

"It's not so bad," remarked Oliver, fearing he was fighting another losing battle whilst trying his hardest to win the war.

He couldn't leave town until he was ready to walk away from Jake's memory and he was far from that point.

He supposed he could give up working behind that bar if the compromise would appease his mother.

"Oliver, I heard all about a drag queen who worked there. Apparently, they were arrested for selling drugs. Four policemen arrested him... her... whilst he... she... it?... was performing a cabaret act about prostitution."

"Well, it sounds bad when you put it like that," he replied. "But we don't know she did for sure. She's been released pending further investigation. Anyway, she wasn't selling them in there. If she did, it would probably have been at Divas."

"Don't be flippant, Oliver. And, whilst we're on the subject, I have also heard rumours that the fire at Divas was not an accident, and this Chris Randall might have killed a couple of the drag queens who worked there. Neither of them has been seen since!"

"That's just gossip. I don't know how the fire started. Anyway, who is telling you all of this? Oh, wait, I think I know; the restless tongues, no doubt!"

My god, she had been there one night and had suddenly become the worst informed guru on the planet!

No wonder if she had been chatting to those small minded creeps, who would happily have told her anything she wanted to know - true or not - for the meagre price of a large white wine or two.

"Oliver, I want you to think very carefully about the moth that is so fascinated by a light bulb shining so brightly it eventually flies towards it only to be burnt and killed."

"What? Sorry, I don't understand what you are trying to say. Are you calling me a moth or a light bulb?"

"And this morning," continued his mother, firmly, "I find you standing outside what is left of that building like it's the most natural thing in the world. It's like you are permanently looking for trouble."

"I just wanted to think about Jake, that's all."

His mother instantly softened and took his hand in hers. "Yes, of course you did, and I understand that.

But your obsession with that place nearly burnt you once and almost killed you."

Oliver nodded. Yes, she was absolutely right but there were certain things he needed to do, one day at a time, and on that particular day he had needed to go and see what was left of the cabaret bar which he had once loved so much and couldn't have imagined his life without.

Now, he fantasized daily it had never been in his life at all.

"Sweetheart, I don't think you being here by yourself is good for you. Will you please consider moving back home? You were going to before."

"That was part of a different plan," choked Oliver, fearing he might burst into tears again as the grief flooded back in yet another wave of pain. "That was a plan for me and Jake, but there is no me and Jake now."

Oliver looked at his mother as she drank in silence; just watching him, loving him, listening. He blinked away the tears he could feel forming in the corners of his eyes, although it would have been okay for him to release them.

He knew she worried about him and understandably so. She didn't trust this town or its people and, truth be told, he didn't either. But Enemy Number One was Chris Randall, and he was firmly locked away behind bars.

As long as he remained locked up, Oliver believed, he was safe.

"Okay, I will think about leaving here," he finally said, though rather unconvincingly.

"Do you promise me?"

"Yes."

But they both knew he wouldn't, and they both knew further excuses would come when the issue was broached again.

"Aren't you lonely here?" his mother asked him. In his situation, she felt she very much would be.

Oliver thought about this for a few moments. Yes, he was lonely there was no denying that but staying allowed him to feel closer to Jake and that stopped him feeling entirely alone. "Okay," he said, this time a little more convincingly, "I will consider moving back or at least leaving here, but it has to be when I'm ready to leave and I'm not yet."

As he said it, his eyes filled up once more and several tears rolled down his face before he had any chance of stopping them. It had been a turbulent, eventful, terrifying year and, somehow, he wasn't quite ready to let go of it.

His mother stared at him and nodded.

She would continue to keep her eye on him, her only son. He was very dear to her, and she loved him very much and, whilst she was not happy he wouldn't just jump in the car and come back with her now, she knew she had to respect his decisions.

She also knew he would always need her, this year more than ever and probably the next one too.

Maybe, in time, she could share the journey of fixing him with another guy who would love him but there wouldn't be another Jake and the possibility of Oliver finding love again seemed light years away.

However, this impromptu trip to see him had confirmed everything she had suspected: everything was not fine, as he had attempted to make out on the telephone.

It was easy to fool someone by putting on a brave voice and saying all the right things but, when standing face to face, the truth was much harder to conceal.

"I will continue to come here and see you, Oliver," she said. "Until I am convinced you are in a better place, both emotionally and mentally. I might just pop in unannounced whenever I'm free or when I'm missing you."

"Okay, thank you," he replied, and he realised to what extent he had been hiding his real feelings.

"I have a bad feeling about you being here and I do not trust anybody around you. I don't think you should either."

"I'll be fine. Honestly, it will all be okay. You'll see."

"Hmmm, well, let's just stay in touch, okay? And if anything changes, anything at all, or you are worried about something, call me and I will come and get you straight away. Do we have a deal, sweetheart?"

Oliver nodded for there was no defying his mother when she was in this mindset, and it was a decent compromise from both sides.

"This cake looks lovely," she said, picking it up and instantly lightening the mood.

With that, she tucked in and asked him how work was going, if he was keeping on top of his bills, and if he needed any extra money - which he always said he did.

Her face no longer showed it, but she was far from happy about him staying there.

She had an ominous, unshakeable feeling that something was going to happen; she didn't know what, when, or to whom but she knew, when it did, it was not going to be good.

She was very concerned that Oliver would be the one to bear the consequences, and it would probably have something to do with this Chris Randall, whether he was behind bars or not.

She had heard all about him from her son and from those relentless gossips in that cabaret bar, and she was very wary of him.

The most logical explanation for her enduring sense of unease was mother's intuition.

CHAPTER 11
Following the Miss Divas Cabaret Bar pageant

"And now, ladies and gentlemen, please show your appreciation for your favourite night-time TV host, the ex-hairdresser turned chat-show star who will always get to the root of the problem and blow your top, the one and only, Mrs Seavers!"

In the television studio, Mrs Seavers stepped out onto the set, which was part hair salon and part reception area with comfortable seating, where she was greeted by a hearty round of applause from her audience. Her stunning brown hair was pulled stylishly forward over one shoulder and trailed down her sequined black dress, which sparkled like a million fireflies flitting over a meadow at midnight.

She smiled widely at her audience and purposefully waved to those in the very back rows who had arrived too late to get a better seat nearer the front. Nearer to her.

Taking a seat in the reception area, she was handed a steaming hot cup of coffee by her 'Saturday Girl' who then wandered towards the rear of the set to fold towels and rearrange the shampoos and conditioners, before eventually disappearing out of sight altogether.

With her legs crossed and the tip of one of her raised high heels pointing outwards, Mrs Seavers pouted seductively at the camera in an attempt to appear a few years younger than she actually was. Deliberately drawing attention to her beautifully manicured nails, she used her right hand to shoo the camera lens away from the extreme close-up it was showing of her face; she suspected she looked considerably better from a distance. That was another reason she made a point of waving to the late comers at the very back.

After taking a sip from her coffee cup, she returned it to the saucer on the table in front of her, ignoring the selection of magazines laid out in a fan shape for her clients to peruse at their leisure. She always ignored them because they were just so predictable: always the same tired old story told ad nauseum.

Boy meets girl.

Boy leaves girl.

Girl has really bad hair and urgently needs a makeover.

Girl eventually discovers contact lenses, shampoo, either wins the lottery or dates a premier league football player, has beautiful children, and lives happily ever after.

"Welcome to the Mrs Seavers show," she purred. "I am, of course, Mrs Seavers and this is my show. Tonight we are being joined by some delightfully fascinating guests, and I'm thrilled to announce a very special first appearance in my salon by a remarkable guest."

Although the audience harboured a modicum of hope these people – particularly the esteemed mystery person – would live up to the hype, they mostly expected them to be averagely dull at best.

"Joining me in the salon later will be everybody's favourite psychic drag queen, Miss April Showers, who will share her predictions for this year's hottest new hairdos including, believe it or not, a new blonde and auburn streaked bouffant for a more elderly member of the royal family.

"But first, we are going to tackle the very difficult subject of people who love younger foreign men and live to regret it.

"Tonight, we are going to hear some very sad tales of lonely, desperate individuals who have reached out to younger foreign men for love, invested their life savings into the relationship and then never heard from them again.

"So, please... let's have a huge round of applause for my very first client in the salon tonight, who is here to tell us all about how their Turkish delight literally gave them the chop."

At first, the audience clapped half-heartedly as they anticipated hearing yet another sob story from somebody who would sit there sipping free coffee, munching chocolate biscuits, and shedding a few tears which would streak the heavyweight makeup that had been slapped on them by the production team, to stop them looking so washed-out.

Another tragic person who would try to convince them all that their nineteen-year-old Turkish lover had been different from all the others and, as they had genuinely been in love, felt they could legitimately give him the twenty thousand pounds he so urgently needed to save his grandmother's leg from amputation.

Same old, same old...

But much to their surprise and delight, there was nothing predictable about the figure that came lolloping onto the set with all the force and grace of a bull in a china shop.

There was nothing samey about the way she crashed down on the sofa next to Mrs Seavers, launching everything that was resting on it – including the host - upwards from the impact!

"Now, Mrs S, less of the 'desperate and lonely' if you don't mind!" she said. "As you can gather from my feminine demeanour and obvious seductive charm, I am neither of those things."

Her guest was momentarily distracted by the magazines resting on the coffee table in front of her. "Ooh, I haven't read this one yet," she announced, picking one up and popping it into her handbag. "You don't mind if I take it, do you? Saves me buying it and after my ordeal with my Turkish lover. I barely have two pennies to rub together anymore."

"Yes, why not," announced Mrs Seavers, slightly amused by the cheek of her guest.

As if she had given the person sitting next to her permission to help herself to the entire contents of the set, she watched agog as several more magazines were hoisted and stashed into the tatty old handbag, along with a few sachets of sugar, and a spoon.

"Oh, I see you are an admirer of my bag. It used to belong to Whitney Houston, can you believe it?"

"No, Dear, I really can't."

"Now where is my coffee?" asked her guest, "I was promised coffee and biscuits too. It's one of the reasons I'm here. That and to meet you of course, but especially Miss April Showers, the psychic drag queen. I adore her! She recently predicted somebody would be presented with a love token and guess what?! One of my fans bought me half a lager, isn't that amazing?!"

Mrs Seavers smiled politely at the over-sized person in front of her, wearing too-tight clothes which were almost bursting at the seams, although that wasn't the reaction she'd have given had the cameras not been on her. Instead, she professionally explained her 'Saturday Girl' would be along shortly with the hot beverage and biscuits she had been promised.

"Now, Miss WolfWhistle, please tell me all about your hideous ordeal and do not miss out a single detail. After all, a problem shared is a problem halved and you are among friends here."

Mrs Seavers smiled with fake compassion; there was a story to be extracted and she was determined to obtain every gory detail because that problem sharing she had just talked about so sincerely translated in to decent night-time ratings and a renewed contract. "Obviously the entire experience has been, well, it's clearly taken a terrible toll on you! I don't know how you coped! Tell me everything, Dearie."

"Well, I suppose it all started this morning when I woke up and it looked like this. Honestly, I haven't been able to do a single thing with it all day."

Her guest fluffed up her hair with both hands and shook her head, disgruntled. Mrs Seavers regarded Wendy's matted wig, she couldn't help but think it looked as though there may have been small wild animals living in there. She half expected a disgruntled mole to poke his nose out at any moment.

Mrs Seavers sat silently and let her guest ramble on. Was this good television or not? Could it be edited into something entertaining? The audience seemed to be loving it.

"Oh, I do like your hairdo, Mrs S. I wonder, could I borrow it after the show? I'm about to take the lead in a high-profile production at Divas cabaret Bar and it would go perfectly with my outfit."

Borrow her hair? Just what was this guest insinuating? "Erm no," she gasped in horror. "This is actually my own hair."

Wendy gave a loud, disappointed sigh at learning this.

Mrs Seavers then exclaimed: "Hey, I'm not a drag queen as well! You do know that don't you?" She made a mental note to tell the producer to edit that part out. "Right, let's get back onto the subject of, er... well... you. Now, you initially met Ibrahim, your Turkish lover, online, didn't you?"

"Yes, that's right."

"And you must still be bereft and utterly devastated by his betrayal, yes? Go ahead, tell me everything, Dearie."

But her guest did not respond. Instead she looked around the studio at the camera man, the boom, and the audience, who were amused by her apparently miniscule concentration span.

Eventually, she turned back to Mrs Seavers and excitedly engaged with the host once more. "Ahhh, it's like we're already best friends chilling together down at Divas Cabaret Bar and having a lovely time, isn't it?"

"Okay look, Miss WolfWhistle, I really need you to pay more attention and talk to me about Ibrahim. *Only* about Ibrahim."

"Oh him," said her guest, moving along the settee until she was practically sat on the poor host's knee and Wendy's broom-sized false eyelashes were literally brushing her face.

"Actually, could you move back a little bit please?" requested Mrs Seavers, wafting the air around her face. "I don't mean to be rude but the smell of wee is slightly overpowering."

"I beg your pardon!" Wendy squawked, as the audience tittered amongst themselves. This alone had been worth finding a parking space for.

"Oui... I think that's what it's called - the expensive perfume you're wearing. It's so strong it's choking me."

"Oh yes, the expensive perfume I'm wearing. It didn't come from a market stall, at all."

Mrs Seavers shook her head in dismay. Seriously, where had they dragged this one in from and could this beast ever be tamed? She hoped, at least, it was making for good television. "Okay, let's continue with our interview, shall we? Right, Miss WolfWhistle, some might say that you were not entirely truthful with Ibrahim yourself, were you? Was it or was it not a picture of Michelle Visage's chest that you used as your profile picture to entice - I believe these were your words - a swarm of bees to your honey making pollen?"

"Oh, everybody tells a few fibs on the internet, it's not like I was catfishing, or anything. In fact, it's expected when you date online. Take my dear friend, Miss Sugar Daddy. She must be doing it because there's no way that moustache of hers suddenly becomes invisible to the camera without a little airbrushing going on! She hasn't been blessed with the fine downy lady hairs we both have that are simply imperceptible to the naked eye." Wendy stroked the hairs on her chin and winked conspiratorially.

Mrs Seavers shook her head again as her audience began to descend into raucous laughter. Downy lady hairs? She didn't have downy lady hairs, imperceptible or otherwise! And her guest had more bristles on her multiple chins than a toilet brush! Oh my god... did her guest honestly think they looked alike?

Whilst she may have been living up to her grandiose promise at the start of the show that there would be fascinating guests, there was almost no broadcastable content by this point, even if the audience was loving it.

"Now, Miss WolfWhistle, Dearie, tell me: is it true you were so mortified by the humiliation you suffered at Ibrahim's hands you haven't been able to confide in anybody about what happened? Are you just too ashamed?"

"Oh no, that's not the case at all. I didn't tell anybody because I was too busy preparing for the Miss Divas Cabaret Bar pageant. It was only a couple of days ago, and I won with a landslide majority. I'm a beauty queen."

Wendy beamed widely as the audience gave her a huge burst of applause and what seemed to be a never-ending cheer.

"In fact, I'm going to headline the show this very weekend," she continued to say once the crew had eventually settled the audience. "I can ask Chris to put your name on the guest list, if it isn't already full."

"No, thank you."

The 'Saturday Girl' returned with a steaming cup of coffee which she put down in front of Wendy, who produced a miniature bottle of whiskey from her handbag with a flourish and poured it in. She picked up the drink and took a big man swig; after all, it was thirsty work being a guest on a popular late night chat show that barely anybody watched.

"Oh, Mrs S, I do love your shoes. I was going to buy the same pair but they didn't come in a slimmer width. Do you like my shoes? They used to belong to Carrie Bradshaw when she was having sex in the city."

Despite the audience howling with laughter once more at the absurdity of this unpredictable and incredible guest, Mrs Seavers turned to the camera, shook her head, and sighed.

"Okay, Miss WolfWhistle," she finally said, once the audience had calmed again, "can we just try and focus on your relationship with Ibrahim? When did you first suspect he was only in a relationship with you for your money?"

Wendy was silently mindful for a moment; when she did speak, she did so in a hushed voice, which she had been advised to do by a member of the production crew in a mistaken effort to garner empathy from the audience. "I think it was when he arrived at my front door and demanded I give him twenty pounds for the taxi fare."

"Oh dear, and I understand Ibrahim wasn't just demanding money from you either, was he?"

"No, he wanted a Chinese takeaway as well."

Mrs Seavers ignored the titters and murmurs that erupted once more from the audience. She finally had her guest on topic, and she was determined to keep it that way. "Now, I understand that this might be quite difficult for you to talk about, but is it true that he withheld sex unless you gave him money?"

"Well, it was not so much withholding sex for money as telling me that no amount of money in the world would make him want to have sex with me."

"And that came as a shock to you?"

"Yes, I was gobsmacked! Especially seeing as I went on to win the Miss Divas Cabaret Bar pageant. Did I already mention that?"

"Yes, once or twice. So, is it true that Ibrahim took so much of your money you could barely afford to buy an outfit for the pageant, and you were forced to wear something a farmer might put out in the fields to scare away the birds?"

Wendy shook her head so violently that her wig slipped slightly to the side and one of her false eyelashes fell off. "Oh no," she squealed, "No. **No**. That wasn't the case at all. In fact, whilst I was backstage Miss Anna Phylactic and Miss Jezza-Belle, who were also competing, shrieked when they first saw what I was wearing."

Mrs Seavers sighed. "Okay, so, what we really want to know - what we *need* to know - is how much money did Ibrahim actually take from you in the end?"

"Haven't you been listening? Twenty quid for the taxi fare. I've already told you that. And you say I'm not paying attention!"

Mrs Seavers was visibly exasperated with her useless guest and her bulging handbag, which looked more like it had come from a council estate tip than the late Miss Whitney Houston's estate. "So, Miss WolfWhistle, are you telling me that Ibrahim went back to Turkey after one date with just twenty pounds of your money?"

"No, not Turkey; West Green Street. It's literally five minutes from my gorgeous bijou apartment and would never have been twenty quid in a taxi to mine! He could easily have walked. That's how I knew he was trying to rip me off… that is the theme of the show, isn't it?"

Beyond deflated, Mrs Seavers turned to the camera crew and production team and said: "I think we've heard enough now. Let's go to a commercial break."

Wendy WolfWhistle stood and took a bow. She may not have been what Mrs Seavers was expecting, and it was questionable how much footage they would be able to use, but the audience had loved her. Perhaps there could be some show, somewhere, where the footage could be used?

"Is it okay if I stick around?" Wendy asked. "I'd love to meet Miss April Showers, the psychic drag queen."

With that Wendy popped her arm through the straps of her handbag, collected her hot drink and the plate of remaining biscuits, and tottered off backstage where she intended to peruse the magazines she had just acquired. This, incidentally, would lead her to read an article about lazy ovaries which she would go on to tell people that she had too, whilst waiting in the wings to swamp Miss April Showers.

She was very much looking forward to meeting this psychic drag queen in person, provided she didn't look better than Wendy, which was highly improbable. Otherwise, she would have to heavy rain on her parade and steal her thunder.

With her dog-eared magazine from which she had already torn a coupon for an oatmeal scrub, a sticky drink spilt over Carrie Bradshaw's old shoes, and a mouth full of biscuits, she dreamt about the myriad opportunities that would surely arise from being on the show.

And the exciting new friendships that would be born from it.

What she couldn't possibly have imagined was just how obsessed she would become with her 'new best friend', Miss April Showers, the psychic drag queen, or how deadly that obsession would become.

CHAPTER 12
Shortly after opening night

It had been a typical dark, wet, and gloomy October day, which had faded into an equally dark night heavy with rain, blustery winds, airborne leaves, and debris.

Tree branches banged against window panes, fence panels rattled in the distance, and James (Tequila) was struggling to sleep in his small bed in his small room.

However, he was relieved that his ordeal with the police was now behind him and decided losing a little sleep due to the outside elements was not the worst thing to endure.

He was glad the whole matter had been dropped from a lack of evidence.

The reality of what had happened and what could have happened was terrifying and he did not want to go through that again. After all, prison was for people like Chris Randall, not him; maybe for the likes of Wendy or Connie too, but definitely not him.

As he lay in his bed staring up towards the ceiling he was annoyed with himself that silly decisions he had made in his past were still affecting his life now.

What had he been thinking selling those drugs for Chris in Divas? How could he have been so stupid? Had he really been that desperate to be a huge star?

Tittie and Connie had tried to warn him not to get involved, but no… he knew better. He had thought, at the time, they were trying to hold him back but he realised now he should have listened to them. He wished he had.

He was relieved it was over but perhaps would not have been had he known the events that had preceded it. He was oblivious to the fact his troubles had barely begun and that the unfortunate incident was simply a warning of what lay in store.

His mind turned to the debts he had run up after starting work at Divas; debts he had not paid back and had run away from. And he couldn't help but think about how the people he owed money to had not managed to track him down... yet.

He shuddered as he thought specifically about the scary loan shark in the Northern Territory - what an absolute horror he had turned out to be. James absolutely did not want to be found by him or his cronies.

Foolishly, he had tried to live the same champagne lifestyle Chris thrived on but had quickly discovered he simply couldn't afford to. He was far from being a Champagne Chris. He wasn't even a Babycham Chris.

He was enormously relieved that nobody had come looking for their money thus far and he hoped they never would, but he lived in constant fear that, sooner or later, somebody would. And he knew, if that happened, it would not be pretty. He couldn't shake off a saying he had once heard: you can run from your past but it will always catch up with you.

Whatever happened, he needed a massive financial injection... but not from a loan shark; he would never make that mistake again.

As he lay there thinking, unable to sleep, he realised just how stupid he had been and how lucky he was to be alive.

There was plenty of time to turn his life around. He was young, good looking, talented, and ambitious. There would always be room for somebody like him in the world, right?

What he needed was to win big on a scratch card or for somebody to give him a tonne of cash, but the only person he knew with loads of cash was Chris – and that was if he still had his money. But that was another mistake he would never make again because he knew now what Chris would want in exchange, what he always wanted in exchange: blood, tears, sweat… and an audit trail that went cold and never made its way back to him.

Why the hell had he trusted him so blindly in the past, always doing as he had been told!

Damn him and his cabaret bar!

Suddenly, James was glad it had burnt down.

He began to wonder if it had been insured… surely, it must have! That meant there would be an insurance pay out, possibly a large one. Chris would have kept up his insurance policy, no matter how dire his financial situation had been. That insurance money would be his new nest egg but Chris wouldn't need all of it, not yet anyway, not where he was.

"No, James," he quickly told himself, in a stern whisper. "Not after the last time."

Chris, the human hurricane who destroyed everything he touched, had ruined too many lives as it was. He would not be allowed to destroy this new and better life that James had created.

Just for a moment, James felt indestructible but it did not last long. As the worry about his own financial situation settled back in on him he realised he needed his own version of an insurance pay out.

Perhaps Martin would give him a pay rise but that was unlikely; he had already asked for one and had been refused point blank. James thought that was very short sighted of his new boss.

After all, he was the (co) star of the show and the punters were spending freely to see him perform as the delectable Miss Tequila ShockingBird (alongside

Father Wendy) night after night. And they were an undeniable success.

Surely, that must be worth some more money in his pocket?

Besides, what else could possibly go wrong? It wasn't as though the likes of Tittie or Connie would turn up unexpectedly and try to reclaim the spotlight; even if they did he would shoot them down, hard.

This was his gig now, he was top of the bill, and he would protect it. Despite everything he had already been through, he was far from done fighting.

He switched on the tiny lamp which sat on the equally tiny bedside cabinet, climbed out from beneath the duvet and stared into the mirror. Looking back at him was a half-dressed young man with one eye open. It was not a pretty sight, especially with the hippopotamus-sized yawn that followed.

Perhaps he should sneak downstairs and help himself to a large-small shot of something and come back to bed? Yes, that might help settle his racing mind and enable him to sleep more peacefully whilst Hurricane Christopher raged angrily inside his head.

Out on the landing, using the flashlight on his phone to guide the way, he could hear both Father Wendy and Martin snoring loudly from within their respective bedrooms, so he felt safe to move freely around the building.

He didn't want to wake anybody, especially not Martin who watched those optics like a hawk. Quietly, he tiptoed down the stairs taking extra care to avoid the creaky step half-way down... better to let Martin suspect it was Father Wendy helping herself to the goods than to advertise it was him by being too loud.

Downstairs, the bar area was eerily quiet as the time approached the devil's hour. Unknown shapes beyond the frosted glass windows cast sinister looking shadows courtesy of the streetlights and it felt as though he was not alone, although he was.

Probably. It was just his nerves and the storm playing tricks on him.

Probably.

He ran the flashlight along the optics until a bottle of *Southern Comfort* caught his eye. That would do nicely! And it did do nicely, so much so he helped himself to a second measure, and a packet of cheese and onion crisps!

Okay… enough now, James… back to bed.

But now he was completely awake and, whilst he knew he should go back up and try to sleep, he wasn't ready to do that just yet. He considered watching some television until he drifted off but he didn't fancy that either.

He left the bar shining his small flashlight towards the stage, appreciating the view the audience must have when they watched him performing up there, in drag.

Ooooh, what about Martin's office, tucked away backstage, well away from the noise and the bar and the restless tongues and the cabaret?

He, along with everyone else, was under strict instruction never to go in there unless personally invited and chaperoned.

Up until that very moment, he hadn't really wanted to go in there: it was not his thing.

Dancing, performing, wearing gorgeous outfits, and receiving thunderous applause from a crowd of smiling faces was his thing… particularly the applause part. But the growing temptation to do something forbidden, to try the door handle to see if it opened suddenly seemed very appealing.

Boring business-related stuff held no interest for him, although all the mind-numbing stuff in there might just help him sleep; it was definitely likely to start him yawning!

James wasn't sure the door would even open. He had seen how obsessive Martin was about locking it even when he was just nipping to the toilet or making a cup of tea and didn't see why this evening would be any exception.

But much to his surprise, when he turned the handle the door opened wide and practically invited him in. Martin's usual vigilance had slipped, it seemed, though when he discovered that oversight in the morning, it would never happen again.

James sat in Martin's luxury executive, leather-effect, black swivel, height-adjustable, lumbar support chair, which had clearly been purchased with the fuller figure in mind – but not before carefully noting its exact position in alignment with the desk, so no one would suspect he had been there.

It reflected badly on James that, whilst he was all alone in there with the time and freedom to search, his mind began to race wondering what he might find. What was it Martin was so particular about locking away in there? Could this somehow lead him to obtaining the money he so desperately needed?

He switched on the desk light and looked around: there was nothing of interest anywhere only a rather dull looking line graph on a white board on the wall.

He was not clever enough to know what it meant, even though there was a colour coded key at the bottom and words had been written along both the vertical and horizontal axes.

He tried to interpret the data in front of him and concluded that the red highlighter pen must be indicating something different to the green one!

Yawn.

Oh, that was a good sign. He must be ready to return to bed. But he pushed himself to stay awake a little longer as he was certain he would not have the opportunity to look around Martin's office so freely again and had a nagging feeling there were still things to search for, even if they weren't immediately obvious. Although the three drawers down the side of the desk were rather inviting; especially as the deepest of the three, the bottom drawer, was firmly locked.

The other two opened though.

One of the drawers which opened only contained a few bits of stationery along with a tin labelled 'petty cash'. The other held two plastic wallets labelled 'Invoices to be paid' and 'Invoices paid' but these only induced further yawning from the nocturnal snoop.

Instinct and unhealthy curiosity kicked in and James returned to the first drawer to open the petty cash tin. According to the original packaging, it had once contained an exquisite range of delicious biscuits but they had long since been eaten, probably by Wendy.

Inside, there were several receipts and a few bits of loose change but nothing that would allow him to run away to a better life in the sun. However, there was one thing of interest in there: a small metal key tucked away in one of the corners... but what was it for? Surely not the bottom drawer?

Only one way to find out...

Success!

Suddenly, sleep was firmly off James's agenda because inside that drawer was a whole bundle of paperwork; paperwork that was so important and private it needed to be locked in a drawer in an office that nobody was allowed to enter unsupervised.

James lifted it out carefully to maintain the impression that nobody, other than Martin, had ever laid their eyes - or greedy little hands - on it.

He was eager to discover what information lay within.

He had better not find out that Wendy was being paid more than him for the mediocre, poorly lip-synced performances she insisted on churning out every night when most people seemed to go to the bar or the toilet.

Unable to find anything relating to their salaries and with the flippancy of a bored seven-year-old, he continued to flick through Martin's private data. Nothing... *yawn*... boring... *yawn*... dull... *yawn*... not interested in that... yawn...

Oooh, but what was this?

Something caught his attention; intrigued, he pulled out a smaller pile of documents that had been fastened together with a bulldog clip. He placed the rest of the bundle onto the desk and began to sift through the separated papers.

Oh my god... Martin, what have you done?!

Alarmed, he scrutinised the contents of the smaller pile several times over, just to make sure he had fully understood the implications of the information he was holding.

Once he felt he had a thorough grasp on what he had uncovered, he sensed a whole new world of possibilities open up to him. One that, ironically, would shut down and restrict Martin's world considerably.

How much might it be worth to Martin for James to keep his gob shut?

Because he really did have a very big gob, unfortunately.

He had not seen this coming at all. What a golden opportunity!

James knew it would be a long time before sleep came to him as his mind worked overtime to process this new information and there was a lot to process as this news was so big there was no way it would just impact Martin alone.

It would affect them all, sooner or later.

CHAPTER 13
The following evening

Martin was sitting alone in his office moving paperwork from one side of his desk to the other. He was good at doing that and he hoped he was convincing at making it appear like he knew exactly what he was doing, even though he didn't.

Most of the time he seemed to be on top of things.

In reality, he was no businessman and he wasn't designed for this type of work at all. He was better at his old job in the police force but those days were over, and this is what he did now.

Thankfully, Wayne was on hand to help with this, that, and the other. He really was a great asset to have on board as he knew how to do things like place orders with the brewery, change barrels, clean out the pumps, empty the slop trays, and put the rubbish out.

It was always with a thumping heart that he regarded the permanently locked bottom desk drawer. He was exhausted from looking at the stack of paperwork it housed and hated thinking about its contents, although he found himself thinking about them a lot. He often wished it was all just a bad dream and that one day he would wake up to find it had never really happened. But he never did and it never would; it was simply a nightmarish reality he was forced to endure.

He realised he had left the door unlocked the evening before although, thankfully, nobody else seemed to have noticed. No one had been in, so he breathed a sigh of relief and believed he had got away with his foolish indiscretion. He had no idea that James had been rooting about in there just hours earlier, or that he now knew Martin's terrible secret, though it still wasn't his worst one; he did not suspect for a moment that James was just waiting for the perfect opportunity to raise the subject for his own advantage.

And it really was something he did not want anybody else to know about. Whatever would they think of him? They would see him for the weak, vulnerable, stupid man he was.

He wanted to believe that, given the circumstances, they might think he had had no other choice.

As he sighed regretfully at the decisions he had made over recent months, he was distracted by Wendy who charged into his office in full drag, this time sporting yellow eye shadow and bright pink hot pants so tight they looked as though they might rip at the seams if she let even the most delicate of farts slip from between her hairy arse cheeks.

"What do you want, Wendy?" he asked, quickly glancing at the bottom drawer to make sure it was locked tight.

He instantly regretted doing so in case Wendy noticed where his eyes had moved to but she didn't. As usual, her mind was elsewhere, preoccupied with curtain up, a long hard screw against the wall (her favourite cocktail), and homemade apple pie.

"I think we need to talk," she whispered conspiratorially, before closing the door behind her, pulling a chair towards the desk and descending delicately in to it with both legs elegantly sloped to the side, and her hands resting in her lap; every bit as graceful as the daintiest Hollywood starlet.

From Martin's perspective, he saw Wendy slam the door as though a hurricane had blown through, lug a chair across the floor with the force of a tug of war team, and bash it clumsily into his desk, before sitting down with the force of ten wrecking balls so that he could hear her barely clothed backside slap against the seat; every bit as graceful as Godzilla attacking the city.

Martin nodded, but only after he had reset his unsettled mind back to that of a professional manager and cabaret bar owner. "So, what do you want to talk about?"

He often found himself having the same conversations with Wendy. Hopefully, this time it would not be about the glass cabinet she felt they should have in the bar area, within which she could display her extensive collection of exquisite accessories that had once belonged to famous celebrities, like the chipped cup and saucer from Beauty and the Beast which had once belonged to Emma Watson; or the bobble hat which had sorted her into Gryffindor.

He knew that one day she hoped to be so famous as to be able to pawn off her own artefacts to an emerging drag queen star on the cusp of stardom, just as she had once been; a struggling artiste who was, perhaps, in need of a wig that had only one or two bald patches, or a pair of stage-ready tights with only a few ladders and the tiniest of skid marks in them, or a pair of shoes with slightly uneven heel heights.

But that day, like so many others, was not this day and Wendy still needed to keep all those items for her own personal use. When she had a little time, she might even rinse some of them through.

"I want to talk to you about Oliver," she replied to him.

Instantly disinterested, he asked: "What about him?" This was another conversation that was beginning to wear thin.

"I'm still worried about him," she replied. "I don't think working behind the bar is doing him any good at all."

"It was his decision."

"After a lot of persuasion from you."

Martin shook his head defensively because he didn't remember it being like that. "Not that much persuasion."

"You were not going to take 'no' for an answer."

"Well, he's young and cute. He's just what people want to look at when they're out drinking. He's the eye candy, the fantasy… much more so than Wayne anyway. No disrespect intended. I know he's your mate from the previous pub but you must agree he's no oil painting."

Wendy shook her head and had to adjust her wig as it slipped sideways. "I've never really understood that expression. All the oil paintings I've ever seen have been of badly dressed, ugly spinsters with bad hair and too much eye shadow. Not something you would ever want to look at."

Martin smiled at the irony and let her ramble on, pleased she had veered off the subject. He knew if she took the conversation back to Oliver it might become difficult and uncomfortable, and he always tried to avoid the subject of Oliver because he had his own reasons for wanting him there.

"Now, an oil painting of me would be quite the masterpiece," Wendy continued, "Stunning! Globally admired, like the moaning Lisa. I would insist on a better title than that, though." She stopped speaking and stared thoughtfully into space. "Hmmm..."

Martin watched her cautiously and braced himself for what might come next. Would she return to the previous subject or could she be distracted with a chocolate éclair if he gave her the money from petty cash to go and buy one?

"Anyway," she eventually resumed, "I really think I should tell him what I know. He deserves to hear it at least."

Martin shook his head firmly in response. "Wendy, we have been over this before. He should absolutely not be told."

"But it might give him hope."

"I hear what you're saying but what you think you saw the night Divas burnt down is not real. I'm telling you, he wasn't there. I was there and I didn't see anything."

Wendy was adamant and refused to give up. "But I saw him, Martin. I know I did. Jake was there, standing behind him."

"You were grief-stricken," explained Martin, exasperated at having to go over this again. "You had inhaled a lot of smoke rescuing your son from the burning building. Your adrenaline was sky high, and you were traumatised at having to save his life at a time when you needed medical treatment yourself."

This time it was Wendy who was firm with the response. "I know what I saw: I saw Jake standing behind Oliver, hugging him."

"You need to forget this, Wendy," warned Martin, sternly. "Your mind was playing tricks on you. Jake was not there."

As usual, Wendy was doubting what she had seen. In her mind when she thought about it, she unfalteringly believed Jake had been there that night. But whenever she broached the subject with Martin, she began to wonder.

"Look," said Martin, more sympathetically, "Jake was not there and he could not possibly have been because his family took his body away and held his funeral."

"Then what did I see?" asked Wendy, finding the strength and determination to fight her corner. "Tell me that?"

"I don't know what you saw but I know it was not Jake. Did you see him again after that?"

Wendy shook her head and had to admit she hadn't seen him again. When she had looked up again, only a few moments later, he was gone.

"I think Oliver has enough to cope with at the moment," said Martin, "without you adding false hope about Jake to the pot. Do you want to push him over the edge completely?"

Wendy was silent. Perhaps Martin was right: saving her son's life had been her priority and the next time she had looked up there were only police and fire fighters swarming the place, trying to help.

Maybe it was one of them she had seen standing behind Oliver, hugging him. A comforting stranger giving Oliver a much-needed moment of love and support, just being there for him when he really needed it. Perhaps it was one of the restless tongues or anybody who just happened to look like Jake from that angle.

Maybe Martin was right. Maybe the stress of the situation had caused her mind to play tricks, in which case it was best not to say anything to Oliver.

"And what about the other thing?" she asked him.

"What other thing?" asked a frustrated Martin, who wanted this over with so he could go back to wallowing in self-pity - his favourite pastime these days.

"What we know happened at Chris Randall's prison?"

Martin shook his head violently. "Oh no, we're definitely not saying anything about that to him. It happened on opening night, so if he doesn't already know by now it's best he doesn't find out at all."

"But don't you think he *should* know?"

"Look, we don't know even know if Chris is one of the prisoners who escaped during the riot. And if he was then there has been no sign of him yet, has there?"

"But he could still come here," panicked Wendy. "He could come in disguise, or on Halloween night wearing a mask. Nobody would even know. Perhaps it would be best if we cancelled it."

Martin shook his head in despair. When was she ever going to shut up? "Now you're just being ridiculous."

She nodded her agreement. Maybe she was worrying unnecessarily. Why would Chris come back to this town, of all places? Surely this would be the first place they would look for him, and there were enough people here that would happily report any sightings of him to the police. "Maybe you're right," she eventually said. "I just worry about Oliver, that's all. He's such a sweetie pie."

"I know you do. We all do. Now stop over thinking it and get yourself ready for the start of the show. Oh, unless that's what you're wearing. Is that what you're wearing?"

Wendy shook her head for there was much she planned to add to perfect her look: more lipstick, a couple of tins of hairspray, a few coats of mascara for good luck, and a stunning one piece that showed off her figure majestically. Martin was right: she was over thinking it so she allowed herself to think about lovely, swirly, girly things instead, like gift receipts, hemlines, and tinsel covered ponies.

Martin breathed a silent sigh of relief as Wendy turned and walked towards the closed office door. Thank goodness, that was over!

Although that couldn't actually have been farther from the truth because, unbeknownst to either of them, James - dressed in full drag as Tequila - had been standing at the closed door listening intently and collecting further ammunition for her much-needed pay out. She carefully gathered every piece of the somewhat confusing jigsaw and stored it away mentally; she was almost ready to burst from all the juicy information she now knew.

Secret paperwork in a locked drawer.

Father Wendy, adamant she had seen Jake alive on the night of the Divas fire, several weeks after he had been knocked down on East Green Street and supposedly killed.

Martin, immovable in the fact she had **not** seen Jake that night.

Martin, desperate to get Oliver behind the bar.

What did it all mean?

Did it mean anything?

And what about Chris?

A prison riot and escaped inmates?

Was Chris out and on the run?

CHAPTER 14
The day of the grand opening of Martin's cabaret bar

They would come for him sooner or later, hunt him down and force him to be part of it making him equally culpable as the instigators, the genuinely guilty ones.

Just to dilute the blame a little and spread it around further.

Not just him though; everybody would be dragged into the mess. Everyone would have to share accountability, no exceptions.

All around him the alarm bells rang relentlessly, just as they had on that final night at his cabaret bar. And, just like on that night, he had no control over this situation and was powerless to change any of it.

Tucked away out of sight on the bottom bunk, he pushed himself up against the cold, coarse wall, both hands pressed hard against his ears to block out as much of the noise as possible. He hid beneath his blanket and pillow, trying to become invisible.

But he couldn't block it out or hide because it was not going away and they were coming for him, whether he wanted to be involved or not.

"United as one!" they would shout. And they would make him shout it too.

But this was not what he wanted. This was ruining everything he had worked so hard to put together. He had his own plans, his own aspirations, and they did not include this or anybody else's expectations of him.

After finally feeling like he was taking control of his life again, this was a severe blow.

It suddenly sounded as though the prison cells near to his were being ransacked, accompanied by cheers and roars from fellow inmates as they united as one.

It was undeniable, unignorable: the revolt was going ahead full throttle and gaining momentum.

The anarchy was moving closer to his cell, and if he didn't move and hide somewhere else he would be swept up in the destruction.

Without warning, images from films and television prison dramas played in his mind: a loud bang followed by an even louder scream accompanied by a river of blood.

Tonight would be no exception, and he did not want the next scream or river of blood to be his.

He was no longer safe in his cell, and had no choice but to move to a better location, if such a place even existed in there anymore.

He had no idea how this had started, where the prison officers were, or what was happening outside his cell door.

Where was Moustache? Was he safe? Did Chris care? In this dog-eat-dog environment, Chris's well-honed self-preservation instincts had kicked in and – once again - his own safety was paramount.

He slipped out from the bunk beds and looked at the few items he owned in there. There was nothing valuable he needed to take, nothing he couldn't live without, and certainly nothing that needed to be destroyed before anybody else could get their grubby hands on it.

He put his ear to the door, but it made little difference.

The noise of the riot could be heard from every direction, and he seemed to be trapped in the centre of it. He just needed to get into the corridor so he could find somewhere else to lay low until it was all over, although that was not going to be easy.

After all, the access doors would be locked, wouldn't they?

Cautiously, he opened his cell door and peered through a small gap. He had thought he'd prepared himself for what he might see but it was much worse than he had anticipated.

There was chaos and destruction everywhere.

Opening the door wider, he saw how cells had been tossed, belongings thrown, and every object had been weaponised.

There were several bodies lying motionless on the floor: meeker, milder inmates who had never stood a chance. Chris had to find a way to survive this.

People were running in every direction, tripping and falling over items that didn't belong where they had landed.

Anxious but determined, he stepped out into the madness and almost immediately was pushed violently aside by an unapologetic body who collided with him as they ran in search of their own sanctuary.

Chris impacted with the wall, banging his head and scraping his hand as he desperately tried to support himself. Apart from a few scratches, some short-lived pain, and a dented ego, he was fine.

He continued haphazardly along the corridor but there was no escape from the endless mayhem unfolding around him.

Seriously, where were the prison officers?

They were nowhere to be seen. Had they been trapped somewhere, taken hostage? Maybe they were under strict instructions to stay away and protect themselves until special back up forces could intervene.

He turned a corner and was surprised but relieved to find the normally locked security door wide open, as was the next one, and the one after that.

He quickened his pace as he negotiated every obstacle in front of him.

He stopped caring about who he had to bulldoze out of his way and inadvertently became as cutthroat and determined as the instigators of the riot.

All he cared about was his own safety and freedom.

He had no friends there, nobody he felt loyal to. As it always had been throughout his entire life, it was him against the world.

Surely the powers that be would put an end to this soon? The dissent would be quelled, order restored, control seized back by those who were meant to wield it.

He imagined his cell had been destroyed by now and was glad he to chose to flee his hiding place; he now needed to determine his next move.

Where would be safest to wait out the remainder of this farce? Outside, probably, where there was more space to move, to breathe, to avoid the makeshift missiles flying around.

But was that even an option?

It could be if the external security doors were unlocked, like the internal ones were. He had yet to find one he hadn't been able to make his way through.

He changed direction and headed for the outdoor recreational space, which was mercifully near to where he was standing.

Where circumstances allowed, he ran quickly towards it; other times, when the way ahead was impassable, he slowed down and carefully navigated the broken furniture, mattresses, and bodies that hindered his progress.

He wanted no part of this and was desperate to keep his model-inmate record clean.

He came to the door that led outside and pushed it hard; it opened easily and he ran through into the clear, clean air. He felt instantly safer, although he could not predict how long that would last.

He was initially surprised to see there was nobody else out there with him but quickly realised why: an escape route out of there lay wide open and completely unguarded.

This was the exact opportunity he had been waiting for since he had been dragged into this hell.

His freedom called to him…

Suddenly, everything changed. Sirens wailed in the distance, heralding their imminent victory. The cavalry had arrived. The authorities were here to impose order and they would do it swiftly.

The atmosphere shifted and so did his chain of thought as the chance to retake his freedom faded by the second.

He sprinted towards the way out. It was now or never.

His freedom beckoned him.

It was within his grasp.

But time was running out. He summoned every ounce of energy he had.

His freedom teased him.

He could hide on the outside, adopt a disguise nobody would see through.

It was his for the taking.

His freedom tempted him.

He raced frantically towards it.

He reached it.

His freedom screamed to him.

He breathed deeply, put one foot in front of the other and stepped forward.

His freedom cocooned him.

Where would he go? To that godforsaken town where his heart and his world had been torn in two?

His freedom dizzied him.

To Oliver... to Martin... to Mark... to the Maniac, and to the countless others who had it coming to them?

His freedom empowered him.

CHAPTER 15
Late October

When Mark escaped from that godforsaken town, he had found some much-needed solitude at the coast, in a sleepy little place not dissimilar to where Oliver had moved from.

A place of serenity, well away from the horrors of his tortured past.

A place of safety, where he felt more invigorated than he had ever been before.

A place of peace, where his only task was taking in as much sea air as possible although, for some reason, it did make him cough in a way he hadn't before moving there.

He assumed it was just his chest clearing itself of all the junk he had previously inhaled. It made him tired - exhausted at times - but he was sure it would ease as he settled into his new cleaner way of living.

He particularly enjoyed walking along the beach in silence, listening to the waves breaking onto the shore.

He loved meandering through the communal gardens shared by the residents of the small seaside town. For the first time, he allowed himself not only to stop and smell a whole array of different flowers but to appreciate their beauty and existence, and to learn their names too.

Finally, his life was completely and utterly stress free. People tended not to acknowledge him and that was exactly what he wanted.

Being on the coast felt right to him; he fancied he could settle there seeing as he already loved it so much, in spite of the temporary health issues it seemed to induce.

True, he would have to settle down and do something at some point but that was a problem for another day, not now.

Right now, he had just one job: enjoy his life as a man of leisure, eating, drinking, sleeping, and actively relaxing.

Who knew how long any of them had left to enjoy?

Who knew what was in store?

He didn't want to leave this place. Ever. He couldn't go back there. He *wouldn't* go back there. Not to that godforsaken town with its unsavoury characters and capacity to destroy lives.

But what if that godforsaken town and his previous life tried to call him back?

What if they slowly began to peck away at him, day after day?

What if his own guilt began to eat him up alive and he couldn't bear to mask it any longer?

What then?

He remained adamant he would never go back there.

Recently, he had spent a few nights in London - a brave move for him. He quite liked it there and had enjoyed visiting in the past, just another face in the crowd, but there was too much going on for him ever to be able to settle.

Too much temptation on every street corner; too many parties; too many opportunities to slip back into his old, risky ways.

He couldn't let that happen. Unlike the coastal sanctum he was presently in, London was not a place he could be happy.

Whilst there, he stepped out of his usual comfort zone and took himself to the theatre. It wasn't that he particularly enjoyed it there - he didn't – and he knew he was unlikely to stay for the whole performance but on that evening he had good intentions and it was something he felt he should do.

It was his conscience that had guided him there, after spending several sleepless nights beforehand deciding whether or not to go.

His previous co-star, Miss Tittie Mansag, was performing in the play, happily immersed in the acting life her male alter-ego had longed to return to.

He had seen the posters advertising the show in his new home town as the play toured through but he couldn't risk watching it then, as it would have been like inviting his past into his new life.

He had even read about it in a local newspaper, immediately recognising the slightly larger than life man he had once known and worked alongside.

After all, they had once sat backstage, as Connie and Tittie, side by side, dressed as both men and women for long enough, although now their names and situations were very different.

He felt he could trust Tittie though and, whilst in London, he had debated at length whether he should present himself at the stage door, the dressing room door, or just to a member of staff who worked there.

He had even contemplated sending an anonymous bouquet of flowers because he'd heard that was what theatre luvvies did. Although no one had ever done that for him after any of his performances.

In the end he decided not to present himself anywhere or to anybody, and thought anonymous flowers were more likely to open the floodgates of confusion and suspicion for Tittie, who didn't need any more surprises in his life.

Ultimately, all he wanted to do was make sure Tittie was safe and happy in his life away from Divas and doing what he loved most: performing. He wasn't sure why but he was certain it wasn't him trying to reconnect with his old life. No, never that… it was just a quick check-up on someone from his past, and it was nothing like 'going back'.

The turmoil that unfolded at Divas had left a legacy of broken hearts and emotional scars; those closest to the situation were still healing and he knew he was partly to blame for that.

In fact, he was largely to blame for that!

If he hadn't been so hell-bent on revenge… if he had been more considerate of others… if he had been less focussed on his own situation then maybe things would have turned out differently for everyone.

For Christ's sake… maybe Jake would still be alive.

Maybe the pressure he had subjected Chris to had worsened his irrational behaviour and contributed to his breakdown.

Mark had his conscience to clear before he could move on and commit to the life of solitude he had discovered.

Maybe the heart of this once frozen bitch was finally beginning to thaw.

So, he had taken himself to London to track down Tittie in this play, and was relieved to discover his former colleague did look happy and gave a professional, convincing performance.

It appeared to Mark that Tittie was just being himself now, free from the horrors of his own past.

As Mark sat unseen in the audience, he was satisfied no lasting damage had been done to the other man. That was enough for him: he prepared to leave and never return.

Perhaps Mark could find some peace now, too.

He craved it.

He desperately wanted to be able to look forward in his life rather than backwards.

Unfortunately, the past did not seem to want to let him go and he could already sense the winds of change were dragging him back in the direction he had come from.

CHAPTER 16
31st October - Halloween

Oliver and Wayne stood behind the bar at The Old Queen's Jugs in their harlequin-style masks and braced themselves for another hectic night of being under-staffed and under-supported by so-called management.

It was the evening of the charity masked Halloween ball and they were expecting a full house. The tickets had sold out in record time; the venue would be bursting at the seams and **no one** was getting in without a ticket.

Masked punters streamed steadily through the doors, heading straight to the bar and ordering bottles of wine and pints of lager in their masses. Oliver could glimpse only random faces in the ever milling crowd but stopped dead when he noticed the stranger with the cap and the hair pulled over his face had returned. The mystery man wore no Halloween mask but then he didn't really need to as the cap and hair did a good enough job of hiding his identity.

Who was he?

There was something familiar about him but Oliver couldn't put his finger on it. He got the feeling it was someone Oliver knew only he looked different in some way. It was infuriating.

Wayne must have served him because he was already nursing a pint of what looked to be lager. Perhaps he had a mask to put on later like many of the others in there, who had realised drinking whilst wearing a mask was far from easy.

Oliver didn't like the masks. They made him feel uncomfortable; anybody could be behind one of them. Any lunatic could walk into the pub that evening with their ticket in hand and a mask on their face, and nobody would know who they were.

What had Wayne said about the stranger the other night? His name was Jay, or something that sounded like Jay.

It couldn't be Jake in disguise, could it? Why would he do that? Who would he be hiding from?

"Oh, idiot!" he told himself. What was he thinking? Of course it wasn't Jake, in disguise or otherwise. He had watched him slip away at the roadside, looked on as his eyes closed when the pain became too much for him to bear. He had heard his final words: "I love you, Oliver. I promise I will always be with you."

Oliver shuddered and snapped himself out of the suffocating memory that had overwhelmed him. He returned to serving the many customers waiting at the bar, all of whom wanted to get their drinks before the guest drag queens appeared, and who seemed to have arranged to meet each other there at that precise moment!

Wayne and Oliver realised they would need help if they were going to be able to serve everyone who was waiting but knew there was no chance of Martin stepping up. He was always too busy giving it the big I am, trying to look as though he was busy, or disappearing into his office for extended periods probably surfing the Net for dates or scouring the personal columns; not for a moment did anyone consider he might be conducting business.

Although he was the owner, he rarely acted like it and Wayne was beginning to feel as though the responsibility of running the place was all on his shoulders, again, even though it was no longer his pub!

As for his so-called mate, Robert (Wendy); well, he was about as much use as a chocolate fireguard - permanently distracted buying things for Wendy, talking about Wendy, becoming Wendy, whilst telling anybody who would listen that garters and girdles were a girl's best friend. To say nothing of explaining how he had bought himself a new apron and baking tray and had found himself with a soggy bottom and an over-sized muffin top on more than one occasion; although, in hindsight, they might have been two separate conversations.

Wayne was not happy with any part of the new arrangement. This had once been his pub, his livelihood, his home. He had lost everything but one day he would find his way again… one day he would be back in charge.

True, he and Robert had been friends for years and had shared many a drink and a chat over the bar but that was different because then it had been *his* bar. The roles had shifted, and he now found himself at the bottom of the ladder. Well, not quite at the bottom: he was still one rung higher than Oliver but only because he was yet to master the art of changing a beer barrel.

It was the fact he had ended up living in Robert's former studio apartment, where they used to play poker with Digger Dave and Plumber Pete whilst Robert had moved into Wayne's old living quarters above the pub that bothered him most. No matter how much he vacuumed or how many lint rollers he bought, he couldn't seem to stop the stubborn bits of Wendy's old wig hairs sticking to everything he owned.

But this phoenix would rise from its ashes and be a success once more. He might even call his next pub 'The Phoenix' because there *would* be another pub;

knowing this was only a stop gap until then kept him going, night after night.

Martin introduced the two guest drag queen cabaret stars and they stepped out into the spotlight to perform their show for that evening. As the audience surged forward towards the stage, with or without drinks, Oliver noticed that the guy who might be called Jay had not joined them but had remained sitting where he was. Just sitting there, watching Oliver across the newly formed void.

Oliver did not want to catch his eye and looked away but the next time Oliver glanced up the stranger was nowhere to be seen. Maybe he had put on a mask and joined the others at the stage. Maybe he had left. Oliver felt extremely uncomfortable about the whole situation.

Just what was this random stranger in the cap all about?

Who was he?

And why did he seem so interested in Oliver?

CHAPTER 17
31ˢᵗ October - Halloween

As the guest drag queen cabaret stars stepped out onto the stage they were greeted with cheers and applause, although some of the bitchier restless tongues clapped with unenthusiastic disdain as they had heard disparaging reviews of the artists' recent performances.

But this was for charity so, surely, they would bring their A-game tonight?

Those not familiar with their act were greeted by one tall and younger drag queen, Whore-Moan, and a wider, older one, Phero-Moan. The taller of the two appeared more glamorous and better put together than the other, who was perhaps fifteen years older and a hundred percent more haggard, but maybe that was intentional. However, any actual family resemblance was entirely absent.

"Well, hello there," said Whore-Moan, the first to step to the front of the stage, with a microphone in her hand. "Welcome to the House of Moan. It's great to see so many of you here tonight at this special charity event."

Whore-Moan beckoned her companion forward to join her. "Come along, Mother," she announced. "Can you walk that far? Say, isn't it nice to see so many people in here tonight?"

"It is," remarked Phero-Moan into her own microphone.

"And can you see them?"

Phero-Moan rolled her eyes and shook her head. "Yes, I can see them. Who'd have thought there'd be so many gay people interested in the old queen's jugs. Lesbians excluded, that is."

Whore-Moan nodded her head and laughed. "Any breast is best right, girls?"

"What even old ones?"

"I guess so."

Phero-Moan looked confused and tried to bounce her own chest up and down, though with little success. "What, even really saggy, old ones, like mine?"

"I don't see why not."

Phero-Moan looked out towards the audience and cringed slightly at what she saw looking back, but only as part of the routine. "So maybe I could get myself a few numbers for home time then. Any hole's a goal, right?"

"Mother, really. No."

"Hey, when you're poking the fire, you don't need to look at the mantelpiece."

Phero-Moan had a quick look around and cringed once more, this time in a far more exaggerated manner, as if she was searching the audience to find the least repulsive of her potential admirers. "Mmmm, maybe you're right. I'm not sure even I'm *that* desperate."

Whore-Moan shook her head. "Actually, Mother, I was warning them." With that, Whore-Moan held her microphone close to her own private lady parts and mimicked it vibrating vigorously, pulling a slightly startled and orgasmic face as she did so with eyes bulging, tongue hanging out, and her body convulsing as though she had ten thousand bolts of electricity running through her. "Any hole's a goal, right?"

"Oi, you be nice," scolded Phero-Moan. "Just because we're not biologically related doesn't mean you won't end up looking like this."

"Oh, I'll never look like you," giggled Whore-Moan, feeling quite mischievous at this point. "Anyway, talking about biology - or at least something that was sloshed around in a test tube - I think one of your actual daughters is here tonight."

"Oh, is it my favourite one?" asked the older drag queen, looking at the faces in the crowd with her hand over her eyes to shield herself from the lights above. "You know the one I mean... she's just like me and brighter than the rainbow flag. Is it that one?"

"Well, it certainly looks like a rainbow flag exploded on her face!"

"So where is she then?"

Whore-Moan pointed at Wendy WolfWhistle, who was standing at the edge of the stage taking what appeared to be notes (not to improve her performance, of course; rather to critique what was wrong with theirs compared to her own high standards).

"Oh yes, there she is," said Phero-Moan warmly. "Come on, let's give her a big round of applause, everybody. She is the star of the show, after all."

"Depending on who you speak to, that is," muttered Whore-Moan. "I bet that Tequila bird has a whole other perspective on that."

The audience gave Wendy a huge round of applause and a cheer, causing her to beam widely and proudly and wave back to her clearly adoring fans, ever hungry for as much attention and appreciation as she could receive. It was, after all, her reason for living.

"Hmmm," said Whore-Moan, winking at Wendy and then turning back to face the audience in front of her. "I bet the last time she had a clap that big she needed antibiotics to clear it up! Only joking, Wendy! I mean, I must be cos you'd need to sleep with somebody to get an STD."

"Ooh, woof woof," said Phero-Moan, "the bitch is out tonight."

"I know, stop me barking, please."

"Actually, I love Wendy. Isn't she fab?"

"That's rude," announced Whore-Moan, slightly shocked. "I would never say anything like that, if it wasn't for fat people who would we complain about for taking up too much arm room on a plane seat."

"Actually, I said fab," announced Phero-Moan, putting her hand over her mouth in shock, and then shaking her head apologetically towards Wendy.

"Oh, I thought you said..."

"Yes, I know exactly what you thought I said, Darling Daughter."

"Anyway, we know it's not true," said Whore-Moan, looking at Wendy in the sympathetic way that people look at an orphaned puppy. "How can she be fat when she's practically a size zero? She told us that, backstage, didn't she?"

"Oh yes, you're right, she did."

"And zeros are round, aren't they?" With that, Whore-Moan drew the biggest circle imaginable in the air, starting at the top and working down in both directions.

Phero-Moan looked at Whore-Moan disapprovingly and Whore-Moan stopped what she was doing. "You know I don't like fat jokes," she remarked. "I'm not exactly a slip of a thing myself. Anyway, I don't think we should be talking about it. I think it's a secret."

"Oh really? And why do you think that, Mother?"

"Well, for starters, I wouldn't have known she was a size zero had she not told me."

Following several mutters from the audience, Phero-Moan added: "Oh right, she's told you lot too, has she? Okay, not so much a secret as a blatant lie, then."

Addressing the audience, Whore-Moan added: "Oh don't worry, we're not being mean; honestly, we're not. You see, Wendy gate crashed our dressing room earlier..."

"Oh, is that when she asked us if we wanted to borrow a handbag that had once belonged to Whitney Houston?" interjected Phero-Moan.

"No, Mother."

"Oh, do you mean when she asked if we thought she resembled Jennifer Anniston, but with better hair?"

"No, Mother."

"Oh, to ask if..."

"No, Mother..." Whore-Moan interrupted, "to ask us if we would like to give her a really massive roasting later on, which, of course, we couldn't resist, could we?"

Upon hearing this, Phero-Moan looked a little alarmed. "Erm, wait..." she hollered. "A massive... roasting, did you say?"

"Yes, that's right."

"Oh, I thought she wanted a massive roast dinner. What the hell am I going to do with these now?" Phero-Moan pulled out a chicken, a selection of vegetables, and two giant sprouts from her bra.

"Oooh, I dread to think where the gravy's being kept warm," muttered Whore-Moan, in mock horror.

"I think I've got a bit of stuffing in here too," added Phero-Moan, pulling the neckline of her dress forward and peering inside.

"Just a bit?"

Phero-Moan crossed her arms and pulled a face at her drag daughter. "Are we done with the fat jokes now?"

"Yes," sighed Whore-Moan reluctantly, but then held up her microphone as a malevolent smile spread across her face. "Wait, no, not quite."

"What do you mean, 'Not quite?'"

"Please could Tequila ShockingBird come to the stage?" asked Whore-Moan, ignoring her drag queen mother. "Paging Miss Tequila ShockingBird to the stage. Wendy WolfWhistle too"

Intrigued, both Tequila and Wendy stepped forward and joined the two guest stars on stage. What was going on? They hadn't rehearsed this earlier.

"So, tell me, Tequila," Whore-Moan began to say, "when you're not dressed up as a shocking bird, is your male name James?"

"Erm, yes, that's right," nodded Tequila.

"Oh look, everybody" giggled Whore-Moan, pointing at the two puzzled people who had just joined them on the stage, "it's *James and the Giant Peach*! Right, now I'm done with the fat jokes, I promise."

Tequila and Wendy both stepped off the stage, resumed their previous positions at the side, and the charity drag act resumed, although Tequila was the only one who was laughing. Wendy wasn't sure what they had meant but the audience had laughed so it must have been gold dust; she wrote it down.

"Oh, don't forget," said Phero-Moan to the crowd, "the more you drink, the more desirable we become."

"Actually," added Whore-Moan, "that works both ways. Can somebody get me a drink?" And with that she grabbed a bottle of beer from the person standing closest to her at the front of the stage and downed the entire contents in one swig before handing back the empty bottle. "Ha, I'm only joking, I can't see how ugly any of you are with those masks on."

Admittedly, the guy she had taken the drink from should have been annoyed by this, but the amazing Whore-Moan had just stolen his beer and drunk it right in front of him. He was officially the most envied person in the building… and the thirstiest!

What a tale he would have to tell people at work on Monday, especially once he had embellished it a little… by the time he was finished, everybody would hear how he had been pulled onto the stage, sat on a chair, and given a lap-dance whilst being serenaded to the adapted version of the *Annie* classic: Your son will come out tomorrow ♪!

Whore-Moan turned to face her drag queen mother and jolted backwards in comical shock. "Nope, a single beer is definitely not enough to make this one look any better!"

"Rude."

"Talking about write-offs."

"I didn't know we were," replied Phero-Moan, as her partner looked her up and down distastefully.

"Yeah… I was," replied Whore-Moan, with a pointed look at her stage mum.

"Are you talking about me? Hey, I'm not a write off!"

"Okay, not so much a write off as an old banger."

"I'll have you know I'm in perfect working order."

"Then what about that oil leak from the front?"

"Once I laughed too hard and I wet myself a little."

"Oh please, you only have to blink and you wet yourself a little."

Phero-Moan addressed the audience: "Front row, please don't worry, she's only joking. There's nothing wrong with this model that a quick waxing won't fix."

"And what about all the gas that comes out the back? None of that is carbon neutral, I can tell you."

"Well, what about you then, you lanky streak of piss?"

"Oh, that's original," mocked Whore-Moan. "Do you have any idea how often I am called a lanky streak of piss?"

"I'm surprised you even wear high heels."

"Any gay man worth their salt knows they're the only things worth going back into the closet for."

"It's a pity some of the guys in here didn't stay in! Oh well, I suppose that's what *Grinder* is for, or masked charity events."

"*Grinder*? Mother, how do you even know that word?"

"Oh, I heard Wendy uses it all the time. I think it's to help us oldies make vegetables more digestible."

"Right, Mother, are you going to sing a song, or shall I?"

"Do you know what, I think I might sing first for a change."

"Are you sure, you are quite flat."

"Darling," announced Phero-Moan, quite proudly. "I haven't been flat since I was thirteen years old. Now, I will sing and they will listen. And who cares if I'm rubbish cos it's all for charity!"

"What is the charity anyway?" asked Whore-Moan.

"I think it's something to do with sending poor disadvantaged gay children to drag school."

"Ahhh yes, because let's face it nobody wants to end up looking like Wendy WolfWhistle, do they?"

"Oh, woof woof, the bitch is back."

A backing track began to play, and Phero-Moan sang a song about broken hearts, whilst Whore-Moan left the stage and stood with Tequila and Wendy.

After the show, as Whore-Moan and Phero-Moan were *untucking* in their dressing room and the audience was still debating whether they had been good or not, there was a knock on the door and Wendy WolfWhistle came barging in eagerly.

"Oh my God," she shrieked excitedly, squeezing herself in between them so tightly that any one of them might have ended up pregnant. "You were so good tonight."

"Ahhh, thank you, Darling," replied Phero-Moan. "Will we see you on stage tonight?"

"Oh yes, I have a few tricks up my sleeve as well. Just in case you were wandering, I wasn't taking notes to steal ideas from your show and use them myself, at all."

"Well, that's good to hear," said Whore-Moan, "because I write all our shows."

"Some more successfully than others," muttered Phero-Moan, but her remark appeared to go unnoticed.

"So tonight," continued Wendy, who wanted to be the centre of attention, "I will be doing my rendition of the *Dying Swan*. I pop on this gorgeous, teeny tiny little wedding dress – it's the size of a cotton bud really and it practically hangs off me… used to belong to Elizabeth Taylor, you know - and then I die on stage. It's such a crowd pleaser."

"I expect you die on stage quite often," remarked Phero-Moan, reapplying her lipstick. Seriously, how had this great lolloping sack of spuds bagged the lead in a cabaret show, whilst she was barely hanging on by her fingertips?

"Oh yes, I do" replied Wendy, too busy memorising exactly how Phero-Moan coloured in her lips to appreciate the sarcasm dripping from them.

It was exactly as Wendy applied it herself: to gently puckered lips, carefully lining the edges, then filling in the plump area in the middle... but Wendy smiled smugly to herself, safe in the knowledge she was so much smarter than this drag queen novice in front of her; yes, *almost* identical but Wendy knew how to multitask so she could eat and drink at the same time. Ha! Amateur!

"Now don't you go and steal my act either," warned Wendy, watching where Phero-Moan put down her lipstick so she could go back and steal it later on when nobody was looking. After all, if she was wearing Phero-Moan's lipstick, and she was in drag and applying it exactly the same way as Phero-Moan did, then surely that would **make** her Phero-Moan?

What a shame it hadn't been Whore-Moan applying her lipstick instead. She looked like a super model. It was like looking in the mirror.

"Oh, you never know," giggled Whore-Moan. "What do you reckon, Mother? Do you want to dress up as a giant meringue and die on stage?"

Phero-Moan pulled a face into her mirror. "Actually, that sounds rather like the last eight shows we've done together."

"Hmmm," responded Whore-Moan, nonchalantly.

"We can be so much better than we have been. We both know that. We had great chemistry tonight and it was a good atmosphere because we winged it. I really miss performing that way."

"I'm not discussing this again," warned Whore-Moan; based on the tone of her voice, this was not the first time the subject had been raised.

"Right, well, I'm off to have few drinks at the bar with the punters and that little cutie I met earlier," announced Phero-Moan, standing up from her dressing table chair. "What was his name again? Oliver?"

"Yes, but be nice to him," said Wendy. "He's had quite the year already. His boyfriend, Jake, was killed in a hit and run right outside his home, but the car was aiming for him. His other boyfriend, Chris, who ran Divas Cabaret Bar, did it. I was in the show there too, you know."

"Oh, wow," announced Phero-Moan, walking towards the door. "Who knew?"

"Oh, everybody knows," explained Wendy. "The restless tongues make sure of that. I won the title of Miss Divas Cabaret Bar, too; can you believe it?"

And, as everybody seemed to whenever she disclosed this information, Whore-Moan and Phero-Moan both shook their heads because they genuinely could not believe it.

Taking no notice of the mood change in the dressing room, or the fact Phero-Moan was clearly trying to get away from there as quickly as she could, Wendy asked nicely – insisted upon pain of death - they had a selfie or six together… or enough until she looked better than they did in at least one of them.

Before anybody could protest, Wendy had rounded up Phero-Moan like a lost sheep to the pen and was faffing around them like an annoying mosquito, snapping away on her camera phone, every which way she could.

"Oooh lovely," she declared, clicking away. "Absolutely drop-dead gorgeous. Sublime. Stunning. What a treat to be photographed with such amazing drag queen talent."

"Ahhh, thanks Darling," said Whore-Moan warmly, assuming Wendy was grateful for the opportunity to be posing with herself and Phero-Moan. Wendy, on the other hand, firmly believed the pleasure was all theirs and she was doing them a favour. After all, she, Wendy WolfWhistle, was the star of the show in this venue, not them.

"You are very welcome," announced Wendy, oblivious as always.

The fans' phones would be ablaze with activity that evening.

#DragQueens
#Fabulicious
#WendyWolfwhistle

She suspected the National Grid would struggle to keep the power supply going once the demand of people sharing these once-in-a-lifetime photos over social media kicked in.

"Now, I'll just follow you both on the socials and you accept my friend requests…" she instructed, frantically pressing buttons on her phone like a woman possessed. "Then I can tag you into all my hashtag posts."

#OldQueensJugsPub
#BeautifulDragQueens
#PsychicDragQueen (so she could check in remotely and see 'her best friend' Wendy, wherever she was.)
#PheroMoan
#WhoreMoan
#WendyWolfwhistle (again) because she was obviously the biggest click-bait.

"Erm, ok…" replied Whore-Moan, reluctantly, as she was not looking for another online stalker.

Phero-Moan agreed too, with some trepidation as she did not want to be publicly linked to this delusional ignoramus.

"Do it now, then!" demanded Wendy, thrusting her phone in both of their faces simultaneously. "I can share all these lovely photos with you straight away - I know you can't wait to see them! I have to say though, Phero-Moan, you don't look anything like your profile picture."

"Oh, we all fib a little on social media, don't we?" she replied, and Wendy had to nod in agreement because she had never heard a truer word spoken.

Left with no other choice, both guest drag queens took out their phones and accepted Wendy's friend requests.

They could always change their mind in a few days' time, when they were miles away in the comfort and safety of their own homes, and Wendy was no longer on hand to strong arm them into connecting with her again. After all, Cyberspace was notorious for 'accidentally' deleting 'friends' on social media. It happened to Wendy all the time! Often, she found herself accidentally blocked, too.

Of course, by that time the photos, messages, and hash tags would already have been published for the entire world to see and the awful consequences they would evoke would already be unavoidable.

No one could have foreseen the magnitude of the chaos this one, simple action would create.

And without warning, The Queen of Broken Hearts edged its way closer to the top of the deck.

CHAPTER 18
Early November

On a different evening, between Halloween and the 5th November, aka Bonfire Night, Tequila was performing an erotic routine on stage. A very erotic routine that Martin thought was way over the top and did not approve of in the slightest. But Tequila convinced him the fans would love to watch her perform it.

It gave her the perfect opportunity to wear the skimpiest outfit she could find to show off her gorgeous, little figure.

Wendy had been very envious when she had first laid eyes on it and was most put out when she was forbidden to go within ten feet of it, in case she stretched it out of all proportion by trying to squeeze herself into it. Wendy most definitely suffered from a severe case of body dysmorphia, only not in the traditional sense: whereas most people looked in a mirror and saw someone much larger than they were, Wendy appeared to see only a fraction of the mass she occupied in space.

♫ *I'm waiting in a dark room*
You'll find everything you need by touch alone
When I'm waiting in a dark room
I'll be in there on my own
But it's better when there's two
Baby, me and you

Step inside…
Leave your inhibitions at the door
Come inside…
You'll be begging me for more

It's never gonna stop
It's never ever gonna stop

Could you want me in a dark room?
Could you love me in a dark room?
You can be anyone you want to be
Your secret's safe with me ♬

But secrets were not safe at all.

And Tequila had a secret too; so far, it had stayed hidden as she was the only one who knew about it.

She didn't think anybody would have believed her if she had disclosed it anyway.

Why would they?

After all, it was all so absurd she barely believed it herself.

♬ *I'm waiting in a dark room*
It's so quiet I can almost hear you breathe
When I'm waiting in a dark room
There's only me and you
And it's better when there's two
Only me and you

Step my way
Can you hear me call your name?
I'm over here
Things will never be the same
Now that you're here
You'll never want to leave
You'll never ever want to leave

Could you want me in a dark room?
Could you love me in a dark room?
You can be anyone you want to be

Your secret's safe with me ♫

Tequila had debated sharing this secret several times but who would she tell?

And was it a secret, or was she simply safeguarding information that may not even be true?

Yet the more she thought about it, the more real it seemed.

Or was it?

She just wasn't sure.

♫ *We're meeting in a dark room*
Should I let you in?
We're meeting in a dark room
Let the hunger games begin

Could you want me in a dark room?
Could you love me in a dark room?
You can be anyone you want to be
Your secret's safe with me

Your secrets are safe with me... ♫

Up until recently she hadn't really thought about it much and had successfully moved it to the back of her mind, where it was gathering dust.

But recent revelations had brought it back, front and centre.

She had pondered it whilst she was recovering in hospital but as the weeks passed by and as she began preparing for the cabaret show, writing songs, perfecting dance routines, and trying to keep Wendy out of anything backless, crotchless or legless, it had just sort of fallen out of her head... life took over.

But now, like a letter with no address, it had made its way back.

And now it had firmly taken root in her conscious brain, immoveable, like a limpet on a rock.

Oh, that night... that blasted night when Divas had burnt down... she had seen him too. Or at least she thought she had.

Wendy had resuscitated her and, as she came to, she was positive she had seen Jake.

Not standing behind Oliver, as Father Wendy had told Martin, but further in the distance. As though he was running away but had turned around for one final look.

From where she had been lying, in her semi-conscience state, it had certainly looked like him.

But then again, she had just been brought back from the brink of death and everything was fuzzy, unfocussed.

But how was she supposed to un-see something she had clearly seen?

And if Father Wendy thought she had seen him too, why was Martin so adamant it had not been Jake? Why was he stopping Wendy from taking the matter any further?

Seriously, what the hell was going on and how much longer would anyone's secrets be safe?

CHAPTER 19
Early November

That very same evening, as Tequila performed her erotic number wearing next to nothing, Wendy sat quietly at the makeup mirror in her dressing room, contemplating the wonderous world in which she was now fully immersed: the glamour, the glitz, the glory. She had always know she was born to this life and was thoroughly delighted everyone else could finally see her shining brightly, exactly as she had told them she would.

After applying the first generous undercoat of impenetrable beige foundation to her porous skin, which soaked it up quicker than a long-distance lorry driver supping his first pint after delivering a truckload of sawdust to the Outer Hebrides, she couldn't help but smile widely to herself; life was amazing now she was in the show.

In her head, she was acting out her scenes, over and over again, each time improving upon her last performance and transporting the audience to places never before visited. A true professional, she commanded the spotlight and had quickly become addicted to its glare.

This egotistical reverie was the entire reason she hadn't yet spotted the envelope that had been placed on her dressing table, waiting to be torn open by her giant sausage-sized fingers with the chipped French tips.

She was far too pre-occupied with her own stunning beauty to have noticed it; over-whelmed with excitement at the new figure-hugging leggings Tequila had left for her to wear whilst lip-syncing to a *Grease* medley - even though she had barely been able to haul them over the voluptuous curves of her giant arse, no matter how much lard she had greased them up with.

So, there it stayed, unnoticed. Her name beautifully calligraphed across the front: Miss Wendy WolfWhistle. Propped up carefully against the vase of plastic flowers she had recently bought herself (claiming were from a fan), which she drenched in air freshener every couple of days for a more realistic experience.

When she finally noticed it, her entire body stiffened with excitement and she clapped her hands joyfully. "Oooh!" she declared to the empty room. "A letter! (Pour moi?! How marvellous! Whatever does it say? Who could it be from? No doubt one of my besotted fans, declaring his love for me!"

She moved aside the car sponge she had been using to apply her make up with and eagerly tore it open. Little bits of paper flew in every direction, rather like gentle kisses blowing in the breeze.

It had to be a fan letter! Why else would someone have gone to the trouble of risking being caught sneaking into the dressing room just to leave it for her to find? Her mystery admirer would surely be waiting with bated breath for her delicate, well-manicured fingers to open it.

It was! It really was a fan letter! And this time it was from a real person, not something she had created herself and purposefully left beside the beer pumps at the bar, for a random person to find and deliver to her.

"Ooh, for *me*?" she would exclaim when the poor - not entirely unsuspecting - mule returned it to her. "How wonderful! I wonder who it's from? Another devoted fan I expect, a lover of my work, no doubt."

But everybody knew who they were really from, especially as they were invariably stained with the exact colour lipstick Wendy slathered on for every performance.

'Wendy your great and soooo pretty to!'

'Love you Wendy, your brill and dead talented.'

'Can't weight to see your next show Wendy, do a pelvic frust just for me, yeah xx'

But this one bore none of those tell-tale signs; this one was genuine! It was thoughtful, charming, and contained not a single spelling mistake - not that she would have been able to spot one anyway.

Wow, she was loved! Really, truly loved! So much so that somebody had taken the time to sit down and tell her just how incredible she was. She would have to show this to Martin immediately. How jealous he would be! He never received any attention at all whilst she, the Wonderous Wendy WolfWhistle, literally bathed in it!

It didn't matter that her face was only partially covered in the much-needed makeup required to make it look marginally better for the show.

And it didn't matter she was virtually naked except for an unstuffed bra and a pair of saggy granny knickers she had not yet *tucked* herself into properly.

It definitely didn't matter her armpits were so hairy monkeys could have swung from them.

The important thing was she had been sent a fan letter and needed to tell somebody **immediately**! Because once she had told one person, they would go on to tell someone else and soon everybody would know her exciting news! That was the one good thing about the otherwise tiresome, querulous restless tongues.

Leaving her dressing room, she charged into Martin's office like a drag queen at a wig sale – screeching so loudly that only dolphins and dogs could hear her. Putting down his paper with a sigh, Martin instructed her to share her news again but this time in a tone that was audible to humans. She did so, gladly, insisting they must frame and hang this important piece of literature in the bar area.

Martin blinked slowly and took the letter from Wendy without question or protest.

He would claim, when asked, that he read the paper to keep abreast of current affairs as all good businessmen did but in reality he spent more time perusing the 'Men seeking Men' page seeking an entirely different kind of affair altogether.

He read Wendy's letter, confused and disbelieving. He read it through a second time, just to be sure. "Wendy," he eventually exclaimed, "my god."

"I know," she responded, proudly, "I'm sure this is just the first of many."

"I hope for your sake it isn't," he replied, a twist of concern in his voice.

Wendy looked most put out. Clearly Martin's green-eyed monster was rearing its ugly head. "Why would you say that? It's a fan letter. Don't you want me to be adored and have fans?"

Martin looked at her and shook his head in dismay. Seriously, what planet did this person live on? "Wendy, this is hate mail. It wasn't a fan who sent this."

"It's not hate mail at all! You're clearly reading it wrong."

"No, *you're* reading it wrong!" exclaimed Martin, in a firm but kindly tone.

Wendy tried unsuccessfully to grab the letter from him . "Look, just give it back. I'm sorry I showed it to you now. I knew you'd be jealous."

"Wendy, you need to take this straight to the police." But he knew she had already stopped listening to him because he wasn't saying what she wanted to hear. "Wendy, listen to me, somebody is threatening you."

"No, they are not!" she squealed, trying to grab the letter from his strong hands once more but still failing. "It's delicious and divine, just like the new wig I purchased from the £10 or less pick and save bin at the market... I'm going to grace the audience with it tonight."

Martin adjusted his reading glasses then quoted a section from the letter aloud. "So, you don't think: 'You are so bad, you make me sick'... and - where is it now – ah, there, 'you need to be killed' are anything to worry about?"

Wendy shook her head and tutted at him in disgust. "Martin, that's how people talk these days. You know, when they're vibing, when they're hanging out. It's cool. You're just behind the times, you dinosaur! 'Bad' and 'sick' both mean 'good', and if you're killing something that means you're great at it. Just ask Tequila... she's always telling me how shit I am. That means shit-hot."

"People may talk like that but they don't write it in a letter..."

"Well, they have this time, Martin."

Martin ignored her interruption. He needed her to listen and stop any thoughts she might be entertaining about romantic weekend breaks away with the author and lace-covered chocolate bars. "...and people who are complimenting you use their own handwriting, they don't cut and paste words from magazines. Wendy, this is really serious."

"No, you're wrong! Now, give me back my fan letter and I will finish getting ready. I don't want you contaminating it with your jealousy any longer."

Martin reluctantly handed it back to her and watched her stomp out of the room, not a pleasant sight in her sagging granny knickers with her lower back hair partially flowing in the breeze and partially brushed down inside them.

Had he interpreted the letter incorrectly? Was it a good thing?

He didn't think so on either count. Okay, Wendy might have a point about the use of modern-day lingo but how could: 'It looks like your face has been covered in acid when you drag up' be taken as anything other than an insult?

Who would have sent such a letter?

Yes, Wendy was a pain in the arse but she was harmless and had a good heart, even if she wouldn't donate her last bit of lip-liner to a destitute drag queen.

He sighed loudly and returned to his newspaper, trying hard to focus on the literary content of something more important. *Middle aged man with nagging wife and more kids than he can count, looking for fun with similar aged man or younger. Local 'celebrity' drag queens with wonky boobs need not re-apply.*

Martin put a circle around that one.

He knew better than most the path to true love was unlikely to be smooth.

Maybe one day there would be love out there for him.

CHAPTER 20
Early November

Mark was sitting on his 'usual' bench in the late autumn sun, staring out towards the sea. This really was the life for him.

Yes, it was all good, although this cough was getting to be quite tiresome now, as were the crushing fatigue and night sweats. Surely they would stop soon; he was frustrated the over-the-counter medicines he had been taking had not helped in any way.

As he sat there that day, slowly munching on a peanut butter and jam sandwich he was not actually hungry enough to enjoy, his mind wandered back to the summertime; to Divas Cabaret Bar, to the drugs, to his previous existence as a drag queen, to the fire, and to the evil Chris Randall, destroyer of lives, hearts, and hope.

He hated that man more than he ever thought possible.

Every single day, Mark was so grateful that Chris was no longer part of his life; he was finally free to live however he wanted.

But that afternoon, for some reason, he was unable to shake off the past in the way he normally could. Unusually, he was focusing on a specific memory of when he had arrived late for the cabaret show at Divas; Tittie and Tequila had helped drag him up as Connie in a matter of minutes, and he recalled how he'd had to go on stage with his false eyelashes hanging off, flapping like broken windscreen wipers across his face.

Tittie asked where had he been to make him so late but he had not responded. He rarely did in those situations and Tittie knew better than to push it any further but had likely presumed he was with some god-awful client somewhere, earning drug money by the hour.

But on that occasion, as on many others, that was not what he had been doing. Sometimes, though, it was easier to let people believe what they wanted to, especially when it helped avoid awkward questions.

On that particular day, he had been in the Northern Territory negotiating with The Maniac. Nobody ever spoke openly about The Maniac because he was a very bad man who you did not want to piss off. An astonishingly bad man who would happily trample all over the likes of Chris Randall before pulling them apart, limb by limb, like a vulnerable gazelle who had found itself stranded from the pack.

The deal with him had been a hard one to agree upon and had taken far longer than anticipated but it had eventually led to his freedom, albeit at a high cost to many others who got caught in the backlash along the way, Tequila included.

But Tequila was not aware of that.

He had made a lot of sacrifices to get where he was today, some deliberate, some not, but it meant he was now able to sit there on the promenade whenever he wanted to, eating sandwiches and watching the ocean; he could breathe in the fresh sea air and live a life without retribution. He could live well, in sobriety.

It had also led Chris to his current existence.

Mark had deftly turned the tables and transformed from being Chris's puppet into the puppeteer. He engineered things so that, in the end, he held all the cards. He had thrown them all in now but that was okay because he thought he had no further use for them.

Clearly, he had forgotten that, sometimes in life, a card could be dealt without warning, when you least expected it, and all you could do was stick, twist, or cross your fingers and hope for the best.

Why oh fucking why could Mark not clear his mind that afternoon?

The past often badgered his thoughts but he had always been able to suppress them before. That day though, he could not push it away, no matter how hard he tried. It just sat there, festering like a bad smell in a confined space without any ventilation to provide release.

And he was not enjoying it in the slightest.

Living life on a knife edge the way he used to meant the people you met along the way tended to be pretty much the same: greedy, obnoxious, and vile. He had never liked them but, as he only ever he dealt with them and their requirements as Connie, he could almost convince himself Mark hadn't really been involved, and he could deflect the shame onto his alter ego.

Connie was the scapegoat and was usually saddled with the messier tasks. Sometimes he did have to do stuff as Mark but it very much depended on the situation.

It had not taken much persuasion from Mark for Chris to change his plans, particularly because he felt he was getting something better out of it. It had also helped that he thought he could trust his cousin. Chris was far from naïve, but his one weakness was greed and Mark had led him to believe the arrangement he was putting in place would make him rich beyond his wildest dreams. And all Mark had seemed to want in return was to be the star of his cabaret show, a small price to pay for a colossal payoff.

Was this what was meant by Fool's Gold? Chris was no fool by anyone's standards but Divas Cabaret Bar had been flagging for ages; the show was tired, the punters had grown bored, and his debts were escalating out of control. This newly negotiated deal with The Maniac was meant to have sorted that out for him but the benefits were slow to manifest. Ultimately, the rewards were unrewarding and the Heavies were heavier than he had ever encountered before.

To make matters worse, they kept raising the bastard stakes too, making more demands and pushing boundaries until Chris could no longer cope with the situation; he became unhinged and dangerous. He had wanted to flee, to find a safe place, but he had nowhere to run to and his unrequited love for Oliver had only blurred the lines even more.

Little did Chris know that his own cousin had orchestrated the whole thing, personally delivering him to the executioner's chair.

Payback for the years of abuse Mark had endured because of him.

The Maniac had not even been the one making demands and changing the rules; that was something Mark had done for his own entertainment.

Mark had pocketed most of the repayments himself, telling the other party that Chris had - yet again - been unable to meet the costs of services rendered.

Having Chris locked in a rancid prison cell was Mark's quickest possible route to freedom. But Mark only knew half the story and was still in a lot deeper than he imagined.

Looking out to sea with tired eyes, he coughed again as he put down his half-eaten sandwich and continued to sag under the weight of his own unbalanced emotions.

He had expected this would happen at some point after he left that godforsaken town; he'd sensed it looming in the depths of his soul and knew it was not something he could escape or avoid. The best he could do was hold on tight as it rose to the surface, burning his throat like bilious acid, and endure as it exploded out of him like a toxin being purged from this body.

He didn't want to go back to that past, but the urge to was growing stronger by the day.

The guilt and regret buried deep in his conscience compelled him and he simply could not ignore his angst.

Damn it. He would have to return. He would never be able to rest if he didn't.

Once more, he would have to walk the exhausting streets of that exhausted town, hiding in the shadows and hoping he would be able to pass unnoticed; praying nobody would spot him, judge him, question him, or even recognise him as he attempted to be invisible.

He had no other choice.

He would not be able to live with himself if he didn't. His anguish prevented him from being happy because it constantly reminded him how own selfish, vengeful actions had stripped the joy from the lives of others.

He needed to make amends.

His actions had almost killed Tequila; she would almost certainly be dead had Wendy not been there to save her.

He did not yet know it, but the next time she was in danger – which would be far sooner than anyone could dream – he alone would be the only one who could save her.

CHAPTER 21
Shortly after the Divas Cabaret Bar fire

The Psychic Drag Queen, Miss April Showers, was holding an evening of mediumship and a demonstration of her psychic abilities.

The whole evening was going to be filmed for the Mrs Seavers Show and televised at a later date.

As usual, many of the people in the audience were hardcore sceptics who had turned up either to cast aspersions on her performance, to be amazed and converted, or just to try to get on television for a fleeting moment of fame.

After all, any exposure was good exposure, right?

Naturally, Wendy had turned up in her most spectacular outfit to support her newly-appointed - but not consulted - best friend and was, in her own words, rocking the arse out of the new super-sized hip and derriere pads she was sporting, which had once belonged to Khloe Kardashian.

Well, sort of... she had recently discovered that cutting out large pieces of sponge in the shape of Africa and adhering them to her person was **the** best way to achieve a perfectly feminine hourglass silhouette.

Unfortunately, that required a lot of effort and she wasn't really sure what shape Africa was so instead, she just shoved a hot water bottle down each side of her moth-eaten shapewear and convinced herself that had achieved more or less the same effect.

Had she not filled both hot water bottles to maximum capacity, perhaps she wouldn't have sounded like an overly full bucket that badly needed draining each time she took a step.

And had she used hot water bottles that were the same size, perhaps her madcap scheme might have avoided detection.

As it was, her poorly executed effort to appear more womanly only resulted in her looking and sounding like some kind of giant, defective water balloon.

That aside, Wendy's motivation for being there that night was not just to wow Miss April Showers with her inimitable style, but also to find out what the future held for her as a professional cabaret star and future drag queen superstar.

After the recent fire at Divas Cabaret Bar, which had caused her so much heartache, her dream of headlining her very own cabaret show seemed to be slipping further away with every passing day.

Yes, there were rumours going around town about a brand-new drag queen cabaret bar that was meant to be opening on East Green Street that autumn, but that was far from definite and only coming from the restless tongues.

If the rumours were true and they were seeking professional cabaret stars such as herself, who were available to start rehearsals at a moment's notice, then her shattered dreams might be salvageable, and she may never need to be branded the queen of broken hearts.

How Wendy hoped April Showers would reveal her fate to her; after all, seeking guidance from a Psychic Drag Queen in a public arena such as this was so much easier than taking a short walk down the same street she lived on to the Old Maiden's Jugs pub to ask what was going on.

That evening, Wendy was her usual deluded self: assuming every TV camera was there for her, she twittered away into each one she passed, telling completely fabricated stories about herself and April, which nobody believed a word of.

"April Showers is my best friend, you know. Oh, isn't she a love?" she said to one camera before wobbling clumsily over to another.

"April Showers and I are the very definition of bosom buddies. In fact, I'm wearing her padded bra right now, although I didn't get round to asking her first, so probably best not to tell her."

She then proceeded to position herself in front of an unfortunate team member who appeared to be at a loose end and blocked their escape route with her bulky frame whilst spouting more nonsense about her and April's 'special friendship'.

"Oh, have you met April Showers yet?" Wendy asked. "She's almost as famous as I am. She's the Psychic Drag Queen, you know. We appeared on the Mrs Seavers Show, together."

She went on to ask if they needed her assistance backstage with any last-minute costume changes or to help touch up her best friend in any way.

"We're proper gal pals, me and April. In fact, we have been inseparable ever since we first met. I'm forever commenting on her socials. Just little tips, you know, handy hints and tricks of the trade. Small enhancements to improve oneself, that's all. In fact, I'm the one who suggested she should pad out her hips like mine."

Once she had finally run out of lies to tell, Wendy tottered over to the buffet table to help herself to just about everything on it.

It was there, whilst sticking her finger into the avocado and chickpea dip to determine whether or not she liked it (she did not), that she came across a formidable creature: standing there was a most striking person with the longest mane of thick black hair Wendy had ever seen.

Her flawless skin glowed beneath the lightest, most natural dusting of makeup - apart from her lips, which were redder than a freshly painted pillar box.

Her dress sense was just as impeccable as her face, her exquisitely fitting outfit accentuating the curves of her body perfectly.

Wendy had never encountered anyone like this before. The designer sunglasses she wore gave her an alluring air of mystery and she exuded an aura that was both intoxicating and suffocating. Sheer confidence and power radiated from every inch of her elegant frame.

There was no denying it, there was something very special about this person and the normally garrulous Wendy fell silent for possibly the first time as she experienced the greatest epiphany of her life: whoever she was, Wendy wanted to be like her - **exactly** like her. To stand erect and proud, just like her; to behave just like her; to command the attention of every single person in the room, just like her.

"Well, I never! You must've thought you were looking in the mirror when you saw me," said Wendy, her mouth full of the tuna vol-au-vent she had almost choked on moments earlier.

"Excuse me?" questioned the ravishing stranger, whose demeanour suddenly altered to one of puzzled irritation.

Did this rancid ogre in a dress, who looked like she had climbed out of a landfill site, seriously believe they were even remotely comparable?

Blissfully unaware of the magnitude of the differences that set them apart, Wendy attempted to calculate how many extra minutes it would take her to achieve this same striking look... two, possibly three if she switched out the vigorous backcombing this beautiful stranger had clearly needed to do and just whacked her wig against the banister a few times instead.

Wendy instantly decided this was her *newest* new best friend.

"Hi, I'm Wendy WolfWhistle," she announced, thankful that the darkened glasses prevented them from making direct eye contact because she wasn't sure she could handle the intensity.

What were they concealing?

Why did she need to wear them indoors?

Showing less emotion than a Botoxed forehead, the stranger acknowledged Wendy with a slight nod of the head.

"I do love your dress," Wendy continued to say. "I have the same one, although I think mine is a bit smaller. Did yours used to belong to Tina Turner, as well?"

"Oh, you're priceless," responded the other person, her face motionless. "You must be an entertainer, of sorts."

"How funny you should say that!" exclaimed Wendy, delighted. "Perhaps you're psychic too. I have actually headlined a cabaret show and am currently considering my options. I was on the Mrs Seavers Show, you know."

Her reluctant companion nodded her head, only marginally more interested than before but definitely listening now.

"And had the cabaret bar not burnt down," Wendy continued, delighting in her underachievement, "I truly believe Chris would have had me on board full time. Do you know Chris? He's very handsome and he's going to be my fiancé, but he's in prison at the moment so that's on hold for a short while. They said he killed Jake but I don't believe it myself. Do you like my chunky necklace? It used to belong to Theresa May, you kn…"

"Okay, I've heard enough now," the siren said to Wendy, cutting her off mid-sentence and reinstating her expression of crushing disinterest. With a pout of her blood-coloured lips she glided effortlessly away from her.

Wendy watched in confused silence as she sashayed away, her peachy perfect backside swaying hypnotically from side to side; the crowd parted to make way as she approached them, affording her very easy passage across the venue with no further interruptions.

Wendy attempted to follow suit, intending to pass effortlessly through the crowd in the same manner as her new muse except, instead of sashaying she stomped; and instead of swishing a peachy bottom to and fro, her giant arse ricocheted into an unfortunate bystander whose pint spilt over her and the floor, causing her to slip and fall, and launch her latest wig creation into the outer atmosphere.

The crowd did not so much part down the middle for her as flee to safety, as Wendy regurgitated the many tuna vol-au-vents she had devoured.

But she didn't care… she barely even noticed, so spellbound was she by the beauty to which she had just borne witness.

Their parting was such sweet sorrow.

What was it about her that had seduced Wendy so easily? Normally, it was only burly straight men that made Wendy go weak at the knees – or drop down onto them.

What on earth was going on?

Their single, brief encounter was enough for her to have made an impact on Wendy that might change her life forever.

Meanwhile backstage, April Showers had been advised by at least two members of the production crew that some oversized Weeble of a drag queen wannabe was going around spreading lies about their friendship and did she want them to do anything about it like pull her disturbingly dusty tights off and shove them in her mouth, or simply just evict her from the venue?

It sounded to April as though this odd character was basically harmless, so she told them to leave things as they were. She had seriously underestimated Wendy and the havoc she was capable of wreaking – a particularly poor move from someone who claimed to be psychic!

Being a Psychic Drag Queen in the public eye, she was used to unwelcome attention; it came with the territory and she still got paid even if there was negative press around her.

Oh, but April, if only you had foreseen what would follow...

If only you had nipped it in the bud, there and then.

If only you had predicted the damage that oversized Weeble was capable of inflicting.

If only you had read the endless social media comments she had left for you.

If only you had met her on the Mrs Seavers Show and severed your connection to her then.

Maybe then, yet another life might have been saved.

CHAPTER 22
5ᵗʰ November - Bonfire night

The fireworks to celebrate bonfire night were about to begin. Eagerly, the punters, the restless tongues, and any left-over drag queens that were still there headed through the exit and out onto the pavement of East Green Street to watch.

No one wanted to miss a single flash, bang, or premature explosion.

Behind the bar, Wayne noticed Oliver watching everybody leave with obvious envy; he wanted to be out there enjoying the firework display and, if he hadn't been stuck working behind that blasted bar yet again, he would have been able to. "Could you change the lager barrel for me?" Wayne asked him, hoping for a different response to the one Oliver normally gave. "It would be a good opportunity for you to practise whilst it's quiet."

Oliver looked reluctantly back at him, shaking his head slightly and scrunching up his face. He had tried to master the art of changing a barrel several times now but, so far, had been unable to. As far as he was concerned, it would be so much quicker and easier if everybody just drank from bottles - or if Wayne changed the barrel, instead.

"Go on, you'll be fine," said Wayne, more firmly this time. "Look, go down, give it a try, and if you really can't manage then I will do it for you. But give it a go, please."

Oliver made no attempt to disguise the fact he really didn't want to but, as it was part of his job and Wayne was his supervisor, he had very little choice in the matter.

He had concluded he was on the wrong side of the bar. He wanted to be served drinks not be the one serving them. Plus, he really hated going down into those dark creepy cellars, which oozed out beneath the streets above. They were vast, eerie, and not improved by the flickering low-voltage bulbs which barely emitted any light at all, never mind the overpowering stench of damp! But the worst thing was the inescapable sensation of something being down there, lurking, scuttling out of sight when someone appeared at the top of the stairs to begin their approach.

Maybe he should just quit; that would be the easiest option. But was it really worth giving up this job just because he couldn't change a barrel and couldn't be bothered to learn how to? Or because Wayne bossed him around? Or because he didn't like going into the cellars because he thought there might be something down there waiting nefariously in the darkness? Probably not.

But, somehow, he just hadn't been able to stop thinking about it that night. Agreeing to work there had been a mistake but was it his worst one?

His life had been joyless for what seemed like such a long time now and he needed to take that first step towards improving his own wellbeing. This job was delaying that. All he ever seemed to do was work: nine to five at his day job, and evenings at the bar. He never seemed to have time to reset, to decompress, to stop and think, or at least try to.

Oliver walked around the bar and stared at the dwindling crowd that was still flocking outside to watch the fireworks. Reluctantly, he headed for the door next to the toilets which led down to the cellar, with a growing feeling this could be his last night working there. He had only agreed to take the job because he hoped it would make him feeler closer to Jake, but it didn't; it hadn't; it never would.

As he stood at the cellar door looking down the stairs and contemplating the bleakness below, the toilet door opened next to him and the guy he had been referring to as Jay walked out and stepped back into the pub. Their eyes met momentarily but Oliver looked away again. Up close, he could see there was something familiar about him, but what was it?

Who the fuck was he and why did he always seem to be there, looking at him, watching what he was doing?

In an effort to shake off the awkwardness, Oliver stepped onto the top landing that heralded the starting point of his slow journey down into the labyrinth below. As the door closed slowly behind him, he walked carefully down the cold stone steps, holding onto the old rickety handrail and taking great care not to fall whilst listening for the sound of unknown movements beyond.

He bloody hated it down there. As his feet found purchase on each step, he thought about quitting again. Why was he putting himself under this pressure? He didn't need to work there and he certainly didn't need the extra money - so why was he still there, making himself miserable?

Maybe it was because Wendy and Martin had been good to him and he didn't want to let them down, especially considering their new venture was still so early in its infancy. But he didn't feel obliged to stay and hoped they would understand his reasonings for wanting to leave; after all, he needed to prioritise himself above everything else, and he genuinely believed doing fun things like standing out on the street and watching fireworks would help his mental health.

On the other hand, he didn't want to leave them high and dry. He was finding the decision very difficult. Many would argue the fact a strange person who looked a little like a dead man kept coming in, staring at him, then disappearing was plenty of reason to leave and never come back. Maybe they would understand that.

The door at the top of the stone steps closed behind him as he reached the equally cold concrete floor below ground. He shuddered, as if somebody had walked right through him or stepped on his grave but reassured himself it was probably just the frigid air and the terrible lighting giving him the creeps.

At least, he hoped it was.

He walked over to the barrels and examined them closely. Okay, this one is lager and this one is cider... I think... but which is the empty one that needs replacing?

He stopped dead in his tracks upon hearing a noise. Oh Jesus, what the hell was that? Was somebody down there with him? He spun round in a panic and looked back up towards the cellar door. What had he heard?

His heart thumped in his chest and his blood ran icy cold.

The noise sounded again but much louder this time.

Oh, of course! It was the fireworks going off outside. He could hear them through the cellar grid that led to the street. So it wasn't a ghost, an oversized rodent, or an axe-murderer after all - thank God for that!.

But even with a rational explanation, this place still scared the crap out of him.

Pulling himself together he returned to the task in hand: barrel changing. And upon conducting a thorough re-examination of the barrels, he realised he had absolutely no idea what was contained within any of them, which was a shame because he really wanted to get the frig out of there.

He could not be arsed with this and once more found himself sorely tempted to march back up the steps and walk the hell out of there, only looking back to see the fireworks.

He took a deep breath and tried to refocus, eventually realising the worst that could happen was he accidentally caused cider to flow through the lager pump... but, on the bright side, that also meant Wayne would have to change the barrels himself and Oliver could definitely live with that!

Although resigning would still be the easiest option. And as another firework exploded outside and Oliver heard the crowd exclaiming in delight, he knew exactly what he needed to do.

It would be a while before anybody realised Oliver had disappeared... once the fireworks were over and the queues had built up at the bar, probably.

Martin would ask where he was.

Wayne would explain he was changing a barrel, but actually... that was ages ago and he should have done it by now.

Martin would check the cellar but would not find Oliver down there.

And the barrel would still need changing.

And, finally, Martin would have to get off his fat arse and muck in for once.

So, what on earth had happened to Oliver? Had he quit and left them high and dry, as he had contemplated doing?

And what about this Jay character?

That evening, he had decided not to leave early; instead, he sat opposite the bar nursing his pint until closing time.

Just sitting, watching, and waiting.

CHAPTER 23
The morning after Bonfire night

The next morning, as they were about to open, Martin looked around the bar with an uneasy feeling that something was off… he just couldn't put his finger on what.

Nothing obvious; nothing seemed to have been moved or broken. Although there was a used glass sitting on top of the bar now, which he felt certain hadn't been there when he had locked up the evening before .

The staff knew Martin expected them to clean and clear everything away before they retired for the night and would have done so even though they had been left short staffed after Oliver did a runner. Foolish boy!

They would not have left a dirty glass on the bar to be tidied up the next morning under any circumstances.

As his eye became keener, he noticed the cardboard display strip that held the peanuts was no longer hanging on the wall; for some reason, it now lay flat on the bar shelf which ran the length of the optics. He went to hang it back up but was unable to as the hook was torn and unusable. He suspected some of the bags of nuts were missing too, but would have to do a count to see if stock levels and recorded sales matched or not.

As if he was playing a slow game of Spot the Difference, he realised next that one of the stools along the front of the bar sat askew from the others. He straightened it.

It wasn't that he was OCD or anal; he just wanted everything in and about his bar to be better than Chris Randall's.

All the other fixtures and fittings appeared to be in order, and looked exactly as they had the previous evening when he headed up after a long, tiring shift.

Maybe Wendy had come down for a midnight snack… again.

He would have to tell her off for doing that… again.

Of course, she would deny it… again.

But this time it would be because Wendy had not done it.

And - unlike previous times - it had not been Tequila either.

CHAPTER 24
The day following Bonfire night

A little after lunchtime, Oliver's mother stepped into The Old Queen's Jugs cabaret bar. She had arrived back in town unannounced to check on her son, as she had said she might.

Her poker face gave nothing away as she looked around in silent dismay at the smattering of faces that stared blankly back at her.

She headed straight to the bar where Wayne, Robert (AKA Wendy), and Martin all stood chatting. Studying each one in turn, she struggled to determine which of them was the oddest!

Wendy WolfWhistle was unmistakable whether she was dressed as a man or a woman; her unique style and features rendered her instantly identifiable. Oliver's mother was not sure who the other two men were but assumed one was a barman and the other was perhaps the owner.

Small groups of friends were catching up here and there on a rare day off, whilst a couple of lonely looking men sat by themselves, keeping a sharp eye out for an opportunity should it coming knocking. There was also one very love-struck couple - planning to move in together after three dates because this time they were **certain** they had found 'the one'!.

"What can I get you, Love?" asked Wayne, not knowing who she was.

She shook her head firmly. "Oh no, I'm not here for a drink," she replied. "I am here to see my son, Oliver. I believe he works here."

"Well, he did," grumbled Martin, "but he walked out last night without any explanation…. didn't say a word to anybody about it, just disappeared."

"Oh," replied Oliver's mother. "I am sorry to hear that. Have you heard from him at all today?"

"No."

"Oh, I was hoping to catch him."

"You could try his apartment," suggested Robert, "it's just down the road. Do you have his address?"

"I've been there already but he's not in," she replied. "That's why I came straight here. I think something might be wrong. You see, it's my birthday today and we were supposed to be meeting for lunch. He hasn't even phoned me. Not so much as a text message. And he isn't answering his phone either. This is very unlike him."

"Happy birthday," said a different voice to the side of her.

She turned to see a young man holding forth his pint in a toasting motion. He wore a cap pulled down low and his hair was pushed over his face. It was Jay; he had been the first customer to arrive when the doors opened that day.

Smiling politely, she thanked him for the birthday wishes, even though she had no idea who he was.

Deciding to go and look for Oliver, she thanked the men for the information and left the venue more concerned about him than ever.

Jay put down his drink, followed her out, and watched her walk down the street.

An hour or so later, Oliver's mother received a short text message from her son wishing her a happy birthday, apologising for forgetting their lunch date, and telling her not to worry.

Instantly, Oliver's mother knew something was terribly, terribly wrong: somebody had Oliver's phone and was using it to message her.

For she had not made plans to meet him for lunch and it was not her birthday.

CHAPTER 25

April Showers' psychic evening, shortly after the Divas Cabaret Bar fire

April Showers needed the evening to be a big success.

Recently, she had been on the receiving end of some bad media attention for making a number of far-fetched predictions that never came to fruition; she could not afford any further cock-ups.

Her options were extremely limited should the event fail and she did not want to be at the mercy of her unscrupulous agent, who would sign her up to go on some shitty TV game show where she would be drowned in custard to raise money for charity.

Before stepping out to face her audience members, each of whom was eager to have a fortuitous future foretold to them, April examined herself in the mirror. After all, if she was doing this for the last time she wanted to look her best. Gorgeous hair and makeup? Tick. Enviable hour-glass figure? Tick. Pert breasts? Tick. Perfect skin? Tick. Hollywood smile? Tick.

She was the ultimate drag queen; should her career continue to take an unwelcome nosedive, perhaps she could become a pageant drag queen instead... although she had not seen it written in her stars.

Upon entering the concourse where the psychic evening was being held, April walked past the stalls selling meditation CDs, healing stones, and sickly-smelling incense sticks. She turned to face her audience and announced she was ready to give her first reading of the night. She had planned the show meticulously and intended for this performance to facilitate her return to the mainstream.

Nothing could go wrong.

Then she heard a voice screaming loudly, "Me first! Me first! **Me first**!" and panicked slightly as this was not part of her preparations. When she saw a flailing oversized person push people out of the way to get to the front, April knew she was in trouble. And before she could protest, Wendy plonked herself down on a seat next to April and insisted on hearing everything the spirit world had to say about her fame, fortune, and romance prospects.

Was this the giant Weeble creature she had been warned about?

Where were Security when she needed them?

Had April realised this was that utter nuisance she had heard about on the Mrs Seavers Show then she might have taken evasive action but it was too late now: all eyes and TV cameras were on her, and she had to perform even if that meant starting with this weirdo who was definitely not the reading she had secretly planned to do first.

Suddenly, April could feel beads of sweat beginning to form on her brow. Soon, they would start to trickle down her face and sting her eyes. Her makeup would streak and, eventually, she would look as bad as the creature who had just barrelled into her professional life like a wrecking ball.

She had to hold her nerve.

Damn it!

She looked around for the actor who should have been sitting next to her, nodding in agreement, and making all the right noises but they were nowhere to be seen. She imagined them trampled to the ground with heel imprints across their back waiting for the Salvation Army to give them a comforting blanket and coffee.

There was nothing else for it: she would have to play the cards she had been dealt and improvise a whole new script.

Perhaps this was the Universe finally getting its revenge because, when all was said and done, she was not much more a charlatan who made a living from deceiving poor vulnerable souls.

Occasionally, she could pick up on small cues from the client she was with and this allowed her to provide a reasonable reading, which would generally be well received and result in them only ever having good things to say about her.

"Oooh, it was like she knew me personally," they would say to their friends. "She knew instantly I was stuck in a love rut. She knew I had money worries, too, and that I want to progress in my career."

"Wow, I must go and see her... she sounds amazing."

But it was easy for her to spot the people who wanted more money, were failing miserably in love, and wanted to focus on work to take their mind off it all: invariably, they would sit before her sobbing and clawing at their bare wedding ring finger, still in the cheap supermarket clothing range suit they had worn to work that day but hadn't had time to change out of (or anything better to change in to). They accidentally wore their heart on their sleeve and revealed what they were hoping - paying - to be told by this mercenary stranger who would be able to fix all their problems in a single evening. More often than not, they longed to travel, felt 'misunderstood', and resented their siblings who had always been treated more favourably than them!

In these instances, all April had to do was offer a few choice words of reassurance and a tissue or ten to the paying customer who was crying uncontrollably at her side. A few sympathetic head-tilts, a gentle pat on the shoulder, and the occasional message that a loved one was nearby and watching over them, followed by some perfectly sincere advice that they had the potential to make all the changes they needed but it had to come from them, and April would watch the gullible sap walk away to be replaced by the next person who was looking for answers in all the wrong places.

In some ways, she was an empath and had built a career on listening and understanding, like a caring friend, then offering guidance and direction, like a trained professional. And if people left her company feeling happier and more hopeful than when they had arrived, how could that be seen as a bad thing?

Some said she gave people 'false hope' and tried to discredit her; but nobody could be one hundred percent sure whether she was genuine or not and that element of doubt was the thing she had learnt to exploit. That evening, she had a lot to prove and a lot to lose. If she was successful, she would have an awful lot to gain.

Perhaps she should have responded to the relentless knocking on the door of her dressing room back when she and the Weeble were on the Mrs Seavers Show, but she hadn't bothered. Maybe she should have gone to the bar in the green room afterwards for a drink and to meet the other guests, Wendy included, but again she hadn't bothered. It could be argued that she should have checked the comments Wendy had posted on April's social media telling everybody how they were 'best friends', but yet again she hadn't bothered to.

And now she was faced with this giant troll beast sitting next to her, about whom she knew nothing other than she looked like something people would have paid to stare at in a freak show carnival from days gone by.

Wendy, on the other hand, had completely bought in to her own fabricated version of reality and fully believed April was as invested in her and their friendship as she was herself. And she wanted her 'bestie' to get on with revealing the intimate secrets only April could know through the strength of their incredible bond.

Feeling at an absolute loss and not knowing where to begin, April noticed the mysterious and striking woman with the long mane of black hair and the glasses watching her in a rather intimidating manner... for reasons she couldn't quite explain, she became intensely uncomfortable.

Was she another one of those nightmare vigilantes who made it their life's mission to expose the truth about people like April? You didn't need to be psychic to see there was danger behind those dark glasses; this woman was formidable.

Gripped by anxiety, April could feel the now fully formed beads of sweat merging into a river as they dripped down her face, shoulders, and back.

She could not understand why she felt so ill at ease, as if some kind of reckoning was underway; like she was somehow next in line to be taken down.

Exhaling heavily, she dragged her attention back to the matter in hand and conducted a rapid but intensive study of the oddity sitting beside her: Wendy WolfWhistle. What could she say about this one?

And as she wracked her brain to find something suitable to say to Wendy, she looked back to where the mystery person had been standing but she had gone.

April's body flooded with relief, but it was short lived; she had simply moved closer. Two spaces forward and one to the side, like she was closing in for the kill. Gaining momentum. What did she want?

She felt the hairs on her arms begin to stand on end, which did nothing to enhance her already offputtingly sweaty exterior. She could also sense the Weeble staring at her, waiting for predictions and affirmations; how she was destined to become an international superstar and befriend Ru Paul; how she would bathe in bank notes with her face on them, whilst being love-bombed by scrummy dream boats; how she would achieve world-domination and unprecedented success, all in an adorable gingham-trimmed petticoat.

Even JK Rowling would struggle to keep up with the narrative Wendy was able to weave for herself!

But April couldn't tear her gaze away from the menacing figure with the long black hair; she felt threatened. Unsafe. As if she was about to be violated. Could this person take whatever it was she had obviously set out to achieve?

And what was she after? April's mind? Her sanity? Her soul? Was she about to deliver retribution for every fake reading April had ever given?

Or was she just imagining it all?

April looked away again, counted to three and looked back, determined to stay calm and in control; but like a chess piece, she had moved again - diagonally this time. Advancing closer.

Check!

She felt like prey. Rational thinking began to wane, and survival instincts screamed at her to run.

Everything about her predator indicated to April she had already lost: her posture, her presence, and that concealed stare... there would not be much left once she had finished feasting on April's carcass. And she looked ravenous.

Whoever she was, April Showers was undoubtedly her next victim. But why? Exposed and defenceless, April kept her aggressor in sight, ignoring all those around her who were waiting impatiently for her to begin.

She had forgotten about the TV cameras and the need to save her dwindling career.

This woman in the crowd, this living chess piece, was distinctly different to the other audience members. She didn't appear to be lacking in male attention, and she certainly wasn't short of money, stuck in a rut, or wearing an anguished heart on her sleeve; so why was she there?

Was she subtly moving forward through the crowd, trying to be next in line after the Weeble? Perhaps April was reading her wrong - it wouldn't be the first time.

The woman raised a small glass to her lips which contained a clear liquid. It might have been water but was more likely gin, rum, or vodka.

April watched her take one sip then another before putting it down, unfinished. Maybe she needed to keep a clear head, although she already appeared invincible, like a Spartan.

April reached for her own glass of water and swallowed a refreshing mouthful of the cool liquid. In spite of the fear that was coursing through her, she felt she was holding her nerve well.

Almost as an afterthought, she looked back at Wendy who was still sitting next to her. "Predictions, please!" she hollered at April, like a caveman placing an order for dinosaur drumsticks at a drive-through.

April realised she needed to say something – she had been silent for far too long now. It wasn't just Wendy who was waiting for her to begin: every single person in the room was watching expectantly, waiting to see if there was any point hanging around to find out what their individual future held; waiting to see if the Psychic Drag Queen was as good – or bad - as they had been told. Or, in some cases, had predicted themselves.

April looked back to where the mysterious stranger had stood sipping her drink but she had moved again. She was just a couple of spaces away! Right next to Wendy; right in her line of vision. There was no escaping her now. She stared at her through those dark glasses, expressionless, motionless, undeterrable.

Check!

April lowered her gaze, unable to look anywhere but down. Her persecutor was almost upon her.

This was so unfair. She could give good and even accurate readings but nothing was worth this amount of shit! She may not have been a natural clairvoyant, but she wasn't a complete charlatan either... she probably fell somewhere in between the two. Her looks, her abilities, and her showmanship all combined to make her a drag queen novelty act who could appeal to minority groups: the LGBTQIA community loved her; paranormal fanatics thought she rocked. Not everybody wanted to see her fail.

April looked back at Wendy and all the while the frightening woman focused exclusively on her, draining her very life force. There were at least a hundred people in the room but not one of them understood what April was going through. They were oblivious to this woman's power. To her oppression. And that was when April lost her grip on reality, and made the biggest mistake of her career so far.

"Why are you here?" she screamed out loud. "Sucking the life and soul out of everything, like an energy vampire! I bet everyone dreads you coming into the room. Nobody wants you here! And you're delusional if you think people care about anything you say or do!"

Check mate!

Gasps of horror and surprise echoed around the concourse. The chess piece retreated, disappearing quickly into the crowd, camouflaged amidst the shock of those surrounding her. Whoever she was, whatever her intentions had been, April had disarmed her, and forced her to abort her mission. But maybe she had already completed it. Or maybe there was no mission in the first place.

"I can't do this anymore," April muttered to herself but nobody heard above Wendy's shrieking cries of disappointment.

"How dare you!" she responded to April, standing up and towering over the diminishing drag queen with all the fury of an angry silverback gorilla. "Everything you said... why, you couldn't be farther from the truth if you tried! Perhaps you are a big fake, after all! If anybody is delusional it's you, thinking you're any good at this! Best friends? I don't think so!"

With that, Wendy stood up and marched off with her head held high, her heels buckling inwards, and Whitney Houston's old handbag swaying from side to side. All April could do was watch her until she vanished amongst the disappointed crowd, all of whom were pointing and whispering in her direction; all of whom wanted an immediate refund.

"Oh, I knew she was a fake!" April heard one of them say.

"Well, they do say you should never trust a drag queen, don't they?"

There was no point continuing or trying to explain what had actually happened that night. It was over. She was done. There was no coming back from this. No one would ever trust her to make a prediction again - not on the television, not on the promenade, not even for free at the local spiritualist church.

As quickly as people had arrived they all left until she was the only one there. The TV cameras had been turned off and the production crew had disappeared, too.

This was the worst media exposure she had ever generated, and they would be all over it. Her reputation as the Psychic Drag Queen was in tatters simply because she had lost her nerve at the precise moment she had needed to hold it the most.

All because two random strangers had come along and not played nicely.

And now it was all over.

April vowed then and there to seek her revenge... as soon as she worked out who either of them were.

What a shame she had not foreseen this happening to her.

But this was just the first in a chain of events she failed to predict that would have an irreversible impact.

CHAPTER 26
The day after Bonfire night

In much the same way Oliver had been just days earlier, Mark was riddled with all sorts of emotions and confused feelings as he stood outside the shell of Divas Cabaret Bar, at the far end of town.

He soaked it all up: the visible destruction and the invisible memories of heartache. This was his doing. Well, his and The Maniac's. But mostly his.

Reconstruction had already begun. Mark could not understand who the hell would do so but someone had clearly put up the money to foot repairs to this burnt-out ruin of a building.

He looked around again before moving on. He had never planned to stand there for long and had seen all he needed to. There was no emotional attachment to any of it; if anything, he felt more disappointed there was still something there.

He had rather hoped there would just be a big hole in the ground. A huge gap between the neighbouring buildings that all the hurt and devastation of the past could fall into so it could be covered over with tonnes of fresh cement and held down, forever, by new iron girders.

As it was, parts of the previous building would be integrated into the new one and Divas would never truly die... pieces of it would live on in whatever structure took its place. It would continue to leech out its poison, just like before.

However, the building was not the reason Mark had returned. It had just been a small detour from the nearby train station. He had lived in this town all his life and knew he would only have to sacrifice a few minutes out of his day to get there. He knew the town too well. He knew how it looked in the sun and the rain. He knew how it looked in the light and the dark. Especially in the dark.

Had he returned home? It certainly wasn't where his heart was. It didn't feel like home, not anymore. If anything, it only felt like some place where he used to exist and, suddenly, he felt suffocated just being there.

No, this was not his town anymore, not his home. It never would be again.

He did not think of himself as a local now but, just for a short while – until he could get the hell out of there again - he needed to pass for one. Just long enough to enable him to go about his business unnoticed.

As he walked from street to street, he found himself deeply conflicted: reminiscing but trying not to remember; regretting but trying not to drown in remorse; lamenting but then catching himself smiling just a little because it hadn't been *all* bad.

Part of him felt he still belonged there but a much bigger part of him didn't want to.

When he checked into his hotel near the train station (specifically selected in case he needed to make a quick exit) the receptionist asked if he was from around there. There was something familiar about the way he spoke: his accent... it was local.

Thankfully, that was the only familiarity she picked up on and, on reflection, that wasn't necessarily a bad thing - it meant he could blend in. It gave him more flexibility to move around town without suspicion. Most people would recognise him dressed up as Connie but not so many when he was Mark. And the few who did know him as Mark were unlikely to be out during the daytime.

But those were the people he needed to find so he could begin to put the past to rights. Unless, of course, it was already too late.

He would check social media later on in the safety of his hotel room to see if anything had changed. He detested social media but saw its value from time to time.

With a bit of luck, people wouldn't even remember him anymore. They'd probably all moved on, too absorbed in their own lives to give him a second thought.

Sure, somebody might occasionally recall those three drag queens that used to be on stage at that cabaret bar when they came across an old brochure Wendy had autographed on their behalf tucked away at the back of a drawer but, otherwise, who would ever really question what had happened to any of them?

It hadn't taken much for Mark to find out what had become of Tequila or Wendy. Quick searches on TwitBook X, or whatever they were called, had revealed they were headlining a cabaret show in a new bar on East Green Street, called The Old Queen's Jugs. Tequila headlining with Wendy; seriously, how the hell had that happened?

Previous internet searches had allowed him to follow Tequila's recovery after the fire. The whole thing had been a big news story at the time and there had been loads of coverage, all available at the touch of a button to those who wanted to know - and he had wanted to know.

The dreaded Socials had also given him a virtual first row seat to watch the unfolding story of The Old Queen's Jugs; he had been concerned to see all the hash tags about the police raid on the opening night.

That wasn't a publicity stunt: that was a warning and a severe one at that.

As for East Green Street... well, he knew exactly where that was. He had walked the length and breadth of it enough times to know it was a street of broken hearts.

He had lived on it for a while, even conducted business there - though more in its alleyways than on the street itself. But he had hardly been the only one working there... he was just one of the many victims dragged up in a town that always pulled them down.

Mark thought he could guess exactly where The Old Queen's Jugs was. The name alone was a big clue. It had to be where that other pub had stood on the corner, along with its pervy landlord, Wayne, who was neither use nor ornament. But it had a different name then... something about a slave or a maid?

That hovel of a boozer might have been a local haunt in days gone by but he had developed higher standards in this new life of his. He would go there to sort his outstanding business if he had to but, once it was concluded, he would leave and never come back.

Mark was adamant he was not a local anymore.

Others would disagree with him about that; after all, he was from these parts and that made him one of them... whether he liked it or not.

Ultimately, as badly as he wanted to turn his back on all the things he did not want to be a part of, there was no escaping his heritage.

There was no escaping his past.

CHAPTER 27
The day after Bonfire night

Shaking his head in despair, Jay, or the one Oliver had been calling Jay, put away his phone, sighed heavily, gritted his teeth, and carried on walking up the road, alone.

All he wanted was to be left alone. It wasn't much to ask.

He didn't need to be reminded what he was supposed to be doing. He knew exactly what was expected of him. He just wanted to be left alone to get on with it.

It wasn't going to be easy – it felt impossible at this point - but the plan was underway and there was no turning back now; he was committed.

The outcome rested solely in his anxious, trembling hands, and the stakes were high: he had to succeed. His poor head was reeling from it all but there was no time to rest or recover.

It was several hours since Oliver's mother had left the pub having voiced her concerns that Oliver was not responding to her calls or messages. If anyone was going to become suspicious and raise the alarm, it would be her. Oliver's colleagues had also noticed he was behaving strangely... Jay was running out of time.

He would have to find a way around these obstacles to make his plan work because what else could he do? It was too late to change or back out now. He was already in too deep; he had to keep going.

Nobody in the bar had seemed overly concerned about what had happened. They had just acted as though Oliver's sudden and unexplained disappearance was perfectly normal. Maybe he had quit, maybe he had found a better job… maybe they thought it was none of their business.

Had they given it any serious thought, they might have realised that a level-headed, vulnerable person, who had been through the toughest challenge it was possible to face, simply vanishing in the middle of his shift was far from normal and was, in fact, real cause for concern.

He walked through a small passageway that had random weeds growing through the cracks in the paving. It was between two apartment blocks, one of which was in a shocking state of disrepair.

Feeling suddenly unsafe, he quickened his pace and found himself back on East Green Street again. Hungry and exhausted, all he wanted was to get back to his new apartment, eat something, and rest. His apartment was in the same block as Oliver's.

Except Oliver had no idea yet that they shared the same building and awful landlord. He had never taken the trouble to get to know any of his neighbours, offering nothing more than a nod and a smile in the stairwell.

Jay used the key to open the door to his permanently chilly home and stepped inside. It wasn't particularly nice but it would do for the short term. It might have felt more homely if he had unpacked even just a few of his personal belongings but he'd never planned on staying there for long.

Right now, he needed to replenish his energy - body, mind, and soul; he hadn't slept well the night before and did not know when he might get the chance to sleep again after today.

There was so much to think about with battle lines needing to be redrawn every time someone new butted in unexpectedly and caused problems. It made his head hurt. He felt exhausted from being permanently at DEFCON 1. He did not need people getting in his way, asking questions, scrutinising him whilst he was trying to give off the impression that nothing was amiss, at all.

Thankfully, his bed was always ready for him and, as he yawned for the umpteenth time, he felt it calling him to its soft mattress, cosy duvet, and downy pillows.

But there was something he needed to do before he could allow himself to succumb to sleep: he needed to remove the mask he wore to conceal himself from the outside world.

So, he took out the coloured contact lenses which gave his eyes a completely different look, then pulled off the cap and slicked his hair back into a more manageable style.

He stared at himself in the mirror – his original, unfiltered self; the man behind the mask... a wolf in sheep's clothing, perhaps? He didn't bother to undress before falling awkwardly onto the bed. He had barely even found the energy to close the curtains.

As he lay there, safe, warm, and comfortable beneath his duvet, he found himself thinking about Oliver and the plan he was entangled in.

And as he drifted away, into a much-needed sleep, he still thought about Oliver, and the plan.

Oliver... are you so lost now that you will never be found?

CHAPTER 28

The day before the grand opening of The Old Queen's Jugs – Late October

Chris felt like he was on the edge of glory. Finally, things were falling in to place and everything he wanted, everything he needed was coming together perfectly - just as he had known it would.

He welcomed the late autumnal sun as it shone pleasantly on his face. It felt like it was warming him from the inside out, reinvigorating him after a long period of bleak stagnation. His eyes sparkled with a restored vibrancy they had long since forgotten.

His whole being was waking up from a long, dreary nightmare… he could feel the thrill of liberty stirring within him.

He had been claustrophobic inside those walls, festering, and forgotten; a victim of his own misdemeanours.

Who was to blame?

The gentle breeze tasted sweet on his dry lips and he inhaled too much too quickly, leaving him slightly short of breath but happy, and very much eager for more.

Eager to experience all the possibilities the outside world had to offer, with its hopes and dreams and demons.

He wanted to indulge in all its temptations, all its excesses.

How could he ever contemplate returning to that dismal place, where he simply existed… survived?

A world of freedom lay before him now but how long would that last?

He wasn't naturally 'good'; he didn't live a clean-cut life as a perfect neighbour, friend, or boss - that was boring and not something he would ever tolerate.

That kind of mediocrity screamed 'vanilla' to him, and Chris Randall *hated* vanilla; it was ordinary, dull, predictable... yawn-inducing.

And he was none of those things.

Whatever people thought about him, no one had **ever** described Chris Randall as average or humdrum.

Chris had never craved a vanilla existence, lacking in excitement and power and control.

Without those things, he might as well be incarcerated.

Without those things, they might as well throw away the key and pad his cell for good measure.

Without those things, he might as well be dead.

CHAPTER 29
Bonfire night

The door at the top of the stone steps closed behind him as he reached the equally cold concrete floor below ground. He shuddered, as if somebody had walked right through him or stepped on his grave but reassured himself it was probably just the frigid air and the terrible lighting giving him the creeps.

At least, he hoped it was.

He walked over to the barrels and examined them closely. Okay, this one is lager and this one is cider… I think… but which is the empty one that needs replacing?

He stopped dead in his tracks upon hearing a noise. Oh Jesus, what the hell was that? Was somebody down there with him? He spun round in a panic and looked back up towards the cellar door. What had he heard?

His heart thumped in his chest and his blood ran icy cold.

The noise sounded again but much louder this time.

Oh, of course! It was the fireworks going off outside. He could hear them through the cellar grid that led to the street. So it wasn't a ghost, an oversized rodent, or an axe-murderer after all - thank God for that!.

But even with a rational explanation, this place still scared the crap out of him.

Pulling himself together he returned to the task in hand: barrel changing. And upon conducting a thorough re-examination of the barrels, he realised he had absolutely no idea what was contained within any of them, which was a shame because he really wanted to get the frig out of there.

He could not be arsed with this and once more found himself sorely tempted to march back up the steps and walk the hell out of there, only looking back to see the fireworks.

He took a deep breath and tried to refocus, eventually realising the worst that could happen was he accidentally caused cider to flow through the lager pump... but, on the bright side, that also meant Wayne would have to change the barrels himself and Oliver could definitely live with that!

Although resigning would still be the easiest option. And as another firework exploded outside and Oliver heard the crowd exclaiming in delight, he knew exactly what he needed to do.

However, he had not noticed the cellar door slowly opening behind him, when his attention was diverted by the noisy fireworks, the identical and unidentifiable barrels, and his own existential crisis!

He had not noticed somebody slipping onto the small landing at the top of the stone steps.

He had not noticed them sneaking noiselessly down into the freezing underworld beneath the pub.

And he had not heard this person approaching him slowly and carefully across the concrete floor in absolute silence, with deadly focus and malicious intent.

Just as the loudest and longest firework screamed through the night sky outside, echoing off the walls of the catacombs within which Oliver was currently entombed, the intruder struck him hard from behind, applying brute force via a weapon which immobilised Oliver instantly.

He fell onto the hard barrels and landed awkwardly but that didn't matter for he had been knocked unconscious. Nobody had heard his cry of shock and momentary pain, except for the person who was in the cellar with him at the time.

Nobody had seen him fall, except for the person who was in the cellar with him at the time.

Nobody had seen him being pulled away and dragged to his own hell, except for the person who was in the cellar with him at the time.

And nobody knew where he was now… except for the person who was in the cellar with him at the time.

CHAPTER 30
Early November

Just before the evening's cabaret show was about to begin, Tequila knocked on the door of Martin's office. James felt more confident with his mask on, so had decided to broach the issues that were on his mind dressed as his louder-mouthed, bolder drag queen alter-ego.

He hoped Martin would find Tequila more intimidating and that he might be persuaded to agree with her demands more easily.

Money! Fame! Truth!

"Come in," said Martin in his monotonous voice.

Tequila opened the door and stepped inside, without speaking a word. It was her first time back in there since the night she had been snooping. The contents of Martin's usually locked drawer and the conversation she had overheard between him and Wendy about Jake, the night of the Divas fire, and what may or may not have happened on the street outside were still fresh in her mind. Along with something that had been said about Chris.

"Ahhh, Tequila," said Martin, almost as if he had been expecting her. "What can I do for you?"

She noticed how he discreetly checked his desk drawers were closed, as usual... he had no idea how far that particular ship had sailed – although he would soon.

"Can we talk?" she asked him, "in confidence."

"Yes of course," he replied, with a slight nod of his head, gesturing towards the seat opposite him. "What's on your mind?"

"The night of the Divas fire..." she began to say.

"What about it?"

Tequila sat staring at him through her beautifully made-up eyes. "When I came round, I… I thought I saw Jake Robinson in the distance, running away."

Point-blank, Martin rejected this revelation. "No," he said, firmly shaking his head. "There was no way you could have. Jake was long dead by then."

Still calm, Tequila continued to sit and stare at the overweight, balding man sitting across the desk from her. So, he was playing exactly the same card with her as he had with Father Wendy. Maybe it was time to shuffle the deck and start a new game? "No," she insisted just as firmly as he had. "I *definitely* saw Jake that night."

"No, you couldn't have done," repeated Martin, more firmly than either of them had been.

How was he having the same conversation a second time in such quick succession? Had Wendy been blabbing to her son about it over a mountain of vol-au-vents, or were they on some kind of mission to piss him off? His life was hard enough without these two drama (drag) queens.

"You were obviously traumatised by the effects of the smoke and the lack of oxygen to your brain," he continued. "That's probably what it was… hallucinations and all."

"Yes, perhaps," replied Tequila, in a softer tone, although she remained far from convinced.

Why was Martin so adamant Jake could not have been there that night? True, he had allegedly died before the night of the fire and Chris Randall had been arrested for his murder - they had all heard him confess to the killing - but still something didn't feel right.

If only she could fit the pieces of the puzzle together. But she had never been good at jigsaws and didn't know to start with the four corners then the edges to provide a robust framework to accommodate the bigger picture within. And, currently, she was missing too many pieces.

Something, somewhere, just didn't add up.

"Was there anything else?" Martin asked, hoping there wouldn't be.

Money! Fame! Truth!

It was all or nothing: she could walk out of there and forever hold her peace, or she could reveal what she knew, as bitty as it was. "I'm sorry, but I truly, truly believe I saw Jake that night and I don't understand why you keep dismissing it. It's pretty shitty of you, if you ask me; especially if he is alive and you know something about it."

Martin stopped looking at her and turned his face towards his computer screen and began tapping away on the keyboard. He may have been pretending. He may have been biding time.

"Shouldn't you be helping Wendy wedge herself into a corset right about now?" he asked, still not looking at her.

Money! Fame! Truth!

"Probably," replied Tequila. "But just so you know, I **did** see Jake that night and I believe Wendy did too! You can't keep fobbing us off because I don't believe he's dead, not for a moment."

"You need to go, now," announced Martin, as firmly as he could without his voice cracking. "And I think you should watch your step very carefully."

"I wear five-inch heels every night," replied Tequila, rather too flippantly for her own good. "I always watch my step."

"I'm warning you, Tequila. I hired you and I can fire you just as easily. Is that what you want?"

And suddenly it felt as though Chris Randall was in charge and she was back at Divas Cabaret Bar, forever fearful of being dismissed whenever she put a foot out of place.

No, that was not what Tequila wanted - far from it - but…

Money! Fame! Truth!

Realising he had taken matters too far and worried that it would only make things worse, Martin calmed down almost immediately. "Right, let's not say anything more about this. Sadly, Jake is dead and there is nothing any of us can do about it, no matter how much we wish otherwise. It's tragic but that's the truth. No one is keeping secrets."

"I know," said Tequila, also backing down slightly. "I didn't know Jake that well but I'm sure he was a really nice bloke. Perhaps you're right. Perhaps, it is just wishful thinking."

But Tequila was still not entirely convinced and, once again, her foolish young head filled with the things she craved.

Money! Fame! Truth!

So she played her trump card. Could she win? Hit the jackpot? Beat the house? "Of course, if I *did* know some secrets, Martin, I wonder how much my silence would be worth…"

"What secrets do you think you know?" asked Martin, reverting to his former police mode, whilst discreetly checking the desk drawers once more, just in case they had sprung open in the last few minutes.

"Well, I know your little secret for a start," she replied, sounding much calmer than she actually felt; her heart and pulse were racing like a speedway as she envisaged her dreams finally coming true.

Money! Fame! Truth!

"My little secret?" he questioned, trying not to sound as though he might be panicking in any way.

"The one you keep tightly locked away inside your bottom desk drawer," she continued.

Had she shown her hand too early?

Martin regarded her as if he could feasibly destroy her in a single movement. "I don't know how you know," he roared angrily at her, "or what you think you know but I will not be blackmailed by anybody, especially some scrawny little shit in heels who I could knock over with one breath."

His whole body was shaking with adrenaline.

He paused. He had to, before he exploded or gave himself a heart attack.

"If I was you, Tequila," he continued to say, "I would shut up now before it's too late. Seriously, I'm warning you: if this subject is ever raised again you will be out of here before your five-inch heels touch the ground. Do you understand me?"

Tequila nodded as she sat there trembling. She hadn't expected this response.

"Now go," said Martin, "and if I hear any more of this stupidity then I mean it, you're out on your arse; homeless, broke, unemployed."

She couldn't risk being in that situation again, not after the last time and certainly not so soon.

This had not gone to plan, at all.

Had she been naïve to think Martin would gasp in horror and pay her thousands of pounds to keep quiet about the secret that lay hidden in his bottom desk drawer? Had she imagined she would be able to continue to live and work alongside him after this, whether he had paid up or not?

Maybe it would have been best if he had fired her but she was relieved he hadn't; well, not yet anyway.

Why the hell could she not be satisfied with the fact she had survived the fire; that she was still alive and kicking; that she was able to perform every night - which she loved to do - and that she finally had quality time with Father Wendy, which was turning out better than she had ever dreamt possible?

Why was she still chasing the champagne lifestyle Chris had groomed her for? Had recent events taught her nothing?

She stood up silently and left the room without daring to look at him. He was right: she had been stupid. She was far too young and inexperienced to play a grown man's game, especially when dressed as a woman.

She thought she was playing to win but she hadn't even qualified. In fact, she had almost lost everything without even realising what she had put at stake in the first place.

Seriously, what had she been thinking?

Money... Fame... Truth...

Yes, she had been stupid and she knew it, but she was nowhere near as stupid as Martin.

Jesus Christ, he had taken stupidity to a whole new level.

Seriously, what was *he* thinking?

Making bottom drawer secret deals with Chris Randall.

Chris Randall of all people!

CHAPTER 31
Mid-August

He had always known Chris would bide his time, summoning him when he was ready. He just hadn't expected it to be quite so soon.

"And what exactly do you know?" asked his visitor.

After all, he could be bluffing, chancing his hand.

"I know you screwed me over," he replied, calmly. "And I also know you have something I want."

His visitor stared at the ground, studying his own footwear... the table legs... the hard, faded red plastic chair he was perched upon.

"Want me to elaborate on either of those things?" said Chris.

"No," he responded quietly.

"I didn't think so," Chris smirked. "You messed with me and this is what we are going to do about it." His visitor listened to every word and did not like anything that was said.

"No," he bravely responded once Chris had finished his well-prepared and overly rehearsed speech.

Chris stared back at him coolly, once more holding his gaze. He had fully expected this kind of pushback but knew it was not an outcome he would accept.

Chris always got what he wanted, and he knew this time would be no exception.

"No," responded his visitor again, trying to sound firm.

Chris glared back at him, his silence, once more, speaking volumes. He folded his arms again, tighter than before and repeated his demands. His visitor had something he wanted and he was going to get it.

"Let's suppose I agree to this..."

"Which you will," interrupted Chris.

"What do I get in return?"

"This may just go away for you. I may even go away for you too. Wouldn't you like that?"

His visitor sat silently for a few moments thinking about it and trying his hardest to look Chris in the eyes. If he could look deep into this monster's soul perhaps he could find the strength to do what was being asked of him, particularly if it meant finally being free from all of this.

Screwed, Martin continued to listen to his inhospitable host, who spoke annoyingly slowly and revealed his instructions in dribs and drabs. "Right, Martin," Chris said, enjoying every moment, "this is what is going to happen:

"You will open your silly little pub on the corner of East Green Street, and you can call it whatever you want; it doesn't matter because it'll get changed anyway.

"You will hire that Tequila drag queen as the lead cabaret star and book in Mrs Slocombe, as well. Between them they'll be good enough to keep the old crowds piling in - especially Wendy. I reckon the fuckers in that town will be pleased to see her get her big break. She's so bad she'll be good.

"You will be the face of the pub in the short term. Do you think you can manage that? Your name will go above the door, initially; not ideal but as long as I'm stuck in here, I'll guess I'll have to go with it.

"You will legally sign whatever lease or contract you have in place for that building over to me but, for now, everybody can think it's yours. Nobody needs to know the truth. When I get out of here and take over, they'll soon figure it out.

"You can all live above the pub, I mean, that's what people would expect, but you'll be out on your arses when I return. You've probably gathered that already."

"Obviously," replied Martin, worn down and longing to be allowed to leave.

"You will need somebody behind the scenes who knows what they're doing to cover up the fact you don't. Find out what the old landlord is doing these days - from what I know about him he'll fit right in there. Okay?"

Martin nodded. This was difficult to hear and even harder to digest. Chris was taking ownership of the pub he was in the process of renovating and reopening, and there was nothing he could do about it. The pub he had purchased with the inheritance left to him by his dearly-departed mother, and after whom he had planned to name it.

Unfortunately for Martin, Tequila, Wendy, and everybody else in that godforsaken town, Chris held the winning cards again, no matter who they were, no matter what game they were playing.

Stick or Twist?

You lose!

Now prepared to be dragged to your hell!

Martin attempted to give the impression he was engaged in what Chris was saying. There was no point provoking him any further. Martin had lost, pure and simple, and there was no point trying to fight anymore. "So, the money for the investment..." he began to say.

"Will continue to be yours," Chris quickly interrupted him. "Until..." his mouth spread into a sneaky smile which sent shivers into Martin's soul and cut him deeply.

Chris was relishing torturing Martin in this way. "Well, as you can imagine, being stuck in here isn't exactly lucrative, although you wouldn't believe what some of the men will do for a bit of cash.

"You know, it's a pity you're not in here, Martin. You could finally get some and even earn yourself a pack of cigarettes at the same time… well, maybe half a pack for you." Chris looked Martin up and down in exaggerated disgust.

"Just get to the point, will you?" snapped back Martin.

He no longer cared for mindless chit chat and being insulted. He just needed to know the facts that were relevant to him. But it was obvious Chris was playing him like a fiddle, plucking him, pulling at his strings, working him harder and harder until something broke.

Chris was looking to create a cacophony of high-pitched noise, not sweet music.

Across the room, an inmate started to go berserk, screaming and shouting before being dragged off by several officers. It was quite unsettling, especially for Chris's guest of honour who was anxious enough as it was.

"I'm guessing nobody bought in his shit and stuff: Heroin. Cocaine. Spice. Have you heard of Spice, Martin?" Chris continued to say. "It's this synthetic crap, like cannabis, and they're going ape-shit for it in here. It's turned some of them mad. I don't get involved myself, I've got too much sense for that. I have my own methods of getting through the day."

"Of course I know it," replied Martin. "I was in the police force."

"But you're not in the police anymore, are you, Martin? Tell me… did you resign before you were thrown out for being a dirty fat pig? Did you take the role of bent copper just a little bit too far?"

"Who told you this? I want to know!"

"No, Martin, you don't get to make demands. I'm the boss and you do what I say.

"Now, tell me, did you do it because you got beaten up outside Divas or was it because you secretly loved wearing your mother's old boots? I reckon it was the latter, personally."

"Right, I've had enough of this," exclaimed Martin, just loud enough for the prison officers to look over but not intervene. "Just tell me what else I need to know and cut the bollocks, okay?"

Chris was still smiling. He was enjoying this so much more than he had anticipated, getting revenge on that rancid old queen who had been undercover in his cabaret bar for so long, watching his every move, trying to get dirt on him.

"Do you miss the police force, Martin?"

Martin looked around the room. He didn't miss dealing with criminals for a second. He didn't miss the verbal abuse and the drama; but, overall, he did miss the job.

And now, as he was trying to rise from his own ashes, Chris Randall had pushed him back down into an ashen pit of despair. Seriously, how was this man still alive? Why had nobody put a bullet in him yet?

For god's sake, he was locked away in prison! He was supposed to be cut off from the outside world but here he was still pulling strings like the puppet master he always had been – and with absolute impunity.

Martin summoned his remaining ounce of inner strength, although he would need to find much more if he was to survive the plans Chris had for him.

"It's going to be so great on the outside," said Chris, thoughtfully. "A new business, a new start, maybe even a new love. Oh, how is Oliver by the way... still alive?"

"Leave Oliver out of this," ordered Martin. "He has suffered enough."

"Oh, trust me," sniped back Chris, "he has barely begun to suffer for the shit he put me through. I want you to give him a job too, something part time, for when you're busy."

Martin shook his head. After everything that Oliver had been through that sounded like a terrible idea. He could not agree to that at all.

But Chris was not taking no for an answer. "I want him behind that bar, and I want to know exactly where he is. Besides, he's cute: the punters will spend their money just to get a closer look at him. That's what I used to think about Jake and it worked, initially. Then one day he just stopped smiling."

Martin exhaled deeply. Of course, Jake had stopped smiling: he had been stuck behind that bar night after night, with the walls closing in on him. They had closed in on all of them, even those who were not obliged to work there. They had all stopped smiling.

Now, he felt as though he might never smile again. He broached the subject of money again. "So, what about the investment for the business? You said: 'until...' Until what?"

"Oh yes," said Chris, rubbing his hands together, gleefully, "I'm glad we're back onto that. So, I know all about the inheritance your mother left you in her will and your house being on the market. That should keep you going in the short-term."

"You're not having any of it," announced Martin bravely or foolishly, he wasn't quite sure which. "It's mine, for my future. You're not having any of it."

"I can have your soul if I want it."

Martin looked down in dismay. Chris was right, he could. "And the investment?" he whispered.

"Oh, don't worry, you won't be out of pocket, not with all the money you have. You pay for the refurbs now and, when I get out of here, you can pay to have it all changed to look better, something more to my taste. I'm selling my house. You should expect a call from my legal team soon - just some paperwork for you to sign."

Martin ignored him. He didn't care about Chris's house, his legal team, or anything else that Chris was twittering on about; he did care about his own assets though. "So, when you eventually get out of here then I no longer have to invest and we're done?"

"Hmmm," replied Chris. "Sort of."

"I don't understand."

"As I said, my insurance pay-out is tied up in the Divas building so that is what you'll get in return for your current investment in the new pub."

"What, so I pay for the set-up, refurbishment, and running of my new bar until you get out, then I sign it all over to you and I get the old Divas building in exchange?"

Chris nodded and smiled. How wonderful it would be when he was finally free of that dump in the arse end of town where nobody ever wanted to go. "Yep. It's yours to do whatever you want with. You can try and sell the lease on... I don't care what you do - I just want shut of the bastard place. Oh, and just one more thing," he added, smiling widely.

Martin looked at him. For fuck's sake, what now?

"Instead of The Old Maiden's Jugs, why don't you call it The Old Queen's Jugs? Seems fitting seeing as you're the one who's going to be looking after it for me until I get out of here."

Martin sighed once more. When the hell would that be? When would Chris Randall walk free from prison?

Eventually, he nodded his agreement. It was worth a try if he could walk away from Chris Randall forever.

Chris got up from his plastic chair and told him it had been a pleasure. He might have said something about returning to his accommodation but Martin had stopped concentrating at that point and everything had become a blur.

He could only remember sitting there watching Chris leave, gob smacked, bewildered, broken.

It wasn't until he had left that awful room in that awful place with its slamming doors, endless shouting, and repressive atmosphere, that he wished Chris Randall dead, again!

His head was awash with worry and confusion; he had no idea how he was going to get through this.

Chris was firmly in charge now, and he knew far too much to ever leave him in peace.

God, he wished that man was dead!

He would have to contact his confidante and let them know about all this.

What on earth was he supposed to do with the old Divas Cabaret Bar other than cut his losses?

CHAPTER 32
The day after Bonfire night

Mark entered the Northern Territory; to say he was anxious was an understatement. He was utterly terrified to be back. It had been a while since he'd had the confidence or the die-hard attitude to brave those dismal streets, and even then he had only done so behind the mask of his drag queen alter ego, Connie.

The Northern Territory was the backdrop to both the best and worst times of Mark's life. It was the sort of place you went to pick up rent boys or a dose of the clap,' instead? x)... or if you needed something very unpleasant to happen to Chris Randall.

It was also notorious for drug abuse but you only ever used in the Northern Territory - you never sold there - because there was only one dealer and everybody knew who that was: The Maniac.

Nobody ever crossed The Maniac, let alone double crossed him.

It was not a nice place and the mere thought of going back chilled Mark to the bone; actually being there was having a physical impact on him. This had once been a huge part of his miserable existence and he was determined to ensure it was the last visit he ever made. But he had already broken so many of the promises he had made so what did one more matter?

This time though he would do what he needed to, get the hell out of there, and never look back. It would always be there, a honeypot for victims and abusers, but he would no longer go there. He hoped, in time, it would all be shut down and moved on, then he would never need to think about it again.

But, for now, it was there, and he knew he had to go.

It was easy to find trouble there: just head towards where Divas Cabaret Bar used to be, take a left at the end of that road by the crumbling old church, and keep going until you could hear the screams and smell the burnt-out cars, or just until you could taste the fear.

Mark spotted his destination and continued his approach, praying he would be able to negotiate a good deal. Even to the untrained eye of some lost unfortunate who just happened to walk past and glance through the window of number 76 North Town Street, there was something different about that place; it stood out from the rest of the terraced houses along the road where all the front doors led straight out onto the pavement.

For starters, it was cleaner and much tidier looking than most of the other houses. The blinds at the window hung with perfect horizontal latitude, and two impressive ceramic flowerpots containing early winter blooms with trailing ivy hanging over the sides graced each side of the doorway; no one ever contemplated stealing them because they were too scared of the consequences.

Mark's first instinct was to stop and smell the flowers; from his limited but growing knowledge they looked like violas or pansies. But he had not come to admire the pretty little faces of some colourful flowers: he had come to meet The Maniac, whose face was far from pretty - although it was often colourful shades of red.

Mark pushed open the front door and stepped inside. As long as somebody was there the door would be open - though just how welcome he would be was yet unknown.

Familiar smells, sights, and sounds flooded his senses and, for a moment, it felt as though he had never been away. There was a permanent aroma of freshly cut flowers and coffee which enticed you in further with their innocent sweetness, concealing the horrible fact that nobody made it out as the same person they went in.

And it had the strangest interior; it wasn't a house in the sense of it being a home nor was it a business. It was merely a destination which many sought out but could not wait to leave – Mark being one of them.

The Maniac was scary and - even at this point - Mark considered walking away. But his conscience would soon overpower him and lead him straight back. It was now not never, and he couldn't wait a moment longer. He had intentionally dragged himself to his hell.

It was a two up, two down mid-terrace with neighbours on either side (who had very quickly learnt never to ask questions), a kitchen and bathroom downstairs, with office space upstairs.

The front room, where Mark now stood, contained little more than painted cream walls, stained wooden floorboards, and white woodchip wallpaper on the ceiling. On a desk in the corner sat a vase of fresh flowers; a Cheese Plant which needed re-staking stood to its side. Mark had never seen anybody sitting at the desk, although he had seen one of the Heavies reluctantly watering the plant and changing the flowers.

Between the two downstairs rooms was a steep flight of stairs which led up to a tiny landing space, just big enough for two doors to lead off in either direction. One door led to the room where the Heavies hung out, which doubled up as a waiting room for those visitors The Maniac felt required immediate intimidation.

The other door led directly to The Maniac himself, and to the other Heavies who were protecting him, drinking with him, or receiving instructions... such as: burn down Divas Cabaret Bar regardless of who is inside. It was a seemingly innocuous space for such monstrous comings and goings, particularly as the downstairs space was mostly unused.

None of it really made any sense to Mark, but this was the world according to The Maniac and he was a visitor there so had to follow the rules. He just hoped he would be permitted to leave in one piece.

Standing on the tiny landing, he pushed open one of the doors and there inside, just as he had expected, was The Maniac, seated behind a grand desk which would have made the American President envious. Mark was unsurprised to see a Heavy looming large on either side of him. Except for the presence of a large metal safe and a silver picture frame facing away from him, the space was identical to the room downstairs.

"Well, well, well," he exclaimed upon seeing Mark entering the room for the first time in months. "I was wondering if I was ever going to see you again."

He turned to his Heavies and gestured for them to leave so they could be alone. Mark watched them pass by and close the door on their way out. It was unlikely they would both be able to stand on the tiny landing to listen in, but one of them might.

The Maniac looked at Mark with disappointment. "Oh," he sighed, indicating towards Mark's now flat chest area. "You haven't brought the twins to see me this time. Such a shame, I used to find them... quite fascinating. Especially on a man."

Mark smiled sheepishly, trying to appear calmer and more in control than he was feeling. His implants were part of his past and had been the first thing to go in his new life. Now, they just formed part of the surgical waste of his history.

"So, what do you want?" The Maniac asked, getting straight to the point. The small talk was over; it was time to get to business.

It had been a while since Mark had placed himself in this kind of arena and the first time he had done so without the confident persona of Connie to hide behind; he missed the mask he had so readily removed from himself and its thick layer of impenetrable makeup. He suddenly missed the shadows where he use to hide.

And suddenly, he wished he was a hundred miles away.

That was how The Maniac and the Northern Territory made even the most determined of people feel: broken.

CHAPTER 33

Early November – between Halloween and Bonfire night

On stage that evening, Tequila was off her game. In fact, she was remarkably quiet and slightly downcast; usually, a bad day for Tequila looked more upbeat than a good day for most.

But today, Wendy had shown her the 'fan' letter she had received; the one that Martin had warned her to be wary of. To be fair, Wendy had not so much showed Tequila the letter as shoved it in her face whilst she was in the process of sweeping off the excess after baking her makeup for the required, much sought after, creaseless effect.

And just like Martin, she knew it was not good.

♫ *Oh, uh-uh-uh, oh*
You are my playboy
Stay, boy
Every night and day, boy

Treat me bad
Treat me good
Treat me like you know you should
You have the power in your hands
You're the emperor of my lands
Touch me there
If you dare
You can have me anywhere ♫

It felt even more menacing because Tequila had also received a letter that day and it had arrived in exactly the same manner as Wendy's: hand delivered through the letterbox of the cabaret bar.

But unlike Wendy, she had not shown it to anybody else. Only she - and whoever had sent it - knew it existed.

And having read the contents of Wendy's letter, hers now seemed much worse than she had initially contemplated.

♫ *But don't tell me that you love me*
That isn't what I'm looking for

I just want some
Pure adulteration
In my room
No complication
Take me as you find me
Take me as I am ♫

'Enjoy your performance,' hers had said, 'you never know when it might be your last one.'

Short, simple, and to the point.

♫ *Oh, uh-uh-uh, oh*

Have you no shame, boy?
Game, boy
Aren't you pleased you came, boy?

Don't stop now
See it through
If you know what's good for you
I know exactly what to do
To make all your dreams come true
You can stay
Everyday
When you rub me the right way ♫

What did it mean? Was her past catching up with her? If so, why was Wendy being threatened too? Was it because they were father and son? Did they come as a package these days? And why were they being targeted?

I mean, who would benefit from them being out of the picture?

♫ *But don't tell me that you love me*
That isn't what I'm looking for

I just want some
Pure adulteration
In my room
No complication
Take me as you find me
Take me as I am

I just want your
Endless need to please me
All the time
'til you release me
Take me cos you want me
Take me as I am ♫

"No, don't take me," she thought. "Not if your aim is to hurt me."

Enjoy your performance; you never know when it might be your last one.

What the hell did that mean?! Was it linked to all the other things she didn't understand too?

There was too much to think about.

No wonder she had developed one of those Tequila headaches she had sometimes heard people talk about

But seriously, what was going on in her life?
When had it all become so complicated?

CHAPTER 34
The day after Bonfire night

Oliver opened his eyes to extreme darkness and became aware of the eerie silence surrounding him.

Panic gripped him as he became more lucid and he muttered something incomprehensible, although nobody heard him… it was possible no one ever would.

He had no idea where he was, how he had got there, or even how long he had been there for. It could have been any time of the day or night; the room was cold, the ground was hard, and it smelt musty and damp.

It was terrifying beyond belief.

His back was sore from lying in an awkward position. His head hurt too but he did not know why. He squinted to try to see something through the pitch dark he had been plunged into but there was nothing.

All he knew was he was lying on a rocklike floor which felt rough and uneven. It might have been concrete but could just as easily have been something else that had weathered over the years.

He could also feel something restricting his mouth; something tight like tape which pulled on his cheeks and skin as he tried to cry out for help.

Instinctively, he went to remove it but found he couldn't as he his wrists had been bound tightly.

His ankles were tied too.

He was helpless - completely helpless. He was trapped and had no way of freeing himself.

How the hell was he supposed to escape?

He didn't even know how large a place he was being held captive in – because, surely, this was a hostage situation. He had been kidnapped, hidden, and left alone, maybe to rot to death.

This type of thing happened in movies or over-dramatized soap operas not real life - and not to normal people like him, who kept themselves to themselves.

Nevertheless, somebody had gone to great lengths to restrict his ability to move around freely and make choices: someone had taken away his freedom.

Who the fuck was that twisted?

Perhaps somebody who'd had those things taken away from him?

But Chris Randall was in prison, right?

He realised he was starving, parched, and had possibly wet himself because his trousers felt cold, wet, and uncomfortable. But that might have been from the damp air that smothered him.

What had happened? What could he recall?

He remembered he had been in the cellar, changing the lager barrel. Okay, fannying around cluelessly with the barrels, whilst trying to make important life decisions as the fireworks went off, outside.

Yes, that's right it was bonfire night. Was it still bonfire night? He listened carefully but couldn't hear anything, certainly not fireworks. There was only silence, darkness, and him.

Where was he? Where had he been dragged to? It felt like his own personal version of hell.

He tried again to look for something that might give him a clue to his whereabouts but could discern nothing.

There had to be a door somewhere: He had clearly been dragged in there somehow, so that meant an opening of some sort.

And if there was an opening, maybe he could escape through it.

But God only knew what lay beyond the door; more darkness?

Rationally, he presumed he was underground due to the air feeling so musty and damp. Perhaps he was still in the cellars.

Realistically, who would have done this to him? The only person who might want to see him suffer like this was Chris Randall and it was unlikely to have been him, right?

But there had been that prison escape recently. He had heard something about it in the bar but, as he did not know where Chris Randall was being held, he had chosen to believe it was not the same place.

And nobody had told him otherwise.

But what if they were one and the same?

Shit, what if Chris had escaped?

Surely, somebody would have told him if there was a risk to his life? Was that why his mother had been so keen for him to leave this godforsaken place?

Had Chris Randall escaped from prison and done this to him?

Working behind that bar he would have been easy to find.

As he lay there panicking, shivering, close to tears, and struggling to breathe, a sliver of light appeared low to the ground near the corner of his eye: was it shining through underneath a door?

If so, it could mean somebody was nearby.

He was going to cry out but decided not to, thinking it through instead. Maybe the person out there was the same one who had done this to him? The monster who had attacked him in the first place and left him to his own torment.

Maybe it was Chris Randall, after all.

In his bound and gagged state, he was defenceless and the person who had done this would already know that; in that case, it wouldn't matter if Oliver did shout for help because he would still be utterly helpless against his enemy. Exposed. Vulnerable.

The terror and the need to be free overtook him and he could not stay silent any longer. "Help!" he yelled as loudly as he could, although it came out muffled and distorted through the tape. Regardless, it was a noise and it was loud enough to be heard by somebody.

But nobody would know he was screaming for help down there, other than the person who had put him there.

Determined, he tried shouting again, louder this time, but nothing that came out made any sense.

He needed whoever was out there to hear him, if indeed there was somebody there. He needed them to find him, to help him… to stop him from being hurt any further.

And if the person out there had done this to him, then so be it. He had nothing more to lose now.

But nobody responded to his desperate plea for help. Nobody said: 'We'll find you!' 'Where are you?' 'Are you hurt?'

Instead, the door began to open and the room he was in lit up from the light of the adjoining room.

Oliver blinked several times. The shift from darkness to light had temporarily blinded him. He could make out the silhouette of somebody standing there staring as he lay helplessly in what he could now see was a small room within the cellars.

He saw their body shape first and then, as he grew accustomed to the light, he recognised who it was.

Standing in the doorway was the man he had been referring to as Jay.

CHAPTER 35
Mid-August

He did not like this one bit and felt uncomfortable in this type of environment, breathless even, as the walls seemed to close in on him and the darkness began to swallow him up from within.

But he needed to do this if he was ever to get what he wanted... and he really needed to get what he wanted.

The smells, the sounds, the other faces staring back at him; how could anybody endure this situation? What would drive anybody to put themselves at risk and end up in a place as terrible as this?

No, prison was no place to be. Maybe there were others like him who also had a plan to get what they wanted. He didn't care either way; he would get what he wanted and reap the rewards forever after.

No consequences for him.

Unlike them, he would get away with it!

And Chris Randall was fully on board to make sure that happened!

Chris was quietly sitting in the prison's visitor room waiting for him to arrive. Hopefully, this one would be more use than the numpty who had visited him the day before. It didn't really matter as they were both going to do exactly as he told them to anyway; they both wanted the same thing... more or less.

With hope in his heart but a sullen look on his face, Chris looked around the room as he did whenever he was in there. It was unimpressive: grim furnishings, faded red chairs, notice boards with nothing on them, and an upswept cobweb, right up high. No wonder so many visitors dissolved into tears and young children descended into high-pitched decibels of distress.

The day before, his goal had been to wear his visitor down and get what he wanted, and he had achieved that. Today would be no different.

He grimaced when a large prisoner winked suggestively at him from the next table. The last time their paths had crossed Chris had performed an unsavoury act on him - something he would never have done in the real world; but he had urgently needed a phone and had no other way of getting one given his circumstances.

Ignoring him, Chris shuddered and looked away. There would be no repeat performance of that with him or anybody else in there, regardless of how good they told him it had been.

It was a high price to pay for a phone he would only need for one call before disposing of it down the toilet u-bend - forever out of sight, forever out of mind.

But his freedom was calling him and that godforsaken town, love it or hate it, was far from done with him yet.

He entered the visitor's room and looked around without really taking anything in. He was searching for Chris Randall, nothing else. There was a deal to be done and that was the only reason he was there. He would lay his cards on the table, and it would be a winning hand with no wild cards or Jokers. The stakes were high – higher than ever before - but until he started playing the game, he did not know what would be expected of him.

Chris half raised his hand to help his latest visitor find him but the newcomer had already spotted him sitting alone amidst a number of tables occupied by other inmates and their visitors.

He sat down opposite and their eyes met, briefly. There was barely any acknowledgment or welcome. There was no small talk.

The game was on.

Chris dealt the first card, face up... would his visitor accept to it?

Yes, his visitor accepted; he was willing to do whatever it took to get what he wanted.

The visitor dealt the next card, face up... he told Chris exactly what he wanted.

Chris agreed to his terms and conditions without hesitation.

Chris dealt his next card face down... he leaned forward and whispered a name into his visitor's ear.

His visitor understood but said nothing, merely giving the slightest of nods in response.

Chris's next card was also laid face down... "In a few weeks' time," he whispered, "I will let you know what to do."

Confused, the visitor looked back at Chris. Was he playing his Joker?

Chris read his mind. "Don't worry," he whispered. "I will tell you everything you need to know." With that, Chris stood up, pushed his chair underneath the table and headed back to his cell.

A short visit that was far from sweet.

Somebody, somewhere, was destined to fall.

Somebody, somewhere, was destined to die.

And all because of Chris Randall.

CHAPTER 36
The day after Bonfire night

On the upper floor of the mid-terraced house in the Northern Territory, Mark stood facing The Maniac. His legs were trembling so hard he thought the floorboards beneath him might start to creak from the tremors he was creating.

He needed to speak but words failed him because he was nervous and drowning in self-loathing just from being there. He could not put his finger on what was upsetting him so.

Was it the room?

The house?

The street?

The Northern Territory?

The Maniac?

His own past?

Yes, that was it. He was scared of his dark and not so distant past catching up with him. He feared how it could change his present and the future he was so looking forward to – if he was allowed it!

That was why he had vowed never to go back. Suddenly, Mark found himself fighting for his own life again and it felt perilous. He would have to play all his Aces to secure the new life he had prepared for himself.

"Well, Kid, what do you want?" asked The Maniac. "Why are you here?"

Mark did not know what to say or where to start? He didn't have much time: The Maniac was busy and impatient. This would be his only chance to speak, or forever hold his peace.

"It's about Tequila," he finally began to say.

"Which Tequila?" asked The Maniac, nonchalant, his face showing no expression. "The drink or the drag queen bitch who screwed me over? I hate them both."

At that moment it could have been about either, as Mark really needed a drink. "The drag queen bitch," he replied, echoing The Maniac's description of her.

"What about it?" The Maniac's mood changed almost imperceptibly at the clarification but Mark could sense it: he had seen it before, this minimal shift in his behaviour, and he knew what followed. First, his teeth would slowly grind together, then his eyes would narrow, and his fists would clench.

Mark was too slow to respond.

"What about it?" The Maniac demanded once more, slamming his right fist violently onto the desk.

A Heavy stepped into the room but was immediately dismissed.

"The police raid on the cabaret bar," Mark began to say, "I assume that was your doing?"

"Course it was" he replied, proudly. "I got that stupid little bitch arrested. I wish I could have seen its face. I hear it was dragged off the stage in front of everyone. Humiliating. Brilliant!"

"But why?"

"Oh, come on, Mark... do I call you Mark these days?" Mark nodded. He never wanted to be called Connie again. "You more than anyone know how much I love to give my little warnings. It helps pass the time... until it's time to get down to business."

Mark braced himself for what might follow. "And have there been any warnings other than the one you organised for opening night?"

"Oh, just a few cut and paste letters, you know. It keeps the Heavies busy when there's not a lot going on." The Maniac laughed out loud, tickled about something.

Mark felt he should laugh too - just to keep the mood up and the momentum going - but it really wasn't funny and instead of laughing he erupted into a sudden bout of coughing, at which The Maniac remarked he should get himself to a doctor because he sounded and looked bloody awful.

He didn't normally care but he'd always had a soft spot for this one.

Mark brushed it off and said it would pass soon enough. He was determined to show no weakness.

The Maniac continued to tell Mark what he had been up to: "We sent a letter to that Wendy bitch, but I don't actually have a problem with that one... I just thought she needed to know how bloody shit she is."

"Fair enough," responded Mark, wondering if that was the fan letter Wendy had gloated about on social media. Only Wendy could take something mean and misinterpret it so badly she could polish it, cover it in glitter, and present it to the world as a New Year Honours List type accolade!

The Maniac started to laugh again: "Now, what was it we said to that Tequila bitch? Oh yes: enjoy your performance, it might be your last one. Well, something like that, anyway."

Although he had not known about the letter Tequila had been sent, Mark was not in the least surprised. He did not react.

"Oh, how we laughed, Mark," he continued to say. "You would have laughed too. I presume they were received safely?"

"I'd have thought so," Mark replied, deliberately not laughing about it.

This was more serious than he had anticipated.

The Maniac turned serious once more. "Right, Kid, what are you really doing here? It's not to catch up or make pleasantries, is it?"

Mark flinched: the spotlight was shining brightly on him, and he was not used to it out of his drag queen disguise. "Please, can you lay off Tequila? He's not a bad lad underneath the slap. He just got a bit caught up in it all. The dickhead believed Chris Randall would make his dreams come true if he did as he was told."

The Maniac listened, saying nothing, and stared intently at Mark who was waiting hopefully for a crack to appear in his hard exterior.

"So will you let him off?" asked Mark.

"No."

"Will you do it for me? For old time's sake?," Mark begged but he already knew the battle was lost.

"No."

Mark was desperate now. He didn't want to resort to playing his wild card but felt he had no other option. Just the thought of it made him sick to the pit of his stomach. "What if Connie was to come out and pay you a little visit, like she used to? Would that sweeten the pot?"

It had helped in the past but he'd had the breast implants then and, in the eyes of The Maniac, that had made it acceptable.

"No. I want Tequila. I don't want you. Not anymore. I never really wanted you anyway." All Mark could do was blink as feelings of failure engulfed his very soul. "I just wanted to get to Chris Randall and you gave me the perfect way in."

"What?"

"I've been after Randall's territory for a long time. Yeah, he did okay out of it but I knew I could do a lot better. His mistake was letting idiot drag queens like Tequila sell gear for him, the knobhead."

"Honestly, Tequila really is a good lad."

Upon hearing this, The Maniac flared up again, reaching a volume that did not necessarily alarm the Heavies, but one which they were not used to hearing.

Mark felt concerned for his own safety. Would he make it out of there alive? He had to; he still had many issues to resolve.

"Tequila is fucking scum who sold some of those dodgy drugs to my son!" roared The Maniac. "I don't care what anybody else does in this town but leave my children out of it! The shit that fucking idiot sold him caused him to have a seizure. He almost died because of that stupid bitch."

"I'm sorry, I didn't realise. I thought it was because he owed you money. You were his loan shark, weren't you?"

"Of course you didn't realise, because all Connie cared about was her fucking self."

"But I'm not Connie anymore," protested Mark, frantically. "I'm Mark."

"Fuck off, you'll always be Connie," snarled The Maniac. "Just because you took off the dress and the makeup it doesn't make you somebody else. The mindset is still the same."

And, to Mark, that was the worst thing anybody could have said to him. Was he the same person? Was Connie still inside him, just suppressed deep in the bowels of his core?

"No!" Mark screamed back, surprising himself as much as The Maniac. The Heavies did not intervene. "I am not the same as Connie. And your war is with Chris Randall, remember? Not with Tequila."

"No. I have now decided it's with Tequila."

"But if your son chose to buy drugs from her then the problem was already there. Tequila didn't start it; she just stupidly added fuel to the fire."

The Maniac clearly did not like what he was hearing. "I want you to go now before you say something really stupid."

Exhausted and defeated, Mark nodded. He had no more cards to play; he had lost. It had been a waste of time... he should have known before he had even tried... it always was.

He turned to leave but stopped and turned back when The Maniac spoke again. "You should know," he said. "I am going after Tequila; I will get her and she will pay for what happened. If you get in the way then believe me I will come after you as well."

Mark nodded, not doubting it for a moment. He already knew Tequila's debt would soon become his own. After all, it was the least he could do to compensate for her almost losing her life in the Divas fire.

He left the building and the Northern Territory as quickly as he could. Damn it, he hadn't helped at all; he had only made things worse.

He should have left it alone in the first place.

So, the real issue had been The Maniac's son. And all this time Mark had felt certain it was because Tequila had loaned money from The Maniac.

This shit was much worse than that.

And now, things would escalate even quicker than they would have if he'd just kept his bloody nose out.

Yet again!

He needed to get to Tequila as quickly as he could. He needed to warn her of the dangers ahead. And to do so, he needed to break another of his new life's resolutions.

He pulled out his phone and swiped until he reached his contacts. And - for no reason other than to know if they had called him - he scrolled through a list of people he had long since vowed never to contact again.

He stopped on one particular name and rang their number without hesitation.

Of course, there was always a chance they had changed it or would not answer but there was also a chance they saved numbers in their phone, so they knew which calls to ignore.

Understandably, Mark had changed his number since fleeing that godforsaken town, so it would probably flash up as 'Unknown Caller', which meant they might just answer.

It began to ring.

When it hadn't been answered by the fourth ring Mark looked at his watch to check the time. Surely, they would be awake, and up and at it by now?

Should he leave a message? Would they call him back? This was important; he needed to speak to the other person urgently.

It rang several more times and then, thankfully, the owner of the phone answered.

He began to plead his case. "Hi, it's me Mark... yes, that's right. Well, no, not Connie anymore but that's irrelevant now... What do I want? Okay, I actually need a massive favour. You're probably not going to be happy about it, but for old time's sake, will you please, please help?"

He was so focused on the conversation that he hadn't realised one of the Heavies was following him, or that he was close enough to overhear every word... which meant he could give The Maniac a detailed recount of what was being discussed.

Without realising it, Mark had placed himself in very grave danger.

CHAPTER 37
Early November

Miss April Showers - now known as the former Psychic Drag Queen thanks to Wendy WolfWhistle's unwanted presence in her life - was at home trying to determine what her future held when she made an unexpected discovery which would have been a much bigger blessing had she not uncovered it.

Her psychic drag queen days certainly seemed to be a thing of the past now, but she still had enough money in the bank to enjoy some time out, rebalance her karma, reflect, and catch up with everyday things like updating her social media pages, visiting friends and family, and indulging in much-needed shopping trips. Something would need to change soon because she could not afford this extravagant lifestyle too much longer.

And so, with a large mug of steaming hot coffee at her side, she picked up her phone.

Casually, she began to flick through her different social media sites - which were far quieter now than they had once been - actively avoiding any posts that suggested she was, in fact, a charlatan, fraudster, or money grabbing manipulative bitch, as some of her disillusioned former fans were saying.

Perhaps, had she chosen to do something else that day, like visit people or go on that shopping trip, the unfortunate event that was about to befall her might have been avoided.

But she did not.

If only April had foreseen the other possibilities that day could have held for her. Maybe if she had switched on her self-professed psychic powers and foreseen the trouble ahead, it might have been averted. Instead, she found herself sitting at home, looking at her phone.

She had no idea what chaos could come from doing something as simple as reaching for her phone and innocently scrolling through the hash tags to see what was happening in the social media world of drag, to see what people still thought of her, and to see whose hurtful comments she needed to block this time.

#AprilShowers

#PsychicDragQueen

Really, there was not a lot to see anymore. Her old fans had grown tired of her desperate pleas for another chance, whilst the trolls and restless tongues had moved on to other celebrities who had been exposed, framed, or caught with their pants down.

April had seen professional drag queen stars Whore-Moan and Phero-Moan performing their cabaret act several times before and had enjoyed their shows so much she had followed them in case they ever returned to her hometown. So, she was delighted to see she had been tagged, *#PsychicDragQueen*, in some photos of theirs. Without hesitation, April started flicking through the comments to see what people had been saying about them, blissfully unaware of the hideous backlash doing so would unleash.

The positive comments about a performance they had given at a recent charity night did not surprise her, as they were hilarious when she had seen them.

She was saddened to see a lot of negativity about their recent tour though... obviously, you couldn't please all the people all the time but she knew the sting of bad publicity first hand.

She started to flick through the photos, many of which were blurry and appeared to have been taken by a three-year-old. She stopped on one of the clearer photos featuring three dragged up faces.

Who was that in the picture with them… some scratty-looking drag queen who looked as though she had just climbed out of a bin lorry.

Was she part of their cabaret act now? Was she the reason the reviews for their last tour were not so favourable? After all, she didn't look well put together or like somebody people would pay money to watch.

Oh, hang on… was that...?

Oh. My. God. It **was!** The giant Weeble woman who played such a massive part in ruining her last ill-fated psychic night!

It was definitely her.

She studied the photo carefully and read the hash tag captions very carefully.

#DragQueens
#Fabulicious
#WendyWolfwhistle
#OldQueensJugsPub
#BeautifulDragQueens
#PsychicDragQueen
#PheroMoan
#WhoreMoan
#WendyWolfwhistle (again)

So, that was her name: Wendy WolfWhistle. April had been trying to track her down ever since she had ripped her career to shreds.

She found the website for The Old Queen's Jugs pub easily on the internet and was assaulted by endless photos of Wendy WolfWhistle: in a wedding dress, in ripped tights… inundating the site, offending the observer.

So, The Old Queen's Jugs cabaret bar…

Wendy WolfWhistle…

East Green Street…
Maybe it was time for April to visit this place.
And maybe Wendy Weeble should watch her back.

CHAPTER 38
Bonfire night

Jay shook himself dry, zipped up his trousers, and washed his hands thoroughly before placing them under the hand drier. He opened the toilet door and stepped back into the bar area of The Old Queen's Jugs.

Oliver was standing right there with his hand up against the cellar door.

Their eyes met momentarily but Oliver looked away almost immediately, firmly pushing open the cellar door and disappearing from view. The door closed slowly behind him.

As it was bonfire night and the firework display was about to begin, almost everybody had gone outside to watch, with just a few remaining stragglers heading for the door.

In a matter of seconds he was the only remaining customer, with Wayne polishing glasses behind the bar his only company. It seemed like the perfect moment to buy himself a drink. "I'll have a pint of lager please."

Wayne shook his head. "Oliver has just gone down into the cellar to change the barrel. He'll probably be a while yet because he doesn't know how to do it. Maybe have a bottle or something else instead?"

Jay quickly scanned the beer pumps in front of him. Most of them he had no idea about, but he knew he quite liked fruity cider, so he asked for a pint of that. Wayne nodded, picked up a clean pint glass, and poured the drink. "That'll be four twenty," he said.

Jay passed over a note and waited for his change. "Thank you," he replied, shoving the loose coins into his jeans pocket without checking them first.

"Aren't you going out to watch the fireworks?" Wayne asked. "I'd like to see them but I can't if you stay in here."

"Okay, I'll go out and watch them," replied Jay, with little enthusiasm.

Wayne locked the till, pocketed the key, and walked around the bar until he was on the same side as this strange guy that came in and stared at Oliver a lot.

They left the building together and quickly lost each other in the crowd. Jay was thankful because he did not wish to stand next to Wayne making small talk about the pretty colours, how cool the rockets were, or how Catherine Wheel would be a great name for a drag queen.

As soon as the first rocket launched and exploded into a blaze of reds and greens to many 'ooohs' and 'ahhhs', Jay turned away and slipped back into the bar. Nobody saw him go as they were too focused on the fireworks, just as he had suspected they would be.

Few people ever noticed him anyway, in the bar, in the town, at the previous charity night, because his appearance did not provoke much interest from those around him; except from Oliver, who had always appeared curious and suspicious of this familiar-looking stranger.

Jay's eyes went straight to the cellar door. It was open but slowly closing, in the same clunky manner it had when Oliver had gone through several minutes earlier to change the barrel.

Maybe he had come back upstairs after completing his task, but he was nowhere to be seen and Jay was confident he had been close enough to the door to notice if he had already stepped outside.

Just to be certain, Jay checked around.

No, he was not behind the bar, and he was not in the men's toilets. Perhaps he had gone backstage? Did he dare venture back there to go and see? Maybe he had gone for change or to look for a spare till key since Wayne had taken his with him.

Surely, he wasn't still in the cellar, was he?

Should he look down there too?

Standing at the top of the cellar steps he listened carefully but saw and heard nothing. Apart from the noise of the fireworks outside, everything seemed peaceful.

But, during a lull in the fireworks, he heard a definite sound. followed by heavy footsteps that seemed to fade away across the cellar floor. As he listened intently for more movement, he heard the tread of someone returning towards the steps where he was standing; in a moment they would appear and know he had been there snooping.

If it was Oliver, he didn't want him to think he had been in there following him like a stalker - he already felt as though he was making the poor guy nervous just being there, which is why he sometimes left sooner than he wanted to, often with his drink unfinished.

Quickly, quietly, he dashed out onto the street once more, whilst watching what was happening inside the venue through the windows.

Jay saw what he needed to and it was exactly what he had been afraid of: it was not Oliver who emerged from the cellar.

He did not leave early that night. Instead, he took a seat opposite the bar and nursed his pint until closing time. He sat and watched and waited, continuously looking around for Oliver; thinking about him, wandering what the hell had happened to him, and desperately hoping he was safe. Praying for an excuse to go into those cellars and investigate what was going on for himself, for his own peace of mind.

Even if it meant he would have to spend the night down there, although he did not relish the idea of hanging out in that bleak, rat-infested space.

Even if it meant he would not sleep until the following day.

CHAPTER 39
The day after Bonfire night

After his ordeal in the Northern Territory and his unsuccessful negotiations with The Maniac, Mark returned to East Green Street - another place he had vowed he would never return to.

Chris Randall had lived nearby, and Mark had often staggered that way, off his head, sometimes in full drag as Connie, ignoring the warnings and offensive dialogue, but always within the darkness of the night. Sometimes looking for his next punter, sometimes for another much-needed fix, or sometimes just to pass on messages from The Maniac, most of which he had made up. And once, to demand he be given the lead in the Divas cabaret show.

At the time he thought he was winning at life, taking full advantage of the unexpected opportunities that had come his way.

Now, he only felt lost again, like everything he had worked so hard to achieve was slipping away.

The harsh words of The Maniac haunted him. Was he still like Connie? Would he always be that person? Did they share the same mindset? Could people never change?

This time he had come to East Green Street to find Tequila, to save her, to rescue her from a debt she did not even know she owed. Maybe, once this task was complete, he could finally leave and never return; but would Tequila even agree to listen to him?

He stood outside the recently renamed pub to look for the improvements he had expected to see, but they were few and far between.

Admittedly, the name over the door was different: Martin Woodward 'licensed to get people intoxicated and find Wendy WolfWhistle more desirable whilst under the influence', and, of course, the pub's name was slightly different too, but that was about it.

Maybe a few bricks had been re-pointed and the Victorian detail around the windows had been painted a different shade, but he had rarely passed this way in the daylight so he didn't really know.

Anxiously, he pushed the door and stepped inside, and that is where he saw the first notable change: although it was relatively early in the day he was astonished to find it crammed from corner to corset.

It looked much better inside now, even with the remnants of its former incarnation, like the lingering odour of stale chips and bad breath, which were probably embedded into the very fabric of the building... or maybe Wendy was just having a pre-performance snack.

The stage was still situated at the far end, albeit much grander than the previous one which had once hosted the meat raffle and the occasional game of bingo. He had never participated in either.

All in all, it was better than it had been and, if Mark was still a local and his circumstances were different, then he might have been quite excited about this new drag queen cabaret bar opening up.

One thing that hadn't changed was the bar itself, still in the exact same spot it had always been, with Wayne the Stain in the exact same place he had always been. In an instant, it felt like the bad old days again.

Mark cringed upon seeing that miserable face there but reckoned he would be every bit as miserable if he had stood behind that bar for years on end trying desperately to make ends meet.

It was unlikely Wayne would recognise him as Mark for their paths had never crossed when Mark was out of drag; but Connie would almost certainly have triggered his memory and prompted some sort of reunion. Thankfully, there was no such spark of recognition.

With his mind on the bigger picture, Mark walked over to Wayne and asked if Tequila was about. He kept it cool and breezy so as not to draw any unnecessary attention towards himself, and purposely did not use Tequila's real name of James because that might also have aroused suspicion.

This way, he would just appear to be a friend or a fan.

Wayne muttered something about him being around somewhere then headed backstage, returning moments later with James, out of drag, nervously in tow. Nobody ever came in there asking for him. Was it somebody wanting money he owed them? Had his past finally caught up with him?

Little did he know just how right he was...

Wayne gestured towards Mark who quickly put his finger to his lips in the hope James wouldn't reveal too much or name and shame him as Connie.

"What do you want, biatch?" James asked him, in only a slightly friendly manner. Towards the end they had warmed to each other and James was relieved it was only him.

Little did he know...

Mark had been unsure what welcome he would receive, and had braced himself for the impact, but was pleased not to be met with outright hostility. "Can we talk?" he asked. "In private. It's important - really important."

"If you're after the lead in the show you can piss off, right now," responded James. "This is my show, and I am the lead act."

"Oh, I thought Wendy was," said Mark, with a cheeky grin. "That's how it looks on the socials and on Wendy's profile pages!"

"No, it's very much me. And I'm a much better lead than you ever were. I kill it out there each night. Unlike you, who used to murder it."

"Listen," replied Mark, beckoning him backstage and away from the prying eyes and ears of others. "There really is something urgent we need to talk about. It can't wait."

"Do you want to have sex with me?" asked James, not picking up on the panicked tone in Mark's voice and making it all about himself, as he always did. "Knowing where you've been, it's a firm no."

Mark sighed. This banter was not getting them anywhere. He was not that person anymore and time was not on either of their sides.

James had always been flaky: too far up his own arse, always out of his depth, and arduously high maintenance. Little appeared to have changed in that regard. Except now, he was the star of the show and that had clearly boosted his ego into the stratosphere.

And to be fair, good on him: it was what he had always wanted. But he needed to come down from his podium before he toppled off and broke his neck.

"I actually have an evening performance to get ready for," James announced, shrugging him off and deciding whatever connection they may have made was not worth exploring.

Mark knew he only had one chance to get James to engage with him before he disappeared backstage altogether. He had to save him - or die trying - and he could only think of one more thing to say that might stop him in his tracks. He stepped forward, leaned in close to the misguided fool in front of him and quietly whispered: "Enjoy your performance; this might be your last one."

Those were not the exact words he had been sent in that letter but they were close enough to make James's face drop. He took a sudden interest in why Mark was there. He hadn't told anybody about that letter so how could this bitch turn up out of the blue and quote it almost word for word?

Mark guessed what James must have been thinking. "I didn't send it," he said. "The Maniac in the Northern Territory did." With that, James allowed Mark to lead him away from the bar area, out of sight and into the back where nobody was around to listen in.

"The Maniac?" repeated James worried, because if that was as bad as it sounded then he was screwed.

The Maniac. He thought hard... was that the loan shark he had borrowed money from and never paid back? He couldn't remember but nobody had come looking for him, so he just presumed he'd got away with it.

Maybe he hadn't.

"Why is this Maniac guy after me?" he asked.

"Look, this is really serious," said Mark, concerned in case James did not yet grasp the gravity of his situation. "Can we talk somewhere more private?"

James nodded. "Come upstairs to my room," he replied, leading the way. "But just so you know, I'm not having sex with you no matter how much you want it."

"Fair enough," replied Mark, humouring him to keep the mood light because, once he had revealed what was happening, fear would be the only emotion left.

Mark followed James up the stairs perhaps a little too quickly because he was left breathless and struggled to control the urge to cough when he reached the top; but he needed to remain silent and calm.

James gestured to the door that led to his tiny bedroom. "So where have you been hiding since Divas came crashing down?" he asked.

"Don't worry about that now," replied Mark, not wanting to disclose where he had been or where he was heading back to, even if he was trying to win James's trust.

"This Maniac?" questioned James, "and the letter..."

Although he had no clue what was going on, he instinctively knew he had to listen to Mark, especially as he had obviously gone out of his way to resurface after all these weeks.

"The Maniac is after you," explained Mark. "He's been biding his time, waiting for the trail to go cold. That's what these people do, they sit and wait before they move in on their prey. And if he knew I was here telling you this he would be after me too."

"Why?"

"It's a long story," sighed Mark, and he told the tale of everything that had happened leading up to the moment that saw them sitting there together in that tiny bedroom, fearing for their lives.

Naturally, Mark omitted things - lots of things - but only the stuff James did not need to know.

What he did reveal was that when James had joined Divas as Tequila ShockingBird, he had replaced Miss Crystal Champagne who, up until that point, had no intention of leaving; Chris Randall had forced her out.

Mark then confirmed The Maniac was indeed his scary loan shark in the Northern Territory.

He described with alarming accuracy how Chris had probably asked Tequila to sell drugs for him, promising whatever he had wanted in return, like the lead in the Divas cabaret show but assumed he had never been given his 'rewards'.

Finally, he explained how Tequila had inadvertently sold dodgy drugs to The Maniac's son, who had almost died from them.

James was visibly panicked at this revelation.

He had always regretted selling Chris's drugs but it pained him even more now. He also regretted not heeding the advice from Mark (Connie) and Tittie when they had tried to warn him.

Clearly, he wasn't as smart or streetwise as he had thought. At least he had the good sense to stop and listen now.

Mark went on to explain that The Maniac had gone after Chris Randall over drug and money issues; it was he who had ordered Divas Cabaret bar to be burnt down.

Mark sensibly left out any details regarding his involvement in the matter.

If James asked how he and The Maniac knew each other he would deal with that question then, but James was not all that bright so Mark felt he was probably safe from interrogation about that for now.

And, thankfully, James did not ask.

He was already only thinking about himself, just as Mark had expected: the spiralling debts from which he was still hiding; his growing fears over The Maniac and what he might do to him; how he was far too young and pretty to be pulverised by such a monster.

He now trusted Mark so implicitly that he never once questioned the veracity of what he was being told.

All the usual paranoia he would typically have harboured - that Mark was only trying to get him out the way so he could take the lead in the cabaret show James had built up from scratch – vanished. He was afraid.

"He has sent you two warnings," clarified Mark. "The police raid on opening night was the first, and the cut and paste letter was the other. You can't afford to ignore them."

But James had been ignoring them, meaning time was running out.

Mark took a chance and assumed he knew what James was thinking – after all, he had been deliberately trying to steer him in one direction throughout the conversation. "Right, we have to get you away from here," he said, "far away. Quickly."

"But I have nowhere to go," replied James, hopelessly. It was the sad epiphany of a foolish young man whose stupid mistakes had left him with no options. In an instant, he realised not only did have nowhere safe to go but that he had no money, career, friends, or home… he had lost everything. And he had worked so hard to establish his reign as the beautiful and much-adored Tequila ShockingBird in a cabaret show everybody seemed to love.

Fame! Money! Truth! It was all gone.

"Don't worry, I have a plan," advised Mark, reassuringly. Then he surprised himself and James by putting his arms around the other man and hugging him, holding him close. And, finally, he felt some of his pent-up guilt release. And, finally, the burden he had been carrying on his shoulders become slightly more bearable. And, finally, he dared to believe he wasn't anything like Connie after all.

But this was about James, not him, and they needed to get him to safety.

"So, what's the plan?" asked James, releasing himself from the relative safety of Mark's embrace… why had he never bothered to get to know him before?

"Okay, this took a lot of convincing but you remember I mentioned that other drag queen from Divas, Miss Crystal Champagne?"

"The one that this shady bitch replaced?"

Mark nodded. "Yeah. She lives on the Costa Del Sol now and runs her own drag queen cabaret bar. She said you can go out there and work for her."

"The Costa Del Sol?" gasped James, stunned. "That's a long way away, isn't it?"

"It's much safer for you."

"Yes, I know," replied James, suddenly overcome with emotion. "It's just such a massive thing to do."

"You did it when you moved here."

"And look at the mess I made of it."

"I understand," said Mark, sympathetically, "but it's by far the best option for you."

James nodded knowing this was true. It also meant he could continue to do drag, the thing he loved most in the world. "And she's okay with me going out there?"

"She is; once I told her how good you are and how committed you are to drag, she agreed to let bygones be bygones. She worked with Chris long enough to know what he was capable of - we all did. He didn't hire drag queens for his show he just manipulated and abused them for a while."

"I'm scared."

Mark smiled at him kindly. "What? Tequila ShockingBird is scared of doing something fantastic like this?"

"No, she isn't, but James is," he explained, trying to come to terms with the sheer enormity of what was happening. An hour earlier he was just thinking he would have some noodles and get ready for the show. Now he was fleeing for his life.

Mark tried to reassure him further. "You'll be okay out there with Crystal, she'll look after you."

"Why don't you come with me? It will be like the old days at Divas, but much better."

Mark calmly shook his head. He didn't want anything to be like the old days at Divas, regardless of how much better it might be. "Unfortunately, I can't. My work here is not yet done."

As the realisation struck him anew, James began to panic once more. "But I haven't got any money to buy a plane ticket! And where will I live?"

"Don't worry about that, I have money you can have, lots of it. And, you'll stay with Crystal until you find somewhere of your own."

"Really?"

Mark nodded. "Apparently she lives in a gorgeous little whitewashed complex with red roofs and a communal swimming pool, with a load of other British ex-pats."

"It sounds nice."

"And you never know, something may come up for rent in the same place. Just think, you can sunbathe every day of the year!"

"It does sound amazing," said James, thoughtfully, "it really does. But I can't take your money as well. You have done enough for me already."

Mark didn't say anything and momentarily bit his bottom lip.

After all the danger he had put them in and Tequila almost dying in the Divas fire, this barely even began to make the amends that were due.

But he could not admit that to anyone. "Okay, as we are being completely honest, would it help if you knew it was actually Chris's money I am giving you? Well, it was his money… it's ours now. Let's call it compensation for the trouble he caused us."

"Oh my god!" shrieked James. "I'm going to the Costa Del Sol."

"You sure are. Right, first of all, we need to book you a plane ticket. I can do that on my phone. And you need to dig out your passport. I hope you have one."

James nodded.

"But what about Father Wendy?" he asked soberly, finding himself unexpectedly hit by a branch from the family tree.

"Crystal only has room for you."

"But we have only just found each other again. I know he's a pain in the arse but he saved my life, and I really would like to spend more time with him… until I can't bear him any longer."

"He could visit you," replied Mark, comfortingly. "And you never know, he may even come and live with you once you're settled. Maybe he could get a job out there too. I don't know what or where, but something."

"Yes, I suppose he could," agreed James, thoughtfully. "Wow, I'm going to live abroad."

"Are you okay with all of this?"

"Yes. Gosh, I can't believe I'm actually going to do this. Wow."

"Right, just to be on the safe side, let's try and get you a ticket out of here tomorrow."

"Tomorrow, okay... gosh, that's really soon. What should I tell people?"

"Don't tell anyone anything. The fewer people who know the better."

"Father Wendy will be upset."

"Yes," agreed Mark, "but then he'll realise he's headlining the show, and his sorrow will turn into glory!"

Mark's guilt lifted a little further when he realised that, through the process of helping James, he was making another person's dreams come true as well.

James laughed a little. "Yes, I think you're right."

As Mark searched his phone for flights he turned to James and spoke: "Do the show tonight, I'm sure everything will be okay; but **do not** leave this building until the taxi turns up to take you to the airport tomorrow. I don't think The Maniac will try anything with other people around."

"How do you know so much about him?" asked James. And there was that question.

Mark smiled and said the only thing that came to mind, which wasn't too far from the truth anyway. "He helped me bring down Chris Randall."

"He deserved it after what he'd done to everybody, especially you," replied James, finally showing genuine care for the other person in the tiny room with him.

"Right, how many cases will you need? The fewer the better."

"I'll probably need three; one for my 'James' stuff and two for my 'Tequila' stuff. Everything else can stay here."

Mark took out his wallet and input his credit card details. "Good. I'll sort out your taxi and I'll need to make a bank transfer to your account too; the wonders of modern technology, eh?"

James smiled at him. And to think he had once disputed every word that came out of this person's mouth.

"Crystal will pick you up from the airport out there, so you won't have to worry about that either. Oh, you *will* have to change your drag queen name."

"Why?"

"Modern technology may be wonderful, but it makes it harder to keep a low profile; you **cannot** afford for anybody to find Tequila ShockingBird through social media from afar, okay? You're only going to get one chance to disappear... you can't waste it."

"Okay," sighed James. "I suppose a reinvention will be good, how about..."

"No! Don't tell me anything about your new life. I don't want to know. Believe me; it's best I know as little as possible."

As Mark left James and the pub behind, he felt pleased he had been able to do this - even if it had meant returning to this godforsaken town.

Very soon James would be safe in Spain.

Very soon Wendy would be the lead in the show.

And soon enough, he would be safely back to his own life, too.

But, as he had said to James, he still had work to do there.

Unfortunately, Mark was so pre-occupied with purging his own guilt, building bridges, and applauding his own success that he lost sight of the bigger picture without even realising.

He had made a fatal error where The Maniac was concerned.

Mark hadn't spotted the Heavy who had followed him from the Northern Territory listening to him plan Tequila's escape, and who was now sitting waiting in The Old Queen's Jugs, monitoring his every move.

The Heavy who would report back to The Maniac and tell him that Mark had completely gone against his wishes.

Stick or twist?

Who was going to lose?

CHAPTER 40
Bonfire night

Jay watched as the staff wiped down the bar and collected the few remaining empty glasses around him. It was closing time but he was not the last one in there; there were still several hangers-on - on the lookout for whatever might come their way, before admitting defeat and walking the short distance back to their homes, mostly on or around East Green Street.

There had been no sign of Oliver anywhere and time, for that evening, was running out. He needed to get down into those cellars to see what was going on and now he'd had more time (and drinks) to think things over, he had a very bad feeling about it.

Oliver seemed to have disappeared into thin air although, rationally, Jay knew he had to be somewhere. The most obvious guess was the cellars.

He watched the chubby older man who usually hosted the cabaret take the till drawer with him into the back, so that was one of the staff members out of the way.

The remaining few gave up their hopes of pulling somebody, including Jay who was clearly not interested, and left the building. Some went straight home, others to the takeaway on the next street, a few to a late-night club, and the rest quietly opened some nasty phone apps that guaranteed them immediate action.

The drag queen called Tequila had disappeared after the show and the dullard of a barman, Wayne, picked up a large bucket of soapy water and headed into the gents.

That just left the dying swan, Wendy WolfWhistle, who was collecting beer mats and wiping down tables. Although still in drag, she was notably even less appealing at this late hour as her stubble was beginning to show, one of her oversized earrings was missing, and the ladder running up the back of her tights was big enough for a firefighter to climb.

So, it was just Jay and Wendy in there and, from his limited knowledge of her, he guessed she could be easily distracted with a bit of flattery or fuckwittery.

He watched her return behind the bar where she removed the drip trays from their respective beer pumps and, with her back to him thinking she couldn't be seen, took a swig from one of them. When she turned around, Jay, the last remaining punter of the night, was standing on the other side of the bar watching her.

Was he her fan? Was he waiting to pick her up? Could this be love? Were the stars aligned for a night of endless pleasure?

"You were great tonight," Jay said to her, happily unaware of any of the erotic thoughts she was having about him.

"Ahhh thank you, Darling" she replied, smiling widely because positive feedback was always wonderful to receive. "I did a pelvic thrust just for you in the finale. Did you see it?"

Jay smiled back at her. He had no idea what she was talking about but felt she was harmless... deluded beyond all measure and probably certifiable but nice enough, on the whole.

Now, how could he distract her?

As if the universe stepped in to help, Wendy asked if he would like her autograph. "I'm sure I have some I prepared earlier... now, where are they? Sometimes Wayne and Oliver throw them away not realising how valuable they are. Hmmm… they might be with my fan mail. Have you seen my fan mail anywhere?"

She hobbled and wobbled around searching the till area but eventually turned to face Jay empty-handed. "I think I have some in my dressing room. Oh, but we're not allowed to leave the bar unattended if there are still people in here."

"Oh, I'm not going to steal anything if you want to dash off and get one for me."

Wendy looked at him for a moment or two. She really wanted him to have her autograph – particularly as she intended to write her mobile number on the back - but she couldn't leave him in the bar alone. "I'm sorry, Darling, but Martin is really strict about this."

"Well, that is a shame," he replied, feigning disappointment, "because I would love to have your autograph. Especially after you gave me such a soul shaking pelvic thrust during the finale."

He cringed inwardly as he said it and felt slightly guilty for deceiving her but he was doing it for Oliver.

"Well, perhaps I could find a pen and scribble it down on something else instead, like your chest?"

"Well, that would be nice," replied Jay, unsure how to respond. Wendy was literally drooling like a rabid dog.

"Oh, here's a pen!" shrieked Wendy joyously, spotting one behind a half-filled bottle of dark rum. "Start unbuttoning your top! Where I used to work in this lovely little place called Divas - I was the lead cabaret star there too - we used to have brochures. I was in the brochure, you know."

She failed to mention how she used to single out a particularly hazy photo of a very sleek, slender Connie and insinuate that it was her. She never hung around to hear people's responses when she autographed what was clearly an image of a completely different person as an urgent (and convenient) photo request from another fan would arise at the very same moment.

She turned back to face him, smiling as she recalled memories of events that hadn't really happened; she had simply told so many people the same fabricated stories that she came to believe them herself.

Jay pointed towards some optics at the very far end of the bar. "I think there is some paper over there."

"Oh, is there?" squawked Wendy, slightly disappointed she was being denied the opportunity to write her name on him as if he was a piece of school gym kit she would get to keep and take home to wash. However, he did still want her autograph and that was something to celebrate, so she waddled off like a duck on poppers, once more turning her back on him.

Upon realising there was no paper there, she turned back around to face him with her pen poised, thoroughly invigorated at the thought of branding him as her own... but he had gone.

Wendy sighed sadly. She had no idea she had been intentionally distracted. Neither did she notice the cellar door slowly closing back into its frame. Nor did she hear Jay's footsteps as he descended into the darkness below.

But she did notice that several of the beer pumps had been switched on and were now overflowing onto the floor. Was there time to stick her mouth under one of them before she had to scream for Wayne to bring his mop and bucket as a matter of urgency?

She switched off the beer pumps but remained despondent. What a shame the cute young man had left. No doubt he was so in love with her he couldn't bear to be alone with her for any longer. Perhaps he was worried she would break his heart.

So sad, she thought to herself, as she picked up the last couple of empties and put them into the glass washer. He would kick himself so hard if he ever found out he had been so much closer to pulling her than he'd realised.

In the cellar with the torch on his phone fully illuminated, Jay tiptoed around looking for evidence of misadventure that might have occurred down there that evening, but everything seemed as it should - not that he was an expert in pub cellars or how they should look.

But there was another door down there and it was padlocked.

What was behind it? Oliver, perhaps? Was Oliver even down there in the first place or had he just set himself on a wild goose chase where he would get locked in the pub for the night?

He listened carefully but could not hear anything. He knocked quietly on the door as he did not want to create a disturbance but there was no response. Suddenly, he felt very foolish: he was acting like he was part of Scooby Doo's gang, playing detective when he didn't even know what he was supposed to be looking for!

He had made a stupid mistake and now he was stuck on his own overnight in these miserable cold cellars in the dark! What an idiot he was!

Oliver couldn't possibly be down there. Why would he be?

He must have left the pub ages ago, unnoticed. He was probably at home right now watching the television or getting ready for bed - just like Jay should have been doing.

But Jay knew he had not seen him leave.

So, he kept looking.

Perhaps there was something behind that padlocked door after all but he did not have a key or anything to force it open with.

He would have to return with some tools if his search for Oliver was to continue past that damned door but doubted there would be anything suitable in the saloon area of the drag queen cabaret bar upstairs. In the meantime, he thought he should get some R&R.

He waited patiently until he felt comfortable everyone upstairs would have retired to their living quarters for the night.

Just before he reached the foot of the stairs, he switched off the torch on his phone... although the bar was probably empty, he didn't want to risk being discovered when he was meant to have gone home.

The already dismal environment immediately became even more dire, and the temperature dropped slightly without the meagre warmth the light had emitted. As he ascended, he hoped the cellar door itself had not been locked. He felt more than a little claustrophobic.

Thankfully the door opened, and he stepped out into the empty bar where he was very much alone.

Hungry, he helped himself to a few bags of nuts, accidentally pulling the cardboard display strip off the wall and damaging the packaging in the process so it couldn't be hung back up. He also poured himself a drink and sat at one of the empty bar stools contemplating what to do next.

He was trapped there for the night, that much was certain. He needed to find a safe place to sleep where he would be well out of the way when the pub opened.

Jay endured a difficult night riddled with hunger and exhaustion, and he found little respite. He chose to head back into the cellar as dawn broke to wait for the place to open so he could sneak up and lose himself amongst the early drinking punters, sometime around midday.

It would be a long wait but he was grateful to get some extra time down there as it gave him longer to explore. Although there was still no noise coming from behind that padlocked door, Jay had a nagging sense it was important for him to find out what it was concealing.

By sheer chance, he found a light switch and dared to switch it on; it would save his phone battery, which was critically low and he needed to save in case of any emergency. It would also give him an opportunity to locate something, anything, that might help him open that door.

For now, he would have to wait until it was time to return – unnoticed - to the bar, where - for the sake of appearances - he would have to have a drink and blend in.

Shortly after that, Oliver's mother would come in and confirm his suspicions that Oliver was missing.

He would watch her leave the pub and then follow her down the street until he caught up with her, when he would explain who he was and tell her his fears for her son.

In time, he would sneak back into those cellars, be victorious against that padlock and see exactly what was hidden behind that door.

And, in time, maybe Oliver could open his heart to him, because Jay's heart was very much open to the possibility of loving him.

CHAPTER 41
The day after Bonfire night

Oliver blinked several times. The shift from darkness to light had temporarily blinded him. He could make out the silhouette of somebody standing there staring as he lay helplessly in what he could now see was a small room within the cellars.

He saw their body shape first and then, as he grew accustomed to the light, he recognised who it was.

Standing in the doorway was the man he had been referring to as Jay.

"Shush," warned Jay, putting his index finger to his lips to encourage him to remain silent. "I'm here to rescue you. Your mother is waiting outside."

Jay quickly released the bonds that held Oliver captive and pulled off the tape covering his mouth as gently as he could before he helped Oliver to his feet who was stiff and sore because he had not moved for many hours. He was also very embarrassed because he had soiled himself but Jay did not care as he had achieved what he had set out to: he had promised Oliver's mother he would find her son and he had.

Jay sent her a short text to say he had recovered Oliver safely from the cellars, but it would not deliver as there was no phone signal. He was confident it would send once they were closer to civilisation.

Oliver's mother had alerted the police as soon as she suspected he had disappeared but Oliver was an adult, and hadn't been missing long enough for the situation to be classed as high-risk. Had his recent past regarding the hit and run on East Green Street, his involvement with Divas, and everything Chris Randall had bought to the table set for two been taken into consideration, it would have been.

"Do you know who did this to you?" Jay whispered, as he led him through the door that had held him prisoner and into the main cellar where Oliver had been attacked.

"Can we talk outside?" replied Oliver huskily; he was very thirsty and the insides of his mouth and throat felt raw.

"Yes, of course," replied Jay, as he led him towards the stone steps that would lead them both safely out of there.

All Jay wanted was for Oliver to know he could trust him and they were on the same side, even if it hadn't always felt that way. He wanted to help Oliver through this traumatic ordeal.

Seriously, why had somebody done this to him? Why would somebody drag him to his hell and then leave him there to die of thirst or hypothermia? Who on earth would want dear, sweet Oliver to perish in such a way?

At the top of the stairs, Jay wrapped his coat around Oliver's waist to give him some dignity, then pushed open the door that led into the pub with such force that it slammed hard and echoed around the room. All eyes turned to see the source of this sudden drama and kept looking when they saw the bedraggled Oliver appear at his side, looking half-dead.

"What were you doing down there?" Martin began to ask Jay, stopping when he saw Oliver.

Oliver paid no attention to the startled faces staring at him or to the phones that had been trained on him, recording his plight for posterity. He focussed solely on reaching the door in front of him that led the way back to East Green Street, to his mother, and to his freedom.

He knew they would talk about him and question what had happened but, as long as they waited until he was out of there, he didn't care. He could not stop the inevitable but refused to be part of the circus.

Whilst he couldn't control the actions of others, he could get himself through that door and out onto the street.

Oliver felt surprisingly safe with his arm around Jay, who suddenly seemed like a dear friend and protector. He held him tighter than any man since he had cradled Jake as he slipped away at the roadside.

Jay held open the door and led Oliver away. The room behind them was silent apart from the frantic clicking of those who were texting and carefully selecting emojis in their effort to distribute news of the bizarre scene that had just unfolded before them.

"Oooh, it must have been Chris Randall…"

"I told you he'd escaped from that prison cell…"

"I knew something like that was going to happen…"

"No, *I* said he'd escaped…"

Outside, the air was cold but felt refreshing on their faces. Oliver's mother was already running towards him with tears in her eyes and, when he saw her there, Oliver welled up, too.

Jay tried to let go of him so they could hold each other, but Oliver's mother wrapped her arms tightly around them both in gratitude and love. This brave young man had saved her son's life; thank goodness he had been around to look after him.

As she stood back, she looked at him as if she was only noticing his battered and weakened state for the first time. "Oh God… you need to go to hospital," she gasped.

"I'm fine. I want to talk to the police first," insisted Oliver, keen to begin the process of putting this behind him.

"Do you know who attacked you?" asked Jay once more.

Now he was safely outside with both of them, Jay hoped Oliver would speak more openly about what had happened. He wanted to know if Oliver said it was the same person he had seen coming out of the cellars.

"Do you mind if we wait until we get to the police station?" requested Oliver, "I don't want to have to do this more than once."

"But do you *know* who did this to you?" asked his mother.

Oliver nodded.

He knew exactly who it had been.

CHAPTER 42
The day after Bonfire night

Mark was feeling trapped inside his hotel room. Although his work in that town would probably never be complete, he had achieved what he had set out to do this time... or so he thought.

The following day, James would be off to a new safe haven, where nobody knew him or cared who he was. Maybe then, he could return to his own safe haven, as he desperately wanted to be free again.

But that night he didn't feel free; he felt like a prisoner within the compounds of the rented room that many had shared before him and many more who were yet to arrive would use after he had finally gone.

He could not imagine anyone having a good reason to visit that godforsaken town. He couldn't wait to return to a place where he wasn't a local and where he would never have to encounter the likes of The Maniac again.

He prayed The Maniac did not encounter him before he was able to escape... what a nightmare that would be!

But Mark had no idea what was happening behind the scenes, where scripts were being rewritten, sets radically changed, and the leading role recast.

Eager to escape the confines of his hotel room for a short time, he slipped into his comfortable faded blue jeans, a white t-shirt, and a cosy black jumper. He then put on his jacket, looked around the small over-priced room where none of the furnishings matched, and closed the door behind him.

He was desperate to leave and, had it been viable to make the journey home that evening, would already have been on his way. At least he could be gone in the morning - one night's sleep. A few final checks and then he could get out of there forever.

That was his plan.

He took the stairs down to the reception area where he smiled politely at an elderly couple who were coming in wearing hats and scarves and rubbing their cold hands together. He was reluctant to stop and make small talk in case they recognised him, so he slipped by them quickly.

They looked like complainers anyway; the sort that were never satisfied with anything anybody ever did for them. He had more pressing matters on his mind and didn't really care whether they were having a lovely stay or not; he certainly had no desire to hear how often their towels had been changed or to know if their tea and coffee sachets had been replenished.

He was a loner... he always had been and he probably always would be. He didn't need anybody and didn't want anybody to need him. Who would want these damaged goods, anyway, even if he ever succeeded in fixing himself?

Maybe in time he would be able to share parts of himself with someone, but he would never be able to admit who he had been, what he had done, and what he had run away from.

Or maybe he would never need to cross that bridge.

On the street outside, the dark November night felt cold, and Mark could not face going any further than the few steps he had already taken. He had wandered restlessly through the shadows of that town too many times already, hurt, alone, sad, and did not want to relive that; besides, he had nowhere to go.

He had already looked at everything he had wanted to see and been everywhere he had needed to go; he probably did need to check on others like Wendy,

Martin, and Oliver – just like he had done with Tittie - but that was not a job for such a cold November night. It could wait for a future visit as he was sure they were all fine.

But at the same time, he really didn't want to be inside his hotel room either.

Perhaps a quick drink in the hotel bar would help ease his mood; a snack too because he was quite hungry and hadn't eaten all day; then maybe an early night and a sharp exit after breakfast… maybe even before.

He felt happy enough with that plan and turned back to the hotel, not knowing that fate was about to dump a whole stack of cards on him and the other unsuspecting players that would change everything about the game.

The Ace of Hearts? Perhaps signalling a new beginning for those that wanted one. Fate was rarely that kind.

The Seven of Swords? Deceit! A card that annihilated trust.

The Moon card? Instantly doubled everyone's problems.

It was a cold, starlit night outside and the moon was shining brightly… and problems were multiplying like bacteria.

The Death card? Would this dreaded omen bring about an irreversible change or see another life cut short? As with the Seven of Swords, its impact would be determined by the other cards that were dealt alongside it.

The Queen of Broken Hearts? God, no. Surely fate would not be so cruel as to bestow the dreaded Queen of Broken Hearts upon them?

Back inside, Mark rubbed his hands together just as the elderly couple had done and made his way towards the bar, which was surprisingly empty. He had barely sat down with his food and drink when another person entered the room.

Mark recognised them immediately.

What the fuck were they doing there?

Immaculately dressed but looking quite tired around the eyes - nothing a good night's sleep wouldn't resolve - the other person took the seat next to his. Mark was very surprised to see them there and could not imagine why they had come.

The Arrival ordered a drink and looked around. "Don't mind me joining you, do you?" they asked, redundantly.

Mark nodded politely. "Sure," he said, although he minded a lot; this person attracted trouble like a magnet.

"Are you staying here?" they asked. Mark was reluctant to confirm it but could think of no other reason why he would be there alone, eating and drinking.

"It's not the best hotel, is it?" his unwanted guest said. "Still, it'll do for a night or two."

Mark nodded again and questioned how soon he would be able to get away from this conversation. "Yes, it could be worse," he finally said, between mouthfuls of food.

They both knew it could also have been a lot better but it was discrete and tucked away, offering the kind of privacy it was difficult to get from a nosey landlady in a B&B; something they both valued above home comforts at that moment in time, especially The Arrival.

They leaned forward and whispered close to Mark's ear, without disturbing his personal space. A question regarding the Eastern Quarter.

Mark listened carefully, then clarified what he thought had been asked of him. When The Arrival confirmed he had heard correctly, Mark reluctantly agreed. The Arrival nodded their appreciation and took a sip of their drink.

Mark looked back at his companion and lamented the peace and quiet he had been seeking out that evening. How had he suddenly become involved in this? He had an overwhelming feeling that slipping away quietly the next day would no longer be an option.

He had a very bad feeling about this.

That bloody Eastern Quarter… it was as big a bane in his life as the Northern Territory.

That night Mark did not sleep well at all.

Tossing and turning, tangled in the bed sheets, he couldn't stop thinking about The Arrival, or Wendy, or Martin, or Oliver, or Jake, or Tequila, or anybody else he had wronged along the way. His conscience was in full-throttle overdrive and he was unsure how it was all going to pan out.

Particularly now with the added complexity of The Arrival turning up.

The next morning, Mark woke early, bypassed breakfast, and headed directly to the Eastern Quarter, to East Green Street, where he intended to wait for The Arrival, so he could try to intercept.

It had been sometime around the devil's hour, when he was far beyond the point of exhaustion, that he decided on his present course of action - if only to make sure there were no problems and he could be free to go on his way again.

Afterwards, he would grab his belongings, check out of the hotel, and return to his new home.

Hopefully, without a hitch.

He hoped the massive sense of dread that was playing chopsticks on his heart strings was purely down to his guilty conscience, but he needed to be sure.

He needed to know that everybody he had wronged was safe. One last task before he could be free of this godforsaken town once and for all.

But like the twisted hands of fate, this godforsaken town had other things in mind and was determined to have the last say.

As those twisted hands of fate scattered cards about with reckless abandon, one card in particular landed on East Green Street for the whole world to see.

The Queen of Broken Hearts had been dealt.

CHAPTER 43

The day after Bonfire night

It was late when Oliver and Jay returned to the apartment block they shared on East Green Street, accompanied by Oliver's mother.

They had spent quite some time making formal statements to the police, who had logged the details and launched an investigation to find the guilty party. They had finally acknowledged that Oliver was vulnerable and were taking the matter very seriously.

Finally, Oliver could start to decompress, shower, change into clean clothes, and eat, although he was not sure if he could stomach anything at that time.

His mother made them a hearty but simple meal as Oliver did not have a lot of groceries in, which was not unusual for him. Despite his reservations, he wolfed down the food as though he hadn't eaten in days, which he hadn't. Jay, who was also ravenous, did the same.

The two men were exhausted. Adrenaline had been coursing through them, fuelling them, keeping them moving; but, now they were finally safe, it had drained from their systems and they had visibly crashed - emotionally and physically. "Right, you both need to sleep now," announced his mother, once she had cleared away the empty plates.

Oliver nodded and yawned. "I'll be okay now if you want to head off. I promise."

"I've heard that before," she replied, frowning slightly, "and look what happened."

"Unless you would like to stay, of course," Oliver added.

"Or I could stay here with him tonight," suggested Jay, whilst Oliver's mother was still thinking about whether she should stay or not. "I'm happy to sleep on the settee. It's not a problem at all."

"Are you sure?" asked Oliver's mother. Oliver also seemed happy with the suggestion. "But you don't have any of your things with you."

"I only live upstairs," he explained. "I'll get what I need and come straight back down."

"You live upstairs?" exclaimed Oliver, very surprised to hear this, "Since when?"

How had they never met in the hallway?

"Not long. Look, it doesn't matter. It's just a coincidence that we both live in the same block, that's all."

He left Oliver and his mother whilst he dashed upstairs to grab the few bits he needed.

In his apartment, he debated whether or not he should remove his disguise and reveal to Oliver who he really was.

Oliver trusted him now and deserved to see who he was.

He took out his fashionable-coloured contact lenses - he couldn't sleep with them in anyway, so removing them was an easy decision to make. He took off his cap revealing his full head of hair, which he ran his fingers through, ruffled up slightly, and pushed back, revealing more of his handsome face.

Perhaps now, Oliver might recognise him.

He looked at himself in the mirror and hoped he was the pleasant-looking man people told him he was.

He particularly hoped Oliver would think so.

Had he not been bombarded by the restless tongues on his first evening in town then he might have felt he could open up to Oliver sooner, tell him why he was there and what his intentions were. But they hadn't been able to contain themselves – simply having to divulge all they knew, or thought they knew, about Oliver's past, his love for Jake, the car crash, and the broken soul he became following Jake's untimely death.

In their opinions, their very much unwanted opinions, Oliver was barely ready to talk to anybody about anything, let alone open the door to the possibility of anything new – especially to somebody like Jay, and especially to anybody who had a name that sounded like Jake's.

Now, Jay wished he hadn't taken on board any of their advice. It was time for him to stop hiding, to no longer keep a low profile; he deserved to be able to show the world the real person behind the masks he had created, and particularly Oliver.

When he returned downstairs, Oliver was already in bed and his mother was standing watching him from the bedroom door as he fell into a zombified sleep.

Jay did not enter the bedroom; he simply stood alongside Oliver's mother and peered inside briefly before making himself comfortable on the settee underneath the bedding he had brought down from his own room.

Oliver's mother gently closed the bedroom door on her son and left him to rest.

He was safe now.

He was warm now.

And she knew exactly where he was.

She was not at all surprised by Jay's sudden change in appearance as they had already spoken openly and she knew exactly who he was, even if her son had not yet recognised him.

"Thank you for looking after him and for being here for him," she said, kneeling down to hug him once more. "I want you to know, if things do work out between you both... well, I think you would make a wonderful son-in-law."

"I hope they do," Jay replied, "because I do have feelings for him and that is why I am here: I need him in my life."

"I know you do," she said, wiping away tears that had formed at the corners of her eyes, "and I'm sure he will know it too, in time. But for now, good night you sweet, wonderful man."

"Good night," he replied, before snuggling down underneath the bedding and closing his eyes.

It had been quite the day for them both but if Oliver cried out in the night or needed him then he would be there, awake, alert, and at his side, ready to help in any way he could.

After Oliver's mother had switched off the lights and closed the front door softly behind her, Jay whispered in the darkness to an unaware Oliver, "And good night to you, you sweet, wonderful man."

He drifted off to sleep with his heart full of hope for the amazing life he might have with Oliver, in time.

CHAPTER 44
Two days after Bonfire night

Robert (Wendy) was up early the next morning. He was most definitely one early bird that wanted to catch the worm that day.

Keep fit, exercise
It helps reduce one's thunder thighs

"Come along, James," he bellowed from the landing, whilst banging on his drag queen son's bedroom door to wake him. "It's a lovely day to embrace the elements. Let's get out there for a bit of a jogging."

"Erm, no thank you," replied a tired and grumpy voice from behind the door, who knew that 'a bit of jogging' was a very literal description.

After all, his father could barely even walk up East Green Street without experiencing heart palpitations and having to stop for breath or to eat cake… there was no way he could run it!

The last time they had jogged, together, Robert hadn't been able to make it past the dilapidated old apartment block he used to live in.

But every now and again he would go through this farce of trying to lose weight.

Back in the late summer he had lost four pounds after a short stint of food poisoning which, when combined with fastening a belt too tightly under his overhanging belly, almost gave the illusion of a waistline.

If anybody dared to mention such extreme weight loss, Wendy would step forward and explain how she had been away on a detoxification boot camp with some celebrities, gushing over the incredible results.

On the other side of the door, inside his tiny bedroom on the first floor of the Old Queen's Jugs pub, James was too busy stuffing just one more magnificent Tequila outfit into one of his three suitcases to even think about keep fit, losing weight, or having a sneaky breakfast at the patisserie in town – if they could even make it that far!

He didn't have time to exercise because he was focusing on closing the cases without any zips ripping open or buckles pinging off! He had to get to the airport safely.

Besides, he had already packed all his man clothes and he had nothing else to wear except what he intended to travel in. Plus, he was very mindful of Mark's warning not to leave the pub until the taxi arrived.

James had already checked his bank account online and, true to his word, Mark had transferred over a generous amount. It was more money than he had ever had before and would set him up nicely for his new life abroad, away from that town which had never felt all that godforsaken to him.

He yawned loudly and widely; he had a lot on his mind and had barely slept the night before, but was sure it would be worth it in the long run.

"Come on, Son," called his father again from the landing. "Get your tracksuit on. Wear the one I bought you that used to belong to that gangly black man at the Olympic Games."

Two, four, six, eight
Exercising's really great

"No, you go on without me," James replied, trying to wrestle a stubborn high heel which refused to point in any direction other than upwards into submission.

He still couldn't believe he would be on the Costa del Sol later that day. It was a dream come true… and if it didn't work out then so be it. He was young, ambitious, talented, and he had a wad of cash to exploit.

After all, you only live once, right?

On the other side of the door, Robert began running on the spot which made everything in James's tiny bedroom shake alarmingly.

He made one final attempt to coax his son into joining him. "Come on, we stars of the show must look after our figures," he exclaimed. "And perhaps when we return, we can enjoy a nice breakfast smoothie together."

Now sitting on his suitcase to close it, James smiled to himself; he would miss all this. Just those little things that made Robert so unique, like the last time he had made them both a breakfast smoothie by liquidizing cereal and pork sausages together.

"No thank you," he said once more.

"Suit yourself," replied Robert, and James heard him running down the stairs, every one creaking violently under his still not inconsiderable weight.

James squeezed the now closed and bulging third suitcase under his bed alongside the other two and pulled down the valence to cover them. There, everything looked exactly as it should and would not raise any suspicion should anyone come in.

He then moved to the small window and looked at the world outside; in a few short hours he would be immersed in a completely new landscape.

Would he miss this town?

There were some good things, like the cabaret shows and the audiences but they would be there in his new life too.

And there were lots of bad things that he wouldn't miss at all, like having no money, being homeless, feeling vulnerable, and almost selling his body for a quick buck just to survive.

He certainly wouldn't miss the likes of Chris Randall or The Maniac.

Down on the street below, he saw Robert run a few steps down the pavement then stop, bend in half, and gulp in a series of deep breaths: the exercise stitch had already struck him.

He stayed there at his window, fondly watching his Father Wendy with love and admiration: he really did live his life without doubt, and James felt sad their time together was coming to an end, albeit temporarily; it saddened him further that his father had no idea of this impending separation.

Yes, Robert was not what you would call a conventional father but James would miss his delusional quirks.

As Mark had pointed out the previous day, he could always come and visit once things had settled down, and it sounded like he was going to be staying in a nice complex which would be good to show off.

Out on the street, Robert stood up with his hands on his hips gasping for air and, as he glanced back towards the pub and scanned the windows, he saw James watching him from the window above.

"Oh, buggar!" he exclaimed to himself and summoned up the strength to run just a few more steps... it made his stitch hurt more.

Five, four, three, two, one

Chuckling, James continued to watch from the window because it was funny to see and he knew exactly why his father had attempted those extra steps during his short-lived second wind.

But invisible and tempestuous winds of change were blowing ever closer, bringing chaos, despair, and destruction with them.

Suddenly, through his window, James saw somebody approach his father and it made him instantly apprehensive.

"Are you Wendy WolfWhistle?" Robert was asked.

"The one and only," he proudly replied.

Another fan and autograph seeker, no doubt.

"Wow, you really don't look any better as a man or a woman, do you?"

Understandably, Robert was disturbed to hear this and he examined the face looking back at him.

He suddenly realised who it was. "Oh my god, it's you!"

Breathing heavily as he sprinted along East Green Street, Mark came into view running to catch up with the person who had joined him in the bar the previous evening.

Unfortunately, he was too late to intervene as the shouting and screaming had already begun, causing curtains up and down the length of East Green Street to twitch.

The whole street would want a front row seat to whatever spectacle was unfolding on its doorstep.

The restless tongues would be messaging each other and, soon enough, the nosier residents would come out for a closer look, getting as near to the action as they could.

The winds of change were now thundering through like a hurricane; unstoppable, unignorable, impossible to withstand.

Destroying everything in their path.

Watch your back
Sharpen your mind
Dust away your paranoia at the door
Someone will soon be dead upon the floor...

CHAPTER 45

Two days after Bonfire night

An almighty racket from the street outside shattered the peace inside Oliver's first-floor apartment and woke Oliver and Jay from their slumber.

"What's going on out there?" asked Oliver, coming into the room where Jay had been sleeping. He was wearing only his underpants and a vest. "It sounds like mayhem."

Wearily, he pulled back the curtains he had not yet replaced and peered out of his window to see what all the commotion was about. He was quickly joined by Jay, and they stood side by side searching for the source of the fuss. Oliver had not yet noticed that Jay looked slightly different to the day before.

It appeared that Robert and another person were outside going at each other hammer and tongs, and airing their dirty laundry for everyone to hear. His, it seemed, were not the only curtains twitching - after all, a full throttle argument in the middle of their street was not an everyday encounter, although it was rarely without drama.

"That's Wendy, isn't it?" questioned Jay, "Out of drag. It looks like he's in trouble. Do you think we should go out and help?"

"Who is that with him?" asked Oliver, staring at the person who was verbally battering him. "She looks familiar."

"She looks familiar to me too," said Jay, unsure. "Oliver, I think it might be the Psychic Drag Queen from the telly."

"I think you're right. What is she doing here and why is she letting rip at Robert?"

"Somebody else is running towards them."

In the distance, Jay and Oliver could both see a third person dashing towards the hot spot. Perhaps somebody trying to intervene?

"Crikey," announced Oliver, surprised to see who it was. "That looks like Mark. He used to be a drag queen at Divas Cabaret Bar."

"Okay," responded Jay, without any indication whether he was aware of who it was or not.

They continued to watch events unfold, with Oliver showing a particular interest in the latecomer, Mark. Was it really him? Was he back? Where had he been all this time? And they watched as he tried – unsuccessfully - to pull the other person off Robert.

"Come on, I think we'd better get out there and help," said Jay, reactively grabbing one of Oliver's coats from the back of a dining table chair, partly because it would be chilly out there and partly because he was only wearing his pyjamas.

Looking down at himself, Oliver realised he was not in any fit state to be seen in public either, but did he have time to change? The vest he had slept in was probably fine but he'd have to put on some jeans and footwear as well. "I'm right behind you," he said but slipped into the bedroom first to make the necessary adjustments.

By the time he was dressed and took another peek out the window, Jay was very much in the thick of it. He fleetingly noticed his hair was pushed back from his face and thought how much it changed his appearance for the better.

Out on the street, the man who had run up was begging the person who appeared to be the Psychic Drag Queen, April Showers, to calm down and go back to a hotel with him.

"Exactly what is going on out here?" Jay demanded to know.

"This Weeble bitch made me look like a psychic fraud!" seethed April, visibly shaking with anger. "He has ruined my career!"

"I did no such thing," protested Wendy. "I just pointed out that you weren't very good with your predictions, that's all."

"So, you *are* the Psychic Drag Queen!" announced Jay, excitedly. April nodded a confirmation - not that it really made the slightest bit of difference who she was anymore.

Oliver ran out onto the street and joined them. "Is everything okay out here, Jay?" he asked. "Oh, wow, you look different."

Oliver stopped and stared at him. How had he not realised that Jay, this familiar-looking and beautiful stranger, had been hiding behind a mask? Without warning, Oliver physically trembled as an extraordinarily strong attraction swept over him, the likes of which he had not experienced since seeing Jake behind the bar at Divas for the very first time.

Oliver was jolted back to reality when James came running into the middle of the fray. "This is James," he whispered to Jay, "also out of drag as Tequila."

"It's quite the morning for drag queens, isn't it!" whispered back Jay.

"Seems so," agreed Oliver.

"Are you okay?" Mark asked Robert, who was now receiving support from his son, James.

"I'm fine," he replied. "Come on, we'd better get off the road."

"And you had better get back inside... *now*," Mark hissed sternly into James's ear.

"Oh shit, is that The Maniac?" James whispered, pointing towards a still raging April Showers.

"No, it's the Psychic Drag Queen," replied Mark. "Now go."

"Ahhh, I love watching her on the Mrs Seavers show," said James. "I'd love to look as feminine as she does."

And a thunderbolt of recognition shot right through Oliver's head. "Oh my God!" he exclaimed at Jay. "I know exactly who you are! You're..."

And that is when it happened again.

Just as it had the last time.

Exactly how Oliver always remembered it - relived it - every moment of every day of his life.

In his thoughts, in his dreams, every time he blinked... he couldn't bear it.

The car came out of nowhere.

The force of the impact against the body caused it to shift quite dramatically, turning, snapping, falling hard to the ground.

There was nothing anybody could have done to help.

There had not been any time to react.

It had all happened too quickly.

It was all out of their hands.

And, again, somebody was dying at the roadside.

CHAPTER 46
Two days after Bonfire night

The car carried on at speed and soon disappeared from sight, leaving screams of horror and despair in its wake.

Just like last time.

Exactly like last time.

The damaged body lay there shuddering, beyond repair.

But whose?

Oliver's?

James's?

Robert's?

Jay's?

April's?

Mark's?

Cries for an ambulance sounded from every corner of the street and curtains began to twitch at the windows of those who had not yet bothered to investigate the noisy drama outside.

What had they missed?

Oh, another car accident! Well, it wasn't as though they hadn't seen one of those before. Still, it was something interesting to post on social media.

People all around fell to their knees crying and screaming, surrounding the victim, who was fading fast. Unqualified passers-by made uninformed judgement calls about what to do and how best to help.

But nobody present was a medic and so nobody knew what to do.

They needed the ambulance.

They needed the paramedics to perform their miracles and breathe life back into this broken heart.

Who had done this?

Who was responsible?

Chris Randall?

The Maniac?

Who?

Blood spread quickly across the asphalt. It was clear that the head had borne the brunt of the damage.

But the body was weak... very weak.

Did anyone see who had been driving that car?

Anybody?

With every second that passed the spark of life dulled; it was almost as if the horrified, helpless onlookers could see the soul leaving the body of the person lying prone on the ground.

The broken heart was losing its battle to live, and they all knew it.

The casualty lay on the ground staring up at the sky, sensing their body as it shut down. They saw angels appear above them, circling, come to collect their spirit, and there was nothing anybody could do to stop it.

This was the end.

And the broken heart could not remember the sky ever looking as blue as it did right then.

An annoying thought was nagging at them: this should not have happened, not like this, not now. Not when life was filled with so many opportunities and new starts.

The broken heart looked at the faces staring down. It was obvious how much they cared... they were going to stay until their spirit passed.

That was a nice thought to die with.

And then the eyes closed.

Never to open again.

A legacy of guilt

Today, could be our final day
So the prophecies all say
If it is written down for all to see
Must we presume it's true?

Another sad love song on the radio
Another life lost on the news
Another storm
Another wave has washed away a town
And the tears that are falling just won't stop falling
down

What are you leaving me?
A legacy of guilt
Are my eyes deceiving me?
I'm blinded by the truth
What are we fighting for?
My strength has all but gone
And half the world is lonely
And half is all alone

Somehow, we're living in fear now
Afraid of the political row
Suddenly, we're numbers now
Stand up and take the blame

Another sad story on the TV
Another desperate heart-felt plea
Another war
Another gone, another bound to die
And the tears keep on falling
When will they all run dry?

Why are you leaving me?
I'm not responsible
Is my heart deceiving me?
I'm not accountable
What are we fighting for?
I'm not invincible
And half the world is hiding
And half is still at war

I can hear the angels sighing
Filling up the rivers and the oceans with their tears
As they sit there softly crying

I can hear them whispering your name
Sweetly in their song
They call you back to heaven
Where you belong

And half the world is lonely
And half will die too young

CHAPTER 47
Two days after Bonfire night

Had it been Oliver lying there, dying on the ground, breaking his heart?

Oliver - who always seemed to take the wrong turning at every crossroads he encountered, and to whom destiny really had a habit of destroying!

Had it been James (Tequila) lying there, dying on the ground, breaking his heart?

James - who was just about to embark on an exciting new adventure abroad and with a pocket full of cash too!

Had it been Robert (Wendy) lying there, dying on the ground, breaking his heart?

Robert - who would soon discover he was finally about to become the sole headlining act of the cabaret show, an absolute dream come true!

Had it been Jay lying there, dying on the ground, breaking his heart?

Jay - who was finally filled with hope at the prospect of a happy future and had been given the approval from Oliver's mother to love and care for her son!

Had it been April Showers, the Psychic Drag Queen, lying there, dying on the ground, breaking her heart?

April - who had a whole new adventure ahead of her, whatever she chose to do!

And then there was Mark (formerly known as Connie) - could he have been the one lying there, dying on the ground, breaking his heart?

Mark - who had escaped, only returning to that godforsaken town to right some wrongs before returning to his life of peace and solitude!

The ambulance arrived.

The paramedics did everything they could but it was not enough.

They were too late.

The victim took their final breath on earth and their soul was carried away to a safer place. The world was a worse place for losing this person, but heaven was a better one for gaining this angel.

Oliver?
James?
Robert?
Jay?
April?
Mark?
Who?

CHAPTER 48

Two days after Bonfire night

"...But first tonight breaking news just in: A man was knocked down by a car which then drove off at speed. The incident happened on East Green Street earlier today.

"He was treated at the roadside for multiple injuries before being taken to the city hospital, where he was pronounced dead upon arrival.

"Police are appealing for witnesses and are requesting for anyone with any information to contact them.

"The man has been named as Jay Galling, the well-known former drag queen entertainer and cabaret star, Miss Robyn RedBreasts.

"The Psychic Drag Queen, April Showers, was with him when the incident happened. April told us: 'I can't believe this has happened. It's an absolute tragedy for somebody so young to die. None of us saw it coming.'

"Our deepest sympathies go out to his family and friends on this very sad day."

CHAPTER 49
Sometime after the car accident

He had instantly become one of Britain's most hated men.

Rightly so.

He had killed a person, taken him away from those who loved him, and who didn't want to be without him.

And now they would never see him again.

All because of That Man.

He had wanted what he didn't have.

He had wanted to reign supreme, to rule the world; but now that dream was over. Because of his bad decisions, many dreams were over.

Everybody who had ever dared to hope for love was hurt by this.

Anybody who had ever dreamt of being accepted for their differences felt exposed.

A role model, an ambassador, a hero, a friend was gone.

And all because of That Man.

Everyone knew who he was.

There had been too many witnesses for him to slip away unseen.

And there were CCTV cameras now, too, strategically placed following the demise of Jake Robinson earlier that year.

The jury would find him guilty of murder and he would be locked away, trapped inside those four walls for many years to come.

The outside world would be free of him.

They would be safe from the impure thoughts which lurked within him.

There would be no repercussions for those who stepped forward and spoke up.

That Man would be lost to the past.

Forgotten, left to rot, alone and broken.

He was arrested shortly afterwards and taken into custody.

He was led along the corridors by an officer with a moustache and taken through doors that shut tightly behind him.

He was led to a cell where he sat down on the bottom bunk and the door was closed behind him.

He would wait there until his trial, but there was no doubt of his guilt on two counts: the first, kidnapping Oliver and holding him hostage, leaving him to die in a slow and painful manner; the second, killing Jay.

All that remained to be seen was the length of his sentence.

A life for a life, most probably.

He stared at the metal sink, the toilet, the television, and the messy walls, his eyes fixed firmly on the graffiti scratched into the walls, in particular the initials CR.

CR for Chris Randall?

This was it… he had lost the game.

Every card from that point onwards would be a losing one.

Every game played would end in defeat.

Pick up two.

Pick up five.

Change direction.

Bust!
Game over!
Go directly to jail!

Suddenly, everything changed. Sirens wailed in the distance, heralding their imminent victory. The cavalry had arrived. The authorities were here to impose order and they would do it swiftly.

The atmosphere shifted and so did his chain of thought as the chance to retake his freedom faded by the second.

He sprinted towards the way out. It was now or never.

His freedom beckoned him.

It was within his grasp.

But time was running out. He summoned every ounce of energy he had.

His freedom teased him.

He could hide on the outside, adopt a disguise nobody would see through.

It was his for the taking.

His freedom tempted him.

He raced frantically towards it.

He reached it.

His freedom screamed to him.

He breathed deeply, put one foot in front of the other and stepped forward.

His freedom cocooned him.

Where would he go? To that godforsaken town where his heart and his world had been torn in two?

His freedom dizzied him.

To Oliver... to Martin... to Mark... to The Maniac, and to the countless others who had it coming to them?

His freedom empowered him.

But Chris Randall had chosen not to take it.

He was not that stupid. If he escaped now he would only be recaptured and it would be years before he would get out of there again.

He walked away from the open door and back towards the prison building.

The riots would soon be over, and it would be safe again inside.

He would willingly help clean up the mess he had not created.

He would be a model prisoner.

The perfect house guest.

Surely that would go in his favour?

The cell door opened and Chris Randall walked in.

The first thing he noticed was That Man sitting on his bunk bed; Chris indicated he should move from there *now*. "Well, you fucked that up," he remarked, shaking his head and scowling as though he had a bad taste in his mouth, which he probably did. "It was Oliver I wanted dead, not some second-rate drag queen he may have mentioned once or twice in the past."

"But I..." began That Man, but the battle was long since lost.

"And don't think you're taking me down with you because there's no evidence. You're on your own, mate."

That Man stared at Chris, incredulous; this had all been his doing. Chris had pulled all the strings, manipulated people, orchestrated everything... but how would he ever convince anybody else of that?

Yet again, Chris Randall would win and evade justice. Who would ever find the strength to bring him down?

That Man felt suddenly claustrophobic with the two of them in there.

He didn't know where to stand or what to do.

Were they really expected to live together and share a cell together?

Did he now have to wash and dress in front of him?

Go to the toilet in front of him?

Sensing his apprehension, Chris offered some words of encouragement, although they brought him little comfort: "You'll get used to it... or you won't, I don't care either way? Besides, you'll be on your own in here soon enough."

With that, Chris flopped onto his bed whilst That Man stood in shock, trying to take it all in.

That Man, a phoenix who would not rise from its ashes.

That Man, who had nothing left except regret over trusting Chris Randall to get him what he wanted.

That Man, who killed Jay Galling / former drag queen Robyn RedBreasts, a person with whom Oliver may have been able to fall in love.

That Man, who would never get what he wanted again.

That Man… who was Wayne.

CHAPTER 50

James Taylor, previously known as Miss Tequila ShockingBird drag queen extraordinaire, had since departed that godforsaken town, and was enjoying his fabulous new life in Spain.

It was sunny, with gorgeous gay men in abundance, he was a cabaret superstar, and he absolutely loved life there.

This really was his happy ever after!

He was well away from the drama and dangers of his past, safe from fate dealing cards that he could neither predict nor control, back in control of his life and its direction.

Life was now full of silver linings and blessings for James, the biggest being that the dreaded Queen of Broken Hearts card had been dealt and could never resurface to hurt him.

Mark had saved him from that along with other fates not even worth thinking about.

But tragedy was never too far away in this game and the worst, most evil card was still lurking somewhere in the pack, biding its time, silently waiting to be found, to be revealed.

Yes, the catastrophic Queen of Devastation still lay in the deck, unseen and unforeseen.

It was so powerful in its nature that it would annihilate the impact of any and all the other cards; it took no prisoners, it knew no mercy, and it offered no peace.

But James was blessed in this arena too; fate had decided he had suffered enough for one so young, and he would not be impacted by this card.

Others were not as fortunate.

Others, fate decided, could take more suffering and rightly so.

Others were not so safe.

Before the year was out, the impact would be known.

Before the year was out, others would be dead.

CHAPTER 51

Mark had fled from that godforsaken town too, but not in quite the same exciting manner as James. Neither had he not gone as far as James, nor as far as he had planned to go.

And regretfully, he had not gone back to the tranquility and solitude he had been longing for either. But, for now, he was warm and safe, and he had a bed upon which to rest his weary being.

Well, for now, anyway.

The universe was still not done with him yet; whilst he had hoped saving James would be enough, it clearly wanted more. It wanted everything it could take from him and cared little for what it might cost.

Perhaps the Queen of Broken Hearts had made its way into his hand? Or the Queen of Deadly Divas had strapped on her stilettoes and dug in her heels? Maybe the Queen of Devastation had him in its sights and was warming up in the wings before taking to the stage for the grand finale?

Maybe this was only the intermission?

But after the awfulness of Jay's death, no one could have anticipated being ambushed by yet another horror - although perhaps it was not a complete shock to Mark... after all, he had played a dangerous game so far, lived precariously and promiscuously, and maybe this was his punishment.

Instead of taking him as they did Jay were the angels pushing him downwards?

What came next for Mark was another ambulance following an unexpected collapse to the ground outside the hotel in that godforsaken town, just after he had finally checked out believing everything was calm and steady once more.

Because that godforsaken town was not done with him either; it had wrapped its seedy underground tendrils around him to keep him bound there, firmly rooted in its dirt.

But perhaps he was not done with it either. Maybe his work was not complete after all.

Maybe his conscience was not yet clear.

A debt was still outstanding between them and it had to be repaid.

And if he was forever destined to be dragged back to his hell, then he would go down fighting.

Because now he had nothing left to lose.

CHAPTER 52

Significant news would come to Martin in two very different forms of communication, at two different times.

The first one came quickly via Chris Randall's legal team, and was of no surprise to him at all. It was expected, and there was no avoiding it.

It was all over. His short yet successful reign at the helm of the Old Queen's Jugs pub had been usurped; a new owner was in place and would change everything Martin had worked so hard to create.

Undoubtedly, he would return to the shadows and become invisible to the whole world again.

But maybe that wasn't so bad?

Maybe the limelight had exposed the cracks beneath the paper?

When it was due, the second piece of news would not be expected. On the contrary, it would come as a complete shock.

That second communication would be absolutely life changing.

Of course, the first change also meant that Wendy WolfWhistle would no longer be the lead cabaret drag queen act and would probably be out of the show altogether.

What would become of her?

The new owner would probably want to hire their own drag queen cabaret acts.

Could she audition? Was she good enough? Or would she set her sights higher, despite barely having two feet on the ground as it was?

Following the sudden and unexplained departure of her drag queen son, James, what effect would this have on a state of mind that was highly questionable anyway?

Would Wendy WolfWhistle be forced to reinvent herself and what would that new incarnation look like?

Probably not very different from the original.

Or maybe fate already had something else in mind for her.

As for Chris Randall, he had been released.

At last, he was a free man and could breathe in all the outside air his lungs could manage, although he still wanted what was rightfully his.

He wanted his dictatorship back, his status, and his life.

He wanted to love and be loved.

And Chris Randall was a free man because, despite the confession he had made in the past, he was not actually the person who had driven the car into Jake Robinson on that fateful summer day.

CHAPTER 53

And then there was Oliver.

Surely the universe was done with dear, sweet Oliver? After all, what else was there left to throw at him?

Surely now it could let him go?

It was December and the weather was much colder than it had been at any other time of the year so far.

As he sat alone on the kerb amongst the dying flowers, burnt-out candles, and poems and messages that had been left for Jay by well-wishers and drag queens from near and far, he once again contemplated the limitations of his own painful life, just as he had often done back on Driftwood Beach.

He was so far removed from the peace and tranquillity of Driftwood Beach here. There were no white horses or gentle waves to lap softly around his soul; no welcome breeze to blow comfortably through his thoughts; nobody would smile politely as they wandered past wishing him a good morning, a lovely day, or a perfect life.

Driftwood Beach - a place he suddenly longed to be.

Morbidly, he stared out at where Jay Galling had died on the asphalt in front of him the month before. Reluctantly, he remembered every single detail of that morning because the graveyard of terror within his head would not let him forget... it probably never would.

Not when it had happened twice on the same street, in almost the same spot, and both times right in front of his eyes.

First Jake then Jay.

Was it him? Was he cursed? Did he make these things happen? Was there a plague upon his heart that would inflict an untimely death upon anybody who dared to want him, to need him, to ultimately fall in love with him?

But if that was true then Chris Randall should be dead too.

Hopefully, in time, he would be.

Jay had not deserved this. Not to die like that, so young.

Jay, the caring and loving man whom he had once met briefly as drag queen Miss Robyn RedBreasts when she had asked him out on a date with her ravishing self in front of all his work colleagues and had accidentally almost 'outed' him before he had readily accepted himself as being gay.

No wonder he had always looked familiar; Oliver had seen the face before but then it had been coated in makeup with a stunning wig framing it.

Jay, the guy who had never forgotten they'd met. He had developed feelings of love for Oliver over time and tracked him down to see if they could start a life together. He had quite literally rescued him - so bravely and selflessly – and had saved his life because of those ever-growing feelings of love.

Jay, the man who could have taught him to love again.

Jay, whose name was forever etched into his thoughts, alongside everything else that ruined his sleep and drained the energy from his crumbling heart.

His mother had been right all along... her intuition accurate: he should not have stayed there a moment longer.

He should have left with her there and then, just as she had wanted him to; right after they had sat together having coffee and cake in the old-fashioned tearoom where the staff looked at least twenty years older than they probably were.

He should have gone straight back to his first-floor apartment, packed up everything he owned, and driven away.

It wouldn't have taken long because some of his stuff was still in boxes from when he and Jake had planned their grand escape that summer.

Yet, he had felt compelled to stay and be miserable there, in that godforsaken town that he had once loved beyond belief.

But why?

Seriously, looking back at everything... why?

Again, his mother had been right: he was like a moth so obsessed by the flame that would eventually entice it in and kill it.

There was no way he could stay there now, not after everything that had happened. There was not a single reason for him to stay there any longer.

His mind was firmly made up.

It was time to go back, pack his remaining things and leave that godforsaken town forever before anybody else died from the evil that laced its streets.

And nothing – absolutely nothing - would make him reconsider.

But the winds of change had not yet blown on, and the universe was far from done with him.

As Oliver looked up and down the street he thought about all the people he had met since he had arrived and his heart became so heavy he couldn't hold it in any longer.

Although he had vowed never to cry again, especially not in this town, he shed some final tears because he had known nothing but heartache since he had moved there.

His hands icy cold, he picked up a glass jar from the roadside shrine which contained the remains of a red candle, held it to his face, and took a deep breath. The wax had run down but there was still a slight aroma of raspberry, both bitter and sweet. And it was red, just like the breast of a robin.

A robin that had flown far, far away to the heavens up above.

This time tomorrow, if not sooner, he would be out of there. Like James and, it seemed, Mark, he would turn his back on this godforsaken town and be free from its evil clutches which held everybody back.

Carefully placing the candle and glass jar back amidst the other objects in the shrine - although he actually wanted to throw it as hard as he possibly could - he screamed out in anguish and despair, not caring one bit who heard. "Why does everybody I care about have to fucking die, and on this godforsaken street as well?"

"Well, hopefully not everybody does," replied a familiar voice behind him.

A voice he knew all too well but had not heard for what seemed to be an eternity.

A voice he had longed to hear every single day and every single night for as long as he could remember.

Startled, because he had thought he was alone, he turned around and gasped out loud when he saw who was standing there. The shock of who he saw was so fierce it knocked him backwards and he fumbled amongst the detritus of tributes that had been left for Jay.

He put out his hands to regain his balance and composure and Jake caught them, pulling him upwards and into a warm embrace.

No, thought Oliver, this couldn't be happening. He couldn't be there... it wasn't possible.

In that moment, the winds of change blew through Oliver so severely he couldn't bear it anymore; he truly felt as though his heart would shatter.

But it was undeniable: there he was, Jake Robinson, standing next to him smiling, alive and kicking every bit as much as he was.

Oliver looked into those brown eyes that no longer looked tired and scared, eyes that seemed to be filled with as much love as they'd always held for him and, as he did so, he saw before him a man who stared deeply back into his heart and soul, and who knew him better than anybody else ever could.

Oliver wondered if he could, perhaps, change his mind about leaving, after all.

He had been so adamant it was the right thing to do.

Standing next to him on East Green Street on that frozen December day, Jake could sense Oliver's conflicting emotions about him being there and instinctively pulled him in for another loving embrace.

But Oliver had already put his barriers up and he pulled away, leaving Jake - who had never anticipated getting such a reaction – at an absolute loss.

For so long, he had ached to return to Oliver, to show him his love, to give him his love, and to make love with him, but Oliver was not reciprocating. In fact, he was positively cold towards him. But Jake had no idea what had happened since the summer.

And, suddenly, the version of Oliver in front of him was nothing like the warm-hearted loving man he had known and never stopped loving. Jake was looking at a man more broken than he himself had ever been; a man filled with only emptiness, desperation, and despair.

Perhaps he had been away too long but that had not been through choice. He knew Oliver needed to hear the story of where he had been and why he had gone but how could he ever tell him when Oliver could barely bring himself to look at him never mind speak to him,?

Had he really been naive enough to believe they could just carry on from where they had left off? Perhaps he should have come back sooner but that had been impossible. Perhaps he should never have come back at all and left Oliver in peace.

Was the price of love just too high?

He desperately needed to be loved by him and had craved nothing else since they had parted company on the roadside that day. Although he had seen him briefly, and fleetingly held him from behind the night Divas Cabaret Bar was burning, it had been nowhere near enough to sate the desire to be near him.

Surely, their names were still written in the stars? Surely, the stars had not stop shining for them?

Jake looked at the flood of dying flowers and memorials that littered the pavement not knowing who they were for or why they had been placed there, though he imagined it was a bad sign that Oliver had been sitting amongst them. "Don't tell me people are still mourning me?" he joked, immediately regretting it when Oliver turned his angry, hurt face towards him.

Jay Galling had saved his life and started to help him heal emotionally after what he had truly believed was a devastating end for him and Jake.

Jake hung his head in shame and apologised for being so insensitive.

"Come with me," said Oliver, quietly, and Jake willingly followed him in silence to a nearby lamp post that had a solitary ribbon tied around it.

On the ribbon were the words Oliver had written when he thought Jake was dead: 'Always be with me.'

Jake read it several times then looked at Oliver. "I will always be with you, Oliver."

"That's what I wrote after your 'death'," explained Oliver. "Day after day, week after week, I mourned you. Some days I couldn't even get out of bed."

Jake put a reassuring hand onto Oliver's shoulder and Oliver allowed him to, just for a few moments. Maybe the electricity was still there? He had certainly felt it once upon a time. "Being away from you for all that time," Jake began, "I might as well have been dead. Some days it really felt like I was."

"I thought you were dead," protested Oliver.

Jake looked at him with hope in his brown eyes. He would never give up. Not now they were back together again. "And now you know I'm not."

"So, what happens now?" croaked Oliver through dry lips. "How can you suddenly not be dead?"

He put his hands over his tired face and closed his eyes tightly.

Was this a dream? Was he still lost inside a restless sleep? This was too much! Jake was supposed to be dead. He had mourned him - he was still mourning him. And now he was mourning the death of somebody else, too.

He couldn't cope.

He should be pleased Jake was alive. He had been the love of his life - or at least he thought he had... now he was unsure.

For the sake of his own sanity, he needed to leave but could he walk away from Jake and this town now he knew the truth?

What was the truth? In all fairness, he still knew very little. Jake had clearly been able to walk away from him and to stay away, so why had he chosen to return now?

Maybe they hadn't been as in love as he had believed they were.

But Oliver did not know Jake's story yet.

Would he feel differently if he knew everything that had come to pass? He had to ask the question.

"Where have you been? Why haven't you been in contact with me? Why..."

It became too much for Oliver and he burst into tears as the emotions of the past few minutes, days, weeks, and months all returned and exploded out.

This damned street! This damned town! Divas Cabaret Bar… Chris Randall… Jay… the cellars… Wayne… now this. How was any of it even possible? It had to a very, very bad dream.

He tried to jolt himself awake.

Without saying a word, Oliver turned away and walked back towards his first-floor apartment. He couldn't look at the roadside anymore. He couldn't look at the memorial to Jay anymore. But most of all he couldn't look at Jake anymore.

"No," he said, when Jake tried to walk alongside him. "Do not follow me. You left me. It's over. It has to be."

"But we need to talk about this," said Jake, still shocked by Oliver's reaction. "We'll sort this out, we have to."

"No, there is nothing to sort out," replied Oliver, clenching his door keys in his trouser pocket so tightly that his hand began to throb with the pain.

Jake was panicking. It couldn't actually be over, could it? "But... what about us? Oliver... please."

Oliver heard the familiar desperation in his voice and stopped to look at Jake.

Time and time again he had imagined looking back into those eyes when he had been crushed by his pain, believing only Jake could put the smile back on his face.

Time and time again he had dreamt they were still together, in love, living freely and honestly in a new place, different to the one outside his window; but every time he had woken up to the harsh, cruel reality that they were not.

And waking up was always the hardest part.

Because reality was the true nightmare.

Now they were both here, together, exactly as Oliver had wished. Looking back at his hopeful face, hearing the desperation in his voice which he had always struggled to resist, it was like facing a ghost. But he could not allow himself to be broken like the last time.

"I'm sorry, I can't do this," he blurted out, before dashing to the front door of his apartment block. "I can't be hurt again, Jake. I'm sorry but I have to go." Even as he said it, he didn't know if he could walk away that easily because he might feel differently in the morning.

He just didn't know... he needed time to think, to reflect, and to decompress.

Oliver turned his key in the lock, stepped inside the hallway, and quickly closed the door on Jake, his past, his present, and what might have been his future.

Jake had returned to him.

But his mind was made up about leaving, wasn't it?

It was clear what Jake wanted. The desperation in his voice had made it explicit.

But the decision had already been made, hadn't it?

But Jake was still alive.

Outside on the street, all Jake could do was stand and watch helplessly as Oliver walked away from him.

There was no point waiting. Oliver wasn't ready to talk yet or face the truth. Understandably, it had been a shock for him but it had been a whirlwind for him too. First, he was running away with Oliver - they were packing and leaving; then he was hurt, mowed down in the road, and it felt like he was dying at the roadside.

Then everything changed. And that meant this could all change too… hopefully.

Perhaps once Oliver had thought things through and once he knew the details he would calm down and be more accepting of the situation. Maybe then he would realise they were still in love and meant to be together.

He would come back the next day and explain everything. He would make him understand but first he could see that Oliver needed space, just a little extra time to get used to the idea of a future together again.

He would come back the next day and they would talk it through and sort it all out. Maybe even go to the old-fashioned tearoom where the staff all looked about twenty years older than they probably were. He would have hot chocolate with cream and sprinkles, and cakes, lots of cakes. They could make a meal out of it and call it tapas, just like they used to.

Damn it, he had really missed those cakes but not nearly as much as he had missed Oliver.

Yes, he would come back the next day and make Oliver understand.

In around twenty hours, or so.

Nineteen hours, fifty-nine minutes, and fifty-nine seconds? Fifty-eight seconds... fifty-seven... fifty-six.

Maybe even sooner if he couldn't wait that long.

The next day he would explain everything from start to finish. He might even put that extra layer of desperation into his voice because Oliver seemed to react favourably to that; although, this time, there would be no other ulterior motive, only love.

He just needed Oliver to hug him back, to love him back, and to need him back.

But when he returned the next day and knocked on the door, would he find love waiting for him there?

THE QUEEN OF DEVASTATION

Book 3 in the Divas Trilogy

The nightmare is far from over…

As old scores remain unsettled and evil walks amongst them, can broken hearts begin to heal, can the weak ones find their strength, and can the Queen of Devastation be repelled?

In the depths of winter torment, as the shortest day approaches and darkness reigns, who will live, who will die, and who will finally escape that godforsaken town?

As some fight for the spotlight whilst others hide away, their remaining secrets are revealed, their futures are determined, and only God knows what lies ahead.

Father forgive them for they know not what they do. But have they sinned?

The Divas Trilogy consists of:
The Queen of Deadly Divas
The Queen of Broken Hearts
The Queen of Devastation

**For author updates and more information on the
Divas Trilogy, follow me:**
TikTok – @rickyjamesrogers
Instagram - @rickyjamesrogers
Twitter / X - @divastrilogy
Facebook – Ricky James Rogers – Author /
facebook.com/rickyjamesrogers1